CASUALTY!

CASUALTY!

HUGH MILLER

Enigma Books

L O N D O N

First published in 1982 by Enigma Books
an imprint of Severn House Publishers Limited
4 Brook Street, London W1Y 1AA

British Library Cataloguing in Publication Data

Miller, Hugh
Casualty!
I. Title
823′.914[F]   PR6063.I/

ISBN 0-7278-3002-3

The names of characters and locations in this book
are wholly invented.

Phototypeset by Tradespools Ltd, Frome, Somerset

Printed in Great Britain by
Hazell Watson & Viney Ltd, Aylesbury, Bucks

NIGHT SHIFT

John Blake – Senior Casualty Officer
Mary Pringle – Sister
Donald Ramsay – Casualty Officer
Glenda Cross – Staff Nurse
Sue McLean – Student Nurse
Claire Doughty – Receptionist
Phil Cowley – Porter

DAY SHIFT

Alan Smedley – Senior Casualty Officer
Rose Harper – Sister
Desmond Owen – Casualty Officer
Iris Cole – Staff Nurse
Maggie Lunt – Student Nurse
Connie Lewis – Receptionist
Miles Campbell – Porter

OVERLAP SHIFT

Jack Lester – Senior Casualty Officer
Jean Boyd – Sister
Elsie Pitt – Staff Nurse
Sarah Bloom – Student Nurse
Isobel Tait – Student Nurse

ACKNOWLEDGEMENTS

I can name only a couple of the people who helped make this book possible. Nevertheless, I want to record my gratitude to the dozens of men and women who put up with me for almost a year and never once treated me as a nuisance, even though the provocation must have been strong.

My thanks to Polly Childs SRN, who was unstinting with her advice whenever it was needed. I am similarly indebted to Maggie Miller for her contribution, which was indispensable.

I don't think it inappropriate here to acknowledge my pleasure in working editorially with David Harsent, who possesses, among his many other talents, the ability to tell me what to do while making it sound like a request.

For my wife, Nettie

Friday

THE public bar of the Bowling Green is jammed. Nowadays most men in the district get their wages, or their dole, on a Thursday, but Friday night is still the time for them to gather in the pub and spend their beer money on each other.

The mutton-chopped landlord and his two barmen are dancing steady attendance on seventy people occupying a space just big enough for forty. At the piano by the fireplace a thin man with his hair in his eyes is making a hash of 'Moon River'. Terry Doyle, standing with his back to the bar and yelling to make himself heard above the music and the noise of other people, is favouring his two friends with his views on a current soccer crisis.

'They want to try entertaining the punters,' Terry says. 'It's a bloody cheek expecting somebody to shell out for a ticket, just so he can go into a stadium and watch a bunch of fairies with permed hair molesting each other. What's happened to guts, fearlessness, all that hard talent we used to turn up to watch?'

The issue has been reported in the evening paper. A local football management has been warning that the team could be in desperate financial trouble if the fans' attendance numbers at matches don't improve. Terry, who has been a taxi driver for thirty years, feels himself well qualified to provide the answer to the dilemma. As he has said more than once, the public is a whore, but it's a whore with strong ideas about what it likes.

'I mean, look at that fiasco the week before last. Pathetic. They'd only been on the field ten minutes and the bloody striker got carried off because the ball hit him in the face. It's supposed to be a game for *men*. In the old days they played with a real ball

1

with a bladder and laces. Get one of them in the teeth and you knew you'd been smacked.' He sighs. 'They're more like ballet dancers these days. They should be wearing frilly frocks and tights.'

As Terry sets his glass on the bar something happens. It's a sensation like a hand moving over his stomach, but on the inside. He touches his forehead and finds it is beaded with sweat. A wave of nausea hits him and he slaps at his belly, trying to belch.

'You all right, Tel?' one of his mates asks. Terry's face has gone white and his eyes look sunken.

'Yeah. Bit of wind.'

The slapping produces more than a belch. Hot bile rises in Terry's throat and as he gulps it back his chest is seized by a tightness that turns swiftly to a clamp, stopping his breathing. Terry coughs once, spilling vomit over his chin and shirt, and then his head is full of ringing and there is a pain like a blade in the middle of his chest. He tries to inhale and sees his mates rise up before his eyes, then they seem to swerve sideways. A thump on the back of his head lets him know he has fallen over. All he can see is the ceiling. The pain is swelling and enclosing his neck. The noise in his head is deafening.

'Jesus Christ!' A barman is leaning across the bar, staring at the very sight he saw ten minutes before he became fatherless at the age of fifteen. 'Give him some room!' In one smart leap he is over the bar and pushing back his sleeves. 'Open the flaming door, somebody!'

The sound of the pub has changed. The music has stopped and the men are mumbling to each other, setting up a background drone to the sudden, frantic telephoning of the landlord.

'Terry!' The barman is loosening Terry's tie and forcing open his mouth, staring at the purpling tongue. 'Can you hear me? Terry, you got a pain?'

Everyone is watching, shifting to make space around the pale, choking man on the floor. Concern and pity are on everyone's lips, but it's the resentment that shows. This shouldn't happen in here. If a pub is about anything, it's about stepping out of reality's line of fire for a while.

The ambulance arrives in less than five minutes. A calm nurse comes in ahead of the ambulancemen, nodding steadily as the landlord gives her a summary of what happened. She kneels beside Terry and lays two fingers on the side of his neck.

'Don't try to say anything,' she tells him, and she puts her mouth close to his ear. 'We know what's happened and we're going to take care of it.'

Terry is in terrible pain. He watches the nurse slip the cover off a syringe and move it down somewhere out of his range of vision. At the same time a mask is put over his nose and mouth. A few seconds later he can feel himself being lifted.

The ambulance is specially stabilised and the ride to Anderson General is smooth by any standard, but every bump and shift in speed sends the pain coursing wildly across Terry's chest. He has lost his sense of himself. Time is a series of flicks, one moment the nurse is smiling down at him on his stretcher, the next he is staring at the cream ceiling of the ambulance, feeling he has been like that for an age. Then the comforting face is back, and she is touching his cold hand, patting it.

'Only a couple of minutes now,' she tells him. 'We'll have you sorted out soon. Just you hang on.'

The driver changes into a low gear and pain flares in Terry's neck and chest. He knows something has happened to his heart, he can feel it labouring. The sensation of loosening is terrible; it's as if he's lost control of something without a name that he's held on to all his life. He thinks about Bella and wonders what she'll do when she finds out.

The nurse has put a cuff round his upper arm and she's got a stethoscope pressed to the skin below it. Behind her, the attendant is taking the wrapper off another syringe. The calmness of them reassures Terry, but he is still frightened and he feels like crying.

'Two more minutes,' the nurse promises, and she is wielding the syringe again.

Two minutes. It seems a long time to wait, and Terry has no idea what for. He feels very insecure, and the coldness spreading in his legs and arms is as bad in its way as the pain. He tries to hold an idea of what two minutes really is. He hopes it won't be too much, for things are slipping. If they don't get him more powerful help very soon, he thinks, he might have to die.

*　　*　　*

The central building of Anderson General was erected at the

turn of the century. At intervals of ten and twenty years since then it has been added to, so that the place has become a sprawling summary of twentieth-century hospital architecture. The largest additions were made in the sixties – four ward blocks finished in a grey concrete that is now pitted and patched, painfully at odds with the dignified dark stone of the main building.

It is a city hospital of average size with fourteen in-patient wards, five outpatient clinics, a casualty department and a district nursing service. Over 500 medical staff serve a large, thickly populated area of South London; on an average day 800 people will receive treatment at Anderson General.

The driveway is long, winding between rows of sparse shrubbery and up over a rise that sets the hospital above its surroundings. The drive forks at the arched main entrance, leading to the laundry and works department at the rear, and to Casualty on the west of the central block.

The Casualty block is a three-year-old structure, joined to the old building by two corridors. The main entrance to Casualty is through a wide, porched ambulance bay, leading into a bare rectangular area flanked by the office and the rear wall of the X-ray department. A smaller entrance, ten feet from the ambulance bay, leads directly to the patients' waiting room.

The Casualty graveyard shift begins in no precise way. Just before 9 p.m. Mary Pringle arrives and says nothing to anybody until she's tracked down the teapot and poured herself a cup. Mary is thirty; she has been a Casualty Sister for four years. Not once in that time has she admitted to liking the work. People assume she does, because she has never asked for a transfer.

Cup in hand, Mary wanders round the department, looking in cubicles, opening and closing cupboards, easing herself into the start of the routine. At the open door of X-ray she stands for a minute, listening to the comforting hum of the machinery. She cranes her neck to catch her reflection in the mirror on the far wall and prods her fair hair more tightly under the edge of her cap.

The stillness of the place doesn't mislead Mary or any of the others on this shift. Friday night is the toe of a Casualty graph and its sharp rise is eerily predictable. This department is the most seriously overworked in the hospital; at the weekend the

4

pressure is higher than at any other time. It's the period when doctors and nurses will struggle hardest to impose order on chaos, a time when professional skill and human stamina will be put to full stretch. Mary Pringle regards the present peace as a small bonus and she is grateful for it – but it won't last.

'Buses,' she says as she walks into the office. It's a one-word code that condemns the entire public transport system. The departing Sister, Jean Boyd, gives her a sharp, sympathetic nod of the head.

'Shut the door and we'll have a puff,' Jean says, and digs a packet of Rothmans out of her handbag.

Elsewhere in Casualty the pace is just as leisurely. The evening has been quiet – two fractures, an overdose and a man with a particle of cigarette-lighter flint in his eye – and the waiting room is empty. There is time for talk.

Staff Nurse Glenda Cross has been out all day with her mother, doing some early Christmas shopping in the West End. She is in the plaster room with two off-duty student nurses, telling them about it. In the small-ops theatre opposite the plaster room, Dr Morrisey is bemoaning weightier matters to John Blake, a Senior Registrar who has just come on duty. Morrisey is an ageing General Practitioner who does part-time casualty work to keep his hand in. He works completely outside the hierarchical structure of Anderson General's medical staff, and thereby enjoys a freedom of movement and immunity from repercussion that has left John Blake, and others, with a chronic mild envy.

'I've seen seven in three years,' Morrisey is saying, and his hands wave to suggest an upsurge of something unpleasant. 'Five borderline nutters, and two who were just thick. But it's seven people dead who'd no need to be.'

What he is talking about is the horrendous death-rate from the abuse of a drug called Distalgesic. Earlier this evening Dr Morrisey has had to wash out the stomach of an eighteen-year-old youth who swallowed ten tablets in a deliberate suicide attempt. The boy is now in Intensive Care. Even if he survives the night, it will be several days before anyone can be sure he will live.

'It's a bloody scandal, John. The stuff ought to have been banned years ago.'

'People have tried.' John Blake is soft-voiced, and blessed with a face that always seems to express a lot more concern and sympathy than he actually feels. He is the cinema-goer's idea of a doctor – tall, blue-eyed, dark-haired with just enough grey at the temples. When John talks he has a habit of looking away every few seconds – a device that adds a lot to what one colleague has described as John's cosmetic profundity. In fact he is a good, plodding doctor, with a physical style that has probably helped to get him where he is by the relatively early age of thirty-two. 'Talking's done no good, though,' he tells Morrisey. 'Neither have petitions.'

'Publicity's what's wanted.' Morrisey has dug his hands into the pockets of his hairy tweed jacket. 'Get it out in the open where the laymen can see the facts and get the wind up them!'

John Blake is putting on his white coat, making a flourish of the job. It is a small disruption of the atmosphere, an attempt to get Dr Morrisey off his high horse. John Blake's reservations about Distalgesic are as profound as the older man's, but this isn't any kind of discussion. Morrisey's just having a moan and it's heading in the usual direction. Another five minutes' talking will have him squarely in the heartland, and he will be into his dirge for departed standards and balanced clinical judgment. John goes to the door and looks out into the passage. Morrisey comes after him.

'Did you see the piece the Birmingham Coroner did for the *Journal*?' He has sidled round to where John can see him again. 'A rundown on twenty-six Distalgesic fatalities in his area alone...'

'And it's not even a good pain-killer,' John says.

'Mm?' Morrisey's flow has been cut. He's looking anxious. 'What do you mean?'

'A couple of aspirin are just as effective. Better, in fact.'

'Where did you turn that up?'

'Oh, there've been a few studies,' John says. 'Federal Drug Administration, Mayo Clinic, Addiction Research Centre. I've got the copies and the fatality figures if you'd like to see them some time.'

Morrisey has turned away and is picking up his belongings from the table and sticking them in his pockets. 'Half our drug manufacturers are hooligans,' he mumbles, glancing at his

6

watch. 'Good God. I'd better be getting myself home.'

John Blake is pretty sure he wouldn't have deflated the old man deliberately, but he will remember the tactic. Morrisey is halfway through the door already, waving a sullen goodbye. No doctor, least of all a pedantic one, cares to be shown that his knowledge is incomplete, especially in an area of personal obsession.

By 9.15 all the late-shift staff have gone and the night-duty team are in control of Casualty. This weekend there are seven people on the team. Sister Pringle is assisted by Staff Nurse Cross and a second-year student, Sue McLean. John Blake's assistant is a Senior Houseman, Donald Ramsay, and an anaesthetist is on call. The seventh member is Phil Cowley, the porter. Phil hasn't shown up yet; he has domestic trouble and is usually late. Nobody complains, because they sympathise and they know Phil always works extra hard to make up for the time lost. The Casualty receptionist, Claire Doughty, is really on the administrative staff, but she pitches in with the others when it's necessary.

Directly opposite the ambulance bay doors, across the fifteen-foot open rectangular area, there is a passage with doors and curtained openings leading variously to the plaster room, a two-bed unit, a cubicle equipped to deal with eye injuries, eight separate bed units with bedside emergency equipment and a sluice room.

There are three operating theatres, one large and two small. The small theatres are designated 'clean' and 'dirty'. In the clean theatre minor surgical procedures, such as stitching and the removal of foreign bodies, are performed under aseptic conditions. The dirty theatre is used when it's known or suspected that a patient is carrying a high-grade bacterial infection. Boils are lanced in there, patients with retention of urine are catheterised, and suspect wounds will be cleaned, irrigated and stitched. The large theatre is heavily equipped to cope with major emergencies, clean or dirty.

Next door to the office is the Casualty X-ray department. This is normally manned by Casualty staff, and in addition to the fixed radiography unit with its screens and posture beds, there is a mobile unit that can be taken into theatres, the emergency area or the cubicles.

7

The largest room of all, thirty feet square, is simply called Emergency. Ten beds stand ready along one wall, to be used in the event of a major crisis – a multiple car crash maybe, or an industrial accident – and bed rolls that can be laid out on the floor are stacked on tables, trolleys and wheelchairs. Nearby stand metal cupboards stocked tight with drugs, dressing packs and emergency surgical equipment; piled in boxes by the door there's a supply of a recent innovation, inflatable splints.

Bolted to the walls at six strategic points through the department, there are lock-up cabinets stocked with emergency injection packs, ampoules of specialised drugs, sterile needles, sutures and catheters. The keys to these cabinets are carried by the doctors, the Sister and the Staff Nurse. Dangerous drugs such as insulin and morphine are kept in a cabinet in the office; only the Senior Casualty Officer and Sister have keys.

Casualty is large, but not large enough. Even in the first year it was opened, the department was sometimes found to be too small to accommodate the weekend accident frequency in the area. Emergency treatment figures have nearly doubled in three years, and at times the staff feel cramped. There are plans to extend Casualty, but there are no funds. The brightest prediction in administrative circles is that it will be four years before the extension can be built.

At 9.30 Staff Nurse Glenda Cross announces, at the top of her voice, that she's made coffee.

'Get it down you while there's a chance!'

Glenda is a short, attractive girl with curly black hair that almost conceals her paper cap. She has the confident movements of a person who is totally in control of herself; Glenda can occasionally lose her temper, but the abiding impression she gives is one of cheerful competence. Swirling the black coffee in the jug a couple of times, she pours a cup then takes it along to Sister Pringle, who is in the office having an impromptu tutorial with Nurse McLean.

'It's a bit too quiet out there for my liking,' Glenda says. 'Just like last Friday, remember?' They had seen two patients between 9 p.m. and 11.15, then they booked another fourteen in the following half hour. It had been close to 3 a.m. before anyone caught breath.

'Stop looking for omens,' Sister says. 'Or patterns.'

8

But there are some patterns to casualty work and they are observed in the procedures. On Friday night there are extra sets of stomach washout equipment to hand; on Saturday the telephone line between Casualty and the Antidote Centre will grow warm as the department makes request after request for information; there will be plenty of respirators and artificial airways within reach on Sunday – a bad day for heart attacks and bedsit suicide attempts.

Nobody knows what it would take to overtax the resources of Casualty. There have been dire emergencies that have filled cubicles, theatres and even the emergency room, but so far the teams have always coped and order has always prevailed. There are new statistics, however, to suggest that the day is fast approaching when casualty departments will have to be totally re-designed and much more heavily staffed if containment is to remain possible.

The hospital's monthly statistical records show no levelling-off in the numbers of patients being treated by Casualty. Street violence, drug abuse, drunken driving, domestic brutality and child battering are all on the upswing. So are suicide, alcoholism and neurosis. Anderson General serves an area which demonstrates every facet of what John Blake calls The New Mayhem. Emergency techniques are being refined all the time and the hardware has reached a point of dazzling sophistication. Even so, there are no longer any doctors or nurses prepared to say that, whatever the emergency, they will cope.

For the moment, though, it is quiet. Dr Blake and Dr Ramsay are in the plaster room, doing the *Telegraph* crossword. Claire Doughty is using the lull to catch up on filing. In the office Sister Pringle is questioning Sue McLean on her knowledge of blood collection by venepuncture, and Glenda Cross is in a cubicle feeding coffee and sympathy to the porter, Phil Cowley, who has come in looking a shade more doleful than usual.

'Bit of a bloody casualty yourself aren't you?' Glenda pats Phil's bald head and wrinkles her nose at him.

'A bit, yeah.' He smiles at Glenda and the deep creases on his face move in a way that makes him look sadder. Work is therapy for Phil. He never quite manages to forget his troubled private life, but the brightness of people like Glenda and the demands of the job divert him.

'Never mind.' Glenda tops up his cup and spoons in the sugar. 'There's cures for everything, if you've got the stomach. Right?'

He nods. 'Right.'

'And don't forget.' Glenda wags a finger. 'You're in very good hands.'

*   *   *

It's 9.50 p.m. An ambulance has brought in an elderly man and woman and a teenage girl. The old couple are shocked and semi-conscious, but the girl is alert and in obvious pain. Their clothes are soaked with blood and there is dirt and gravel in the wounds on their hands, arms and faces.

While Dr Ramsay makes a rapid initial examination of the patients, assisted by Sister Pringle, Glenda Cross and Sue McLean are clearing three cubicles. John Blake gets a sketchy history from the ambulance driver.

'They were at a bus stop halfway down Guild Road. A car veered out on an overtake fifty yards from them and went out of control. Wallop. Hit these three and tore up the barrier.'

'What about the driver?'

'Outside in the little wagon, waiting to be declared DOA.'

'Right.' John follows the ambulanceman out to the bay. They climb inside the one-berth ambulance and the attendant pulls back the blanket from the body.

'It won't strain your powers of diagnosis, will it, doc?'

The car driver is very smartly dressed. He is wearing a dark grey wool suit, a fawn broadcloth shirt and a deep red tie. From the lower margin of his nose to the hairline his face has been obliterated. Shards of white bone glint in the deep lateral trough that has been ploughed halfway through his skull. One eye hangs down by his ear, almost touching the rubber sheet he is lying on.

'He was still behind the wheel when we got to him,' the attendant says. 'Must have shot up at a helluva lick and smacked his head on the window margin.'

'That's exactly it,' John Blake says. The disrupted face is a typical deceleration wound. Travelling at a speed of even twenty miles an hour, the driver's effective weight at the moment of impact would be two tons. John has often seen cases where the forehead has put a huge bulge in the forward curve of the car's

10

roof. 'Do we know who he is?'

'Not yet. The police are on to it.'

John takes out his notebook and scribbles down a summary of findings he will have to put in his report.

> *Deep, ragged lacerations and incised wounds on face, with extensive fracturing and fragmentation of facial bones from mid-parietal region to lower zygomatic.*

John leans forward and presses the dead man's chest, then his abdomen. There are muffled scraping sounds, and air leaks from the throat in a soft groan.

'The steering wheel didn't do him much good.'

'The column was bent,' the attendant says.

> *Extensive fracturing of sternum, ribs and pelvis, with massive leakage of blood into thorax and abdominal cavity.*

'Comprehensively dead,' John says, and he signs the slip of paper declaring that the faceless man was dead on arrival at the hospital.

Back in Casualty, the girl has been transferred to the clean theatre. Her wounds are superficial, but she has severe pain in her chest. Sister Pringle has already cut away the patient's clothing and with Nurse McLean's help she is using swabs and forceps to pick the grit and other debris from the wounds. Dr Ramsay has made a tentative diagnosis of lung bruising: in impact accidents it is common for the victim to inhale sharply and hold on to the air, so that any sharp blow to the chest or back can cause the pressure to build suddenly around the lungs, tearing open the superficial blood vessels. Ramsay's diagnosis is supported by the fact that the girl has twice coughed up frothy, blood-stained mucus.

'No sign of impending coma, no shock syndrome, and she's alert and coherent,' Dr Ramsay tells John Blake when he comes back from the ambulance.

'No panic?'

Ramsay shakes his head. 'She's a touch hysterical, but that's the pain.'

Blake's question about panic relates to a persistent feature of serious chest injuries. If the aorta – the large vessel carrying blood from the heart to the rest of the body – is torn, the patient will always be extremely anxious and animated, with a clear terror of dying. The same thing happens with injuries to the heart – there are signs of panicky foreboding overlying the distress caused by the pain. The patient's eyes bulge with fear and he begs breathlessly for help, without knowing why it seems so urgent.

'And what about the other two?'

'The old man has a clean fracture of the right femur,' Ramsay says, 'and he's concussed. There are superficial wounds on the arms, legs and back, and there's a cut on his forehead that'll need stitching. The woman's got no serious injuries I can detect. But she's old...'

John Blake goes to the theatre to examine the girl. She is obviously attractive under the bruising and cuts and the smudgy discoloration of the dirt under her skin. She is wailing and calling out for her father while Sister Pringle works methodically with her swabs and forceps, making soothing sounds as she would to a baby.

The girl is called Wendy, and John Blake keeps murmuring the name, reassuringly, as his hands move over her rib cage, checking for any misalignment or area of special tenderness. It is customary, when examining the chest, to watch the patient's face, not the part being felt. That way, no undue suffering occurs if a cracked rib or torn muscle is touched. John Blake smiles and nods and murmurs to Wendy, but all the time he is watching her eyes.

There are no injuries other than the one that is causing Wendy all that pain. John Blake didn't expect to find any. His assistant, still in his mid-twenties, has a flair for casualty work and his talent for making a clear, unambiguous diagnosis is reinforced by two years of steady, exhausting work in three different casualty departments. But in the scheme of things, Dr Ramsay's word can't be taken for anything in potentially serious cases; John Blake is Senior Casualty Officer, so he must check.

The diagnosis of lung bruising is entered on Wendy's folder, and Sister Pringle makes arrangements to have her admitted to a surgical ward. There she will be given a pain-killing injection and her respiration will be carefully monitored. She is lucky that when she was hit by the car, she was not standing near a wall, a lamp post or a tree. Road accident victims who are thrown at speed against nearby, immovable objects can have arms and legs torn off, or sustain fractures to every major bone in the body, or, as often happens, have their brains literally dashed out against a wall. In this case the impact was dissipated by the girl's uninterrupted movement across a wide space.

'We'll get you something for your pain, Wendy,' John Blake tells her. 'You're going to be all right. Rest, that's all you need. Lots of rest. Your Dad will be here soon, the police are fetching him.'

Reassurance is a component in the pattern of care, and it must never be left out. Even those beyond the help of medicine must be reassured. In the training of doctors and nurses great emphasis is placed on the therapeutic value of removing fear and apprehension from the patient. The severity of shock can be reduced, dangerous tension can be eliminated in cases where there is internal bleeding, and patients will always co-operate more readily when they are made to believe that everything is under control. Reassurance is a clinical tool.

By now Casualty has developed what Sister Pringle calls a nice tickover. Everybody has something positive to do, and there is pace without pressure. The worst times are when the place has been quiet for an hour or two and a difficult emergency suddenly arises. Staff have to whip themselves and each other into top gear from a standing start, and that inevitably leads to friction and mistakes. For the moment, the tempo of activity is ideal.

On his way to look at the old man and woman, John Blake is hailed by the receptionist, Claire Doughty. She is standing by the swing door to the waiting room, waving a rolled-up case sheet. Privately John calls her Mother Hen, and at the moment she is doing a good hen impression moving jerkily from foot to foot, darting her eyes from the waiting room to John and back again.

'What is it?'

'In there.' Claire points with her paper truncheon.

In the waiting room there is one person, a young woman, sitting awkwardly on a plastic chair with her hand pressed to her forehead. She is enormously pregnant.

'She just walked in and sat down. Says she's not feeling well.'

John introduces himself to the woman. 'What's the trouble, then?'

'I was walking back to the house and I came over all sort of dizzy. Weak.' There's a distinct smell of beer on her breath. Her

13

coat and dress are grimy and rumpled. John recognises something; the cumulative evidence of the woman's unkempt hair, dishevelled clothing, grey-white skin and weathered, grubby hands points to one clear fact. Pregnant or not, she has been sleeping rough.

'Do you live near here?' John asks her.

She nods, avoiding his eyes.

'Where, exactly?'

'Over that way.' She points at the door.

Claire Doughty is behind her window, getting a blank case folder together. She is entitled to ask a whole barrage of questions in the interests of proper documentation, and John Blake knows they will fluster this patient. To avoid that, he sits down beside her to elicit as many facts as he can, so that he can fill in the questionnaire himself.

'Can I have your address for the record, Mrs ah...'

The girl blinks at him. Close up, she looks younger than John had supposed her to be. 'Lawson,' she says. 'It's Miss.'

'First name?'

'Alice.'

John has run a check on her general health already. Her dry, spiky hair and cracked, spoon-shaped nails signal iron-deficiency anaemia. That's serious enough, especially in a pregnant woman; other signs – redness around the eyes, swollen ankles and a difficulty with her speech that might be caused by a swollen tongue – indicate that the condition could be well established.

'Do you have a proper address?' John asks the question bluntly, to reduce the chance of the girl lying to him.

'I'm at The Rock...'

John nods calmly, letting her see that he isn't there to moralise, but simply to get the story straight. The Rock is a group of derelict warehouses half a mile from Anderson General. It is home for transient winos, meths drinkers, vagrants and others who have slipped through the net of the welfare state.

'Do you have anybody close, Alice? A boyfriend, maybe...'

She shakes her head firmly.

'I see. How long have you been at The Rock?'

She shrugs and folds her hands across her swollen belly. 'A month or so.'

14

'Were you at home before that?'

'Yeah.' Her face grows wary suddenly. 'I don't want nobody getting in touch with them.'

Again, John shows her calm acceptance. 'Fair enough. Now how long have you been pregnant?'

'I'm not sure.'

'But you must have some idea.'

It is disheartening to watch her struggle with the question. In a life lived without the normal awareness of margins like weeks and months, pinpointing a duration can be desperately hard.

'Never mind,' John says, 'we'll find that out later. Tell me about what happened tonight, when you felt yourself going weak.'

'Well, like I said, I just felt myself getting, I dunno, *weak* like.'

John has reached his own conclusion. She is a tough little character, the independence shows in the tautness of her mouth and the stubborn angle of her chin. She has gone it alone for reasons John doesn't yet know but has probably heard before. Now illness and the advancement of the pregnancy have forced her to surrender to help. And this is her way of doing it.

'I think we should have a look at you, Alice, then if you don't mind, we'll get you into a warm bed for the night.'

She manages to look reluctant before she agrees. John tells Claire Doughty that he will fill in the case questionnaire himself, then he gets hold of Sister Pringle and tells her he wants Alice Lawson put into a cubicle and undressed. Sister delegates the order to Nurse McLean with a jerk of the head.

Phil Cowley is wheeling Wendy away to Women's Surgical as John Blake goes back to check on the old couple. Dr Ramsay has already put a temporary, immobilising splint on the old man's broken leg. A plaster cast will be made when the X-rays have been taken. Oxygen and warm blankets have reduced the shock.

'I'll leave him to you,' John tells his assistant. 'Give it another half hour, to be sure there's no repercussion from the shock, then let him have a shot of morphine. Staff Nurse can line up the X-rays in the meantime.'

In the next cubicle the old woman is lying very still; she looks deathly pale. It has been established by now that she and the other patient are, as was suspected, married to each other. Relatives have been contacted by the police, but in the meantime there is just the desolate sadness of it all; two old people who have weathered a long life together and have come to this. Neither one will ever be the same. The disruptions of trauma run deep in the elderly and they make permanent changes. For this woman, John thinks, life will certainly be a lot shorter than it would have been.

John is checking her dressings when she opens her eyes. They are pale, flat blue discs and John keeps watching them, performing the double act of diagnosis and reassurance. She blinks once and then the eyes clench shut for a second. There is severe pain somewhere.

John puts his mouth close to the woman's ear. 'Where does it hurt?'

Her tongue appears between bruised lips, moistening them. 'Hand,' she croaks.

For a moment he's baffled. The larger injuries would normally mask the discomfort of the smaller ones on her hands. When he touches the right hand gently she winces and cries out. John sees it at once. The nail of the middle finger is deep crimson. It could easily be mistaken for an old injury, but brushing the fingertip lightly he can feel the tension and the abnormal heat. The patient has suffered a fracture of the terminal bone of the finger, and a welling of blood has collected beneath the nail. It's called a subungual haematoma, and it is always excruciatingly painful.

John calls for Staff Nurse Cross and tells her to bring him a spirit burner, forceps and a paper clip.

'Sounds like you're going to do a conjuring trick,' she says.

'I am, sort of.'

The reduction of pain is of primary importance with the older patient, and in America a number of swift expedients have been developed by people specialising in emergency work. John Blake keeps in close touch with the American developments and he puts them into practice whenever he can. The small operation he is about to perform is still relatively new to doctors in the United Kingdom.

When Glenda Cross comes back to the cubicle John beckons her inside. 'Stand there,' he says, 'and learn something.'

He lights the burner and proceeds to straighten out the paper clip for half its length. He then gently eases the old woman's hand forward, making her moan.

16

'You won't feel a thing,' he promises. 'And I guarantee the pain will go away.'

Bemused, Glenda Cross watches Dr Blake grip the straight length of paper clip in the forceps and hold the end in the flame of the burner. While he is doing that, he changes his position so that the patient won't be able to see what his next moves are.

'You know all that stuff about evacuating haematomas with drills?' he murmurs to Glenda.

'Puts my teeth on edge,' she says.

'Unless it's performed very carefully, it can do more damage than it sorts out. This way, the field's aseptic, the job's quick, and there's no danger of going too deep.' John removes the red-hot paper clip from the flame and lowers the end firmly on to the old lady's fingernail. She doesn't flinch. There is some smoke as the wire burns through the nail; John draws his hand away smartly. Blood spills through the neat hole and the patient gives out a sigh.

'Better?' John asks her, and she nods.

'Very slick,' Glenda says as she wraps a gauze pad around the finger. 'What book was that in, then?'

'*Surgery on Ten Cents a Day* if I remember rightly. Now be careful with that finger. It's fractured. Can you handle it for me?'

'Yes. Bind in the position of function, cushion, aluminium splint. Right?'

'Right.' John blows out the burner and steps outside the cubicle. Nurse McLean comes forward to tell him the Lawson girl is ready.

'Good. Stay with me while I examine her, then get on to Gynaecology and see if they can find her a bed.'

Alice Lawson is lying flat on an examination bed with a sheet over her. She looks apprehensive as John walks in.

'This won't take long,' he assures her. 'Nurse will pinch a drop or two of your blood so we can run some tests, and I'll try and figure out just how long it'll be before your baby puts in an appearance.' He draws the sheet back and, to cover Alice's embarrassment, says, 'What do you want, a boy or a girl?'

'Don't mind, so long as it ain't a Toby jug.'

Ten minutes in hospital has brightened her. John smiles as he spreads his hands over the high, firm mound of her belly. The last time he heard a wisecrack answer to that question, it came

17

from his own wife. 'Boy or a girl?' she said, staring at him deadpan. 'Well of *course* I want a boy or a girl.'

The baby feels fine, a paradox John has grown accustomed to. The girl is undernourished, ill, and she has probably done nothing to protect herself or the foetus from the thousand-odd dangers peculiar to pregnant women. Yet the baby appears to be normal. Other women can take controlled iron therapy, go on special diets, lay off smoking and drinking and think nothing but beautiful thoughts but still land in the kind of trouble it takes a whole gynaecology team to clear up.

'Feels fine,' John murmurs to Alice. From her size she is certainly over six months, so he digs out his tape measure. Nurse McLean watches, as mystified as Staff Nurse Cross was a few minutes ago. John runs the tape down over Alice's lower abdomen, stretching it taut over her bump. He peers at the figures on the tape for a second, then stares at the wall, calculating.

'All right, is it?' Alice asks.

He turns to her, nodding. 'Eight months, approximately. That'll give us time to feed you up and put you right. If you'll let us,' he adds, in deference to her independent nature.

Later, when Nurse McLean has taken a sample of Alice's blood and labelled it for the laboratory, she asks John Blake how he estimated the duration of the pregnancy.

'We were taught a different way,' she tells him. 'And it's complicated. That looked pretty simple.'

'When you know how,' John says airily. 'I didn't pick this stuff up without a lot of sweat, you know.'

'I was just curious...' Sue has a childlike voice that some people find irritating, others engaging. John Blake likes her and her voice, just as much as he dislikes the medical convention that insists doctors should stay aloof and try to give nurses the impression they have special powers.

'If you're sure the patient's gone past the six months' stage,' he tells Sue, 'you measure the distance between the fundus of the uterus to the top edge of the pubic bone, in centimetres, then divide the answer by three-point-five. That gives you the number of months.' He winks. 'Smart, eh? It's called McDonald's rule.'

Sue McLean goes off to telephone Gynaecology looking as if

she's been given a present. John goes to the waiting room to write out Alice Lawson's case sheet. The waiting room is empty.

'We might have a quiet night,' John says to Claire Doughty.

'I hope so.' She reads the name he is entering on the sheet. 'Bit of a scruff that one, isn't she?'

'She's all right,' John says. 'Not much going for her, but she's held herself together.'

Claire sniffs. She does that a lot. She has a good heart and she can work as hard as anyone on the team, but her views on the lower orders have put John Blake's back up more than once. 'There was a smell of drink off her, Doctor. Did you notice that?'

'Yes, I noticed.' He looks up from the paperwork. 'I've noticed it before with people in Miss Lawson's position.'

'It's their solace,' Claire sighs.

'Maybe; I don't know. What I think is that she went down to the pub and had one or two, and she got thinking. Drink isn't always an escape, you know. A couple of jars can settle the mind and make a person face up to reality. For all we know, the drink gave her the courage to come in here.'

Claire goes silent. It isn't likely that the gentle reproof in John's tone or the plausibility of his theory have done anything to change her opinion of Alice Lawson. Claire has often said she can weigh up a person quickly, and when she forms an opinion, she sticks to it. John watches her for a moment, tight-lipped as she lays out her orderly stacks of file cards, then he gets on with writing the report.

Glenda Cross has made more coffee. When Sister Pringle points out that it's less than an hour since the last lot, Glenda tells her she's fighting off sleep.

'I'll drop in my tracks if I don't keep pumping caffeine into myself.'

They are in the sluice, where Glenda usually makes coffee. She pours two cups then puts down the pot and hoists herself on to the edge of the worktop. At every opportunity, a Casualty nurse will get her feet off the ground, even if it's only for a few seconds.

'It's been a lousy day,' Glenda says, and she swings her legs disconsolately.

'I thought you went Christmas shopping?'

'I did. I should have stayed in bed.' Glenda stares reflectively at the far wall. 'Twelve-fifty for a bottle of aftershave. It smells terrible, too. Like bottled joss sticks.' She droops the corners of her mouth and clutches her stomach, aping nausea. 'Mum says it's the old man's favourite. He's got no taste in ties, either.'

'I can't stand the smell of scent on a man,' Sister Pringle says. 'Don't care for it much on women, come to that.'

'My Barclaycard's up to the hilt,' Glenda sighs. 'My feet are giving me gyp, and I haven't been to bed all day. I'll be knackered by two o'clock.' She sniffs the aftershave on the back of her hand, the residue of one blast from the Boots tester that has resisted three applications of soap and water. 'Christmas,' she says, and sounds just like Sister Pringle did earlier, when she said 'buses'.

Sue McLean comes in and tells Sister there's a call for her. When Sister Pringle has gone, Glenda pours Sue a cup of coffee and has a second one for herself.

'You know the pregnant girl, Lawson?' Sue says. 'Dr Blake did something with her that was really clever...'

'Don't tell me,' Glenda says flatly, massaging her ankle. 'He delivered the baby with two rubber bands and a pipe cleaner.'

Casualty is slowing down again. The old man's leg has been plastered and soon he will be taken to Men's Surgical. The old lady is in a ward already. Soon Alice Lawson will be bedded down in Gynaecology and Sue McLean will have only one cubicle and the plaster room to straighten out. Sister Pringle is filling up her admissions register in the office and John Blake has practically finished making out the preliminary record on Alice Lawson. Dr Ramsay is washing plaster off his hands. A lull is beginning to settle on the department. Nobody is hurrying. Glenda Cross whistles softly as she washes the coffee cups. In the waiting room, Claire Doughty is pinning up a new Cancer Fund poster.

The general alert bell goes off. It's a sudden, jarring clangour that startles Phil Cowley so badly that he drops the spanner he's been using to tighten the gauge on a gas cylinder. Glenda Cross comes running with her hands still dripping water, and nearly collides with Sue McLean, who's coming charging out of the plaster room. The bell is a summons to all Casualty personnel and within the minute they are standing outside the office, asking each other what's up.

Senior Nursing Officer Parker arrives seconds after the bell stops. The rules require her to take charge of the nursing team in the event of a major emergency. She is a pneumatic, motherly looking woman who nevertheless has a fearsome reputation. During the war, the joke runs, she was booted out of the Gestapo for cruelty.

'Three ambulances are on the way,' she announces. 'So far as we can determine, they're full of burns victims. I want the Emergency room set up and all three theatres put on standby. We'll have three more doctors and half a dozen extra nursing staff, in addition to myself.'

She turns and looks pointedly at Sister Pringle, who immediately starts giving orders to her staff. Glenda Cross is to oversee the preparations in Emergency and the porter will help Sue McLean to lay out burns packs. Sister, together with Miss Parker, will see to getting the theatres ready, helped by the extra nurses when they show up. The doctors, it is tacitly understood, will be deployed by John Blake.

'Just my sodding luck,' Donald Ramsay mutters to his chief. 'Burns. If there's one thing I can't stand . . .'

'It's haemorrhoid operations with me,' John Blake says. 'I can't watch one. Not even on film.'

They go to the gowning and scrub-up area, behind the sluice, where packs of sterile gloves are stored. Infection is a massive hazard with burns patients, and gloves will have to be changed each time a doctor goes from one open-wound case to another. As they are bursting open the cardboard containers, Sister Pringle comes in.

'We think they're petrol burns,' she says. 'It's a petroleum store that's caught fire, anyway.'

John shrugs. 'Burns are burns. It's just a case of coping, Sister. They're never too predictable.' All burns, except for those caused by certain chemicals, are treated on the basis of their severity, not their cause.

'Bang goes breakfast,' Dr Ramsay mutters. 'I can't even glance at a full-depth burn without wanting to throw up. I'd sooner face a busload of sawmill emergencies. I can cope with blood.'

Someone calls Sister and she hurries off in the direction of the office. She is back again a minute later.

'The police just phoned,' she tells John Blake. 'That place the

21

ambulances are coming from – there's been another explosion. They think maybe fifteen or sixteen more people have been injured.'

'Aw, Christ,' Donald Ramsay groans.

*　　*　　*

At 10.45 p.m. the first nine burns cases come in. Four are gravely serious.

'These men to Emergency! The others in cubicles One to Five!' Miss Parker stands in the area by the ambulance bay waving her arms as she calls out her orders. 'Staff Nurse Cross and Nurse McLean, take charge in the cubicles. I'll send three or four more nurses to help as soon as I can. Dr Darblay from Men's Surgical will be along shortly.'

Glenda Cross stamps off mumbling to the cubicles with Sue McLean behind her. The resentment is automatic and shows itself in the way Glenda jerks back cubicle curtains and strips the covers off beds. Miss Parker's presence is a disruption. A Casualty team is close-knit, its members develop a special kinship from being the most bedevilled unit in the hospital, and intruders, especially those with authority, always upset the team's underlying rhythm.

'We've got four doors! Use them!' Trolleys have been coming through a double-door opening in single file. Miss Parker is unbolting the other doors and simultaneously yelling at the ambulancemen. 'Through here, then! Hurry it up!'

The four serious cases are already in Emergency. They have been transferred to wheeled beds set in a row along the left wall. John Blake is cutting the clothing from a man with deep burning on his chest, face, arms and legs.

'Check his airway, Sister.'

The man is making gurgling sounds through the plastic S tube that has been inserted to keep his throat clear for the passage of air. Sister Pringle unhooks a suction probe from the emergency unit by the bedside and puts the end in the mouthpiece. She draws out some mucus and the man starts to breathe more easily.

'Keep an eye on it,' John says. 'There's a respiratory compromise of some kind. I'll get round to it when I can.'

Three nurses requisitioned by Miss Parker arrive and Sister

22

Pringle appoints one to assist Dr Ramsay with a man whose entire back has been burned. The other nurses begin helping Sister to remove the clothes from the remaining two serious cases. Both have multiple burns on their arms and legs.

'Some mess, this,' John Blake murmurs. His patient's hair has been scorched to stubble and the tissues of his face have been stiffened. He appears to be grinning. As John is removing the shirt, strips of slimy, detached skin come with it. The man groans, but not from any additional pain John Blake is causing him. The surface of a full-depth burn is insensitive, even to a pinprick.

At the fourth bed Donald Ramsay is having trouble staying objective. His patient is lying flat on his stomach with his head turned on one side, breathing with the aid of a ventilating machine. Ramsay and the nurse have removed most of the charred clothing from the man's back, revealing a stiff, toughened, dark brown area of burning that extends from the shoulders to the buttocks.

'Ten per cent coverage, full-depth,' Ramsay announces. The early estimation of the area and depth of burning is important, as it provides a guide to the amount of fluid replacement that will be necessary.

'Right, Nurse,' Donald Ramsay sighs. 'Stage two.'

Above all else, above even the emotional reaction he has to serious burning, it's the smell that bothers Ramsay. It goes beyond a mere odour, and although the thing it resembles most is burnt rubber, there is another element, a pungency that evokes a memory in the young doctor. It recalls something unpleasant from childhood, but he can't pin down what it was. As he prepares to administer intravenous fluid to the patient, the smell rises again, a fierce wave caused by the simple movement of one of the patient's arms as the nurse lifts it to remove a fragment of burnt clothing. Ramsay clamps his mouth tight and tries to keep his breathing shallow.

Dr Roarke arrives and without prompting starts to help with the leg and abdomen cases. Roarke is a Registrar in Paediatrics, a tall, thin man with the easygoing patience typical of people who have to work with sick children.

'They've diverted the other ambulances to St Bride's,' he tells John Blake. 'Our Miss Parker isn't without compassion, after all. She got on the blower and told the powers we've too much to cope with.'

'She's probably got a grudge against somebody over at Bride's,' John says. 'Thank God she swung it, anyway.' He glances along the row of beds and smiles at Donald Ramsay, whose face has become a picture of relieved tension.

In John Blake's opinion, the marked improvement in working pace, and the enhanced quality of the work over the next few minutes, has nothing to do with the ordinary response of people who are told they will have less to do. Rather, John believes, the Casualty staff are responding to the removal of a threat, a threat he calls fragmentation. To be faced with making decisions and taking action that will seriously affect one human life is strain enough; when a doctor or a nurse knows that the strain will go on for hours, involving dozens of endangered lives, the stress leads to a temporary breaking-up of the personality. People begin doing things that are untypical, they make bad mistakes and suffer lapses of memory, and it happens because they are preoccupied with the coming log-jam. They know their skills will be hampered, and the knowledge alone is enough to create dangerous inefficiency. John has plans to develop the subject into a paper, if he ever finds the time.

Within ten minutes of the burns patients arriving in the Emergency room, the first three stages of emergency treatment have been carried out. Their airways have been checked and reinforced. Following the removal of obstructive clothing, catheters have been inserted into the shoulders of two men and the legs of the two others, to permit the passing of a liquid called Ringer's Solution into their bloodstreams; in addition to replacing lost body fluid, the solution contains vital salts – sodium, potassium, calcium and chloride – that are destroyed or diminished in burning accidents. The third procedure has been to draw off blood from each patient for typing, cross-matching, a corpuscle count and chemical-level checks.

Out in the cubicles, things are further ahead. Glenda Cross and Sue McLean, helped by four nurses called in from the wards, have already passed stage four – anti-tetanus injections – and are administering pain-killing drugs. Their five patients have only superficial burns on arms, legs and hands, but unlike the four men in Emergency, none of them has suffered surgical shock and its attendant semi-consciousness, so they are harder to handle.

One man has twice threatened to hit Glenda Cross. He has a large burn on his upper right arm that is obviously causing him a lot of pain, but the major spur to his anger, Glenda believes, is drink. From the coming and going of police in the department over the past ten minutes, Glenda has learned that this patient is under suspicion of having caused the fire. He was seen smoking a cigarette five minutes before the outbreak, and he has a record of rule-abuse and surreptitious on-the-job drinking. The information hasn't improved Glenda's shallow sympathy for him, and when he threatens her a third time, while she's trying to get a needle into his left arm, Glenda steps back and delivers an ultimatum.

'Just you shut it, bugger-lugs!' She snatches up a steel bedpan and waves it at him. 'Lift one finger to me and I'll stiffen you with this!' She approaches the bed again, still brandishing the bedpan. 'You'll lie quiet and do what you're told!'

In one agonising flash Glenda knows she has made a bad mistake. She's applied too much shove. The big man in the bed is the kind who responds best to some pleading. He pushes himself up on his elbows, wincing at the pain it causes him. His raw-edged eyes are full of the certainty of his next move.

'Now I've warned you . . .' Glenda backs as he comes down the bed at her.

'Fucking mare!' One big hand swings in a scything arc an inch from Glenda's nose. Up on his knees, the man tries again and strikes Glenda's shoulder. She falls back against the locker, yelling.

'Leave it out, George!' a man shouts from one of the other cubicles.

Dr Darblay, arriving late from an emergency on his ward, pokes his head into the cubicle and blinks at the tableau. Glenda is cowering in the corner with the bedpan at her feet. George is kneeling on the edge of the bed, aiming a punch at her. Darblay, a permanently apologetic-looking Indian, steps to the bottom of the bed and raps the rail with his stethoscope. 'Stop this, now.'

George takes one look and then re-directs his fist, swinging it sideways. The doctor is small and nimble and he dances aside, grabbing George's arm at the same time. One sharp pull has

George on the floor with a bump.

'Stinking wog bastard!'

Fright has put sudden speed into Glenda. She is across the bed and kneeling on George's chest a second after Dr Darblay has pinned the big man's arms to the floor.

'I'll do the sodding pair of you! Gerroff me!' George's struggling is useless and it only causes him more pain, but he's not the kind to acknowledge defeat. He goes on jerking and threatening until the cubicle is full of people, all intent on suppressing him.

It takes less than a minute to get George back into the bed, and a few more seconds for a big Scots police constable to warn him into silence.

'You're in enough trouble as it is, pal. Just settle yer arse and wait for the CID to land on you. If there's a squeak out of this cubicle I'll be back and put a dull one on you.'

Glenda Cross goes to Reception, where Claire Doughty makes an entry in the red book labelled ASSAULTS ON STAFF. The book has 200 pages, each with space for three or four entries; it was started twelve weeks ago, and already Claire is writing on page sixteen.

'It was my own fault,' Glenda tells Claire. 'Handled him wrong.' She rubs her bruised shoulder and glumly examines the tear in the knee of her tights. 'We should have realised he was that kind of bloke and shoved some Valium in his backside the minute he came in.'

By 11.15 the serious cases in Emergency are almost ready to be transferred. Each man has been given intravenous morphine to suppress the pain, and bladder catheters have been inserted so that the urine output can be collected and measured. The wounds have been washed with a mild soap solution and the dead and loosened skin has been cut away.

In the case of the man with the burned chest, John Blake has had to perform an emergency operation called an escharotomy. It was discovered that the taut, inflexible skin of the chest was clamping the patient's rib cage and seriously interfering with his breathing. The corrective operation was simple and took seconds to perform. John inserted the point of a knife through the skin and underlying tissue just below the patient's left armpit and drew the blade down towards the waist, making a long cut that

26

released the pressure on the ribs immediately. Because of the insensitivity of the burn, no anaesthetic was needed. Bleeding was no problem either, since the blood supply in a deep burn is minimal.

All four men are now on ventilating machines and two of them – the patient with chest wounds and the man whose back is burned – will go straight to Intensive Care. After supervising the dressings – layers of fine gauze impregnated with antibacterial cream – John Blake goes to the office and discusses progress with Senior Nursing Officer Parker.

'Three of them are stable enough,' he tells her, 'but the chap with the burnt back is shaky. He coughed up some carbon particles and his blood pressure's completely haywire. I've alerted the duty surgeon in Intensive Care; he might have to do a tracheostomy.'

Miss Parker sits with hands folded on the desk, nodding. In the old days, when women of her rank were called Assistant Matrons, she would have required a written report from the Senior Casualty Officer. Now, an informal passing-on of information is enough.

'The other five are straightforward,' Miss Parker says. 'Two of them will be going home, one we'll keep overnight, and the fifth one's being taken into custody by the police as soon as we've finished patching him up.'

'Panic over,' John Blake says. 'Heartfelt thanks, incidentally, for diverting the other wagons.'

Signs of gratitude make Miss Parker gruff. She stands up and moves around the desk. 'St Bride's has a properly equipped burns unit,' she says. She picks up her cloak and swings it over her shoulders. 'When I saw there were such serious cases among the injured, I thought it was best to keep numbers as low as possible in here.' At the office door she pauses. 'I mustn't take credit for too much. I asked for only two ambulances to be diverted. It was someone else's decision to divert them all. Next time, I'm sure we won't be so fortunate, Doctor.' Miss Parker pauses by the door for a second to let the gloomy prediction sink in, then she makes a fractional nod that serves as a farewell and strides off towards the ambulance bay.

Donald Ramsay comes across from Emergency, drying his hands on a paper towel. He tells John Blake that the patients they have worked on are being moved now by the porters.

'You look like you could use a drink,' John observes.

Ramsay shakes his head. 'I couldn't tackle anything that would go near my stomach.' He looks genuinely ill. His lips are dry and pale and there are shadows under his eyes. 'I'll have to put in some work on my objectivity.'

'Nonsense.'

John Blake goes back into the office and Ramsay follows him. They sit down and Ramsay lights a cigarette.

'I was feeling wórse than I looked in there, you know,' Ramsay says. 'Queasy, like a kid at his first dissection.' He sends a stream of smoke towards the ceiling. 'Not entirely professional, is it?'

'Think of it as a bonus,' John Blake says.

Ramsay looks at him. After a couple of seconds he smiles. 'Like in those inspirational articles, you mean? Tracts like *Cancer Can Be a Blessing* and *How My Weak Bladder Taught Me to Pray.*'

'I'm serious. You feel concern when you're handling burns, don't you?'

'Enough to sicken me, yes.'

'Well then, that's a very human response to the most devastating accident that can happen to anybody,' John says. 'At the risk of making you dimple prettily, I'd say you're steadily gaining a high degree of medical expertise at no expense to your humanity.'

Ramsay smiles again. 'You've got a silver tongue, Squire. I'd love to believe all that.'

There is a single tap on the door and Sister Pringle comes in. 'There's a cardiac case on the way,' she says. 'It's a man in his fifties, he collapsed in a pub. Sister Young from Cardiac Care went out with the ambulance ten minutes ago.' As the doctors are getting to their feet, she adds, 'And the police are bringing in a rape case.'

On his way to the Emergency room to pick up the cardiac box, John Blake sees Glenda Cross heading for the cubicle area, carrying a sterile catheter pack. She rolls her eyes as she goes past. 'I've got a bladder-daddy,' she mutters.

Glenda's patient is lying in a cubicle, wearing a hospital gown and looking deeply anxious. He is an old man, as the so-called bladder-daddies usually area, and he's arrived at Casualty at an

28

hour when it's common for people with his disorder to seek medical attention.

Nobody really knows why old men's prostate glands swell, but they frequently do, and the swelling constricts the opening of the bladder. The nerves within the urinary tracts of the elderly are less sensitive than other people's, so an old man may go all day without feeling the need to pass urine. At the end of the day, a couple of pints of beer can create enough pressure to alert him, but when he tries to pass water he can't. As the build-up gets worse so does the distress. Even so, shyness will keep a lot of men away from the hospital until they are in virtual agony. Shyness is not this patient's reason for delaying, however. In his entire life he has only seen a doctor twice; he distrusts medicine and its practitioners, and if there had been any alternative to coming to Casualty, he would have taken it.

'Soon have you fixed now, Mr Haddow,' Glenda says cheerfully when she comes into the cubicle.

'What're you going to do?' He props himself on an elbow, eyeing the catheter emerging from its wrapper as if it's a reptile. Glenda's rubber gloves, squeaking about their business, are doing nothing to reassure him.

'We're going to clear the passage through to your bladder and get rid of that ostrich egg you've got on your belly.'

Mr Haddow looks at the catheter again and lies down, sighing.

Sue McLean comes in with an enamel jug and puts it down beside the bed. She smiles at Mr Haddow, who begins to look more apprehensive than ever.

'It needs two of you, does it?'

Glenda nods. 'Makes for a tidier job,' she says.

For a minute Mr Haddow watches Glenda smoothing the lubricant along the catheter. When she turns to him with the nozzle gripped between her finger and thumb, he puts up a hand to restrain her.

'Look love...' He swallows hard and points at the catheter. 'Can't I take the tablet?'

Glenda frowns at Sue McLean, then at Mr Haddow. 'What tablet?'

'I was told there's a tablet you take. It makes the water come away...'

'Oh, I get you. Yes, there is a tablet like that, but it wouldn't

29

help.' The tablet Mr Haddow is referring to is a diuretic, often called a water pill, which stimulates the production of urine by the kidneys. 'It would just top-up your bladder with more water.'

Apprehension and discomfort are nudging for control of Mr Haddow's face. 'Will it hurt?'

Glenda smiles and pats his arm. 'The state you're in now,' she says, 'this is going to make you feel like you've died and gone to heaven.'

It takes less than two minutes. When it's over the jug is half full and Mr Haddow is lying perfectly still with his hands crossed on his stomach.

'How are we feeling then?' Glenda asks him.

'Just like you said, dead and gone and one of the angels.' He grins at Glenda and grasps her wrist. He shakes it playfully, like a man fussing a favourite grandchild. 'I'll tell you something, love.'

'What's that, Mr Haddow?'

'That was the best leak I've had since I pissed in a German trench at Tripoli.'

* * *

Terry Doyle is wheeled into Casualty, unconscious, at 11.30 p.m. Sister Young walks alongside the trolley with her hand clasped over the patient's.

'He looks bad,' Phil Cowley murmurs as he turns the trolley smoothly towards the door of the Emergency room.

Sister Young nods. 'Bad enough,' she says. She moves her fingers to the patient's wrist, feeling the weak, erratic pulse.

They are less than ten feet from the Emergency room when Terry goes into the first stages of cardiac arrest. He begins choking and his face turns deep blue. Phil Cowley runs across and hits the cardiac button by the office door. It sets off a squealing electronic signal that alerts any medical staff within reach.

John Blake and Sister Pringle are on the scene within seconds. John has the cardiac box. It is crammed with the equipment and the drugs that provide the most effective life supports for a patient with a heart emergency, until he can be transferred to the more elaborate protection of a Cardiac Care Unit.

'How long has he been like this?' John asks Sister Young.

'Less than a minute,' she tells him. She has pulled the short plastic airway from Terry Doyle's mouth and is inserting a longer one.

'Give him four good blasts,' John says. He hooks his stethoscope to his ears and puts the end on Terry's chest.

Sister Young has pinched Terry's nostrils shut and is blowing sharply into the airway. As she does this she watches his chest from the corner of her eye, to see how effectively the mouth-to-mouth technique is inflating his lungs.

'It's still moving,' John says. He has heard the heart clearly, giving off the irregular, thudding signal of ventricular fibrillation; the lower chambers of the heart are contracting rapidly and out of beat, and if the condition isn't controlled quickly the pump will fail. It takes only four minutes from the time a human heart stops beating for the disastrous spread of brain damage to begin.

Sister Pringle has opened the cardiac box and is already undoing the roll of pre-packed injectible drugs. The roll is designed for an extreme cardiac emergency. It contains a variety of drugs that can be administered as a cocktail, one after the other, until an effective one is found. Inexperienced doctors can confidently inject the drugs in any order, because no harmful combination is possible.

'Xylocard, four mils,' John murmurs. Sister Pringle pulls out the appropriate syringe and hands it to him. John pushes the needle deep into the muscle of Terry's upper arm and presses the plunger smoothly until the complete dose has been administered. The drug is a local anaesthetic that John has found to be powerfully effective in acute, sudden heart attacks like the one Terry has suffered. It settles the rhythm of the fluttering heart and can, occasionally, even restore a normal beat.

'He's had ten thousand units of heparin,' Sister Young tells John. 'The spasm was bad when we got to him, so I thought it was just as well.'

'In two doses?'

'Yes.'

Nurses specialising in cardiac work are invariably a great comfort to Casualty Officers. They have regular, prolonged contact with a limited number of ailments and their instincts are consequently sharp and accurate.

'Looks like it kept him going, Sister,' John murmurs as he starts monitoring Terry's heart again.

Heparin, which is a substance that occurs naturally in the body, has the prompt effect of reducing the blood's ability to clot. Sister Young saw the clear signs of coronary thrombosis when she looked at Terry Doyle, so her first step was to attack the blockage that was threatening his life. But she was properly cautious. A less experienced nurse or doctor might have administered the whole dose of heparin at once, in order to shift the clot with maximum speed; that course of action could be very effective, but it could also cause massive internal bleeding.

Terry groans and the muscles at his neck tighten. His heart is still struggling. The drug John injected has had some effect, but the signs are that the dangerous fibrillation is persisting.

Sister Young has been checking Terry's pulse. 'It's irregular and feeble,' she says. She is holding up Terry's eyelids and examining the pupils while John Blake continues to listen to the heart.

John straightens suddenly. 'Get him on the floor!' he yells, reaching forward and grasping the patient round the waist. 'He's arrested!'

The two Sisters, the porter and Dr Blake lift Terry off the trolley and lay him flat on the floor. John throws his stethoscope to Sister Pringle and kneels beside Terry.

'Phil, wheel over the shock box!'

John clenches his right fist and delivers a hard punch to Terry's chest. Opposite John, Sister Young is on her knees, feeling for the carotid pulse at Terry's neck.

Phil Cowley has brought across the trolley with the electric heart stimulation equipment on it. He plugs it into the wallpoint beside John and stands back.

'Anything?' John asks. Sister Young shakes her head. John punches Terry two more times, then he puts his left palm flat on the chest and with stiffened arms he starts to press downwards with the right hand on top of the left, making his movements sharp and rhythmic. The hard floor offers solid resistance and the chest compresses deeply each time John thrusts against it. His fingertips are raised clear of the area, so that all the pressure is directed right over Terry's heart.

'It's started again,' Sister Young says.

John nods. 'It's time to consolidate, I think.'

Sister Pringle is unhooking the paddles from the defibrillation machine. When John Blake looks up she hands them to him.

'Right. Everybody well back.' John puts one paddle under Terry's right collarbone and the other just below his left breast.

Sister Pringle is standing by the control unit, waiting for John's instructions.

'Four hundred watt-seconds,' John says. When Sister adjusts the dial and nods to him, he presses the discharge button on the back of one of the paddles. Terry arches up off the floor as the current surges through his chest. John lays down the paddles and reaches up to Sister Pringle for his stethoscope. He listens to the heart for a couple of seconds, then picks up the paddles again. He puts one more jolt of electricity through Terry, whose chest lifts even more violently this time and slams back against the floor. John listens. 'That's it,' he says.

Terry is put back on the trolley with his heart beating almost normally. The electric current momentarily stunned the nerve bundles in the heart, eliminating their disruptive tendency to act independently.

A mobile respirator is wheeled alongside and the mask is fitted over Terry's face.

'He's all yours,' John tells Sister Young, and watches as Terry Doyle is wheeled off to the Cardiac Care Unit.

'I think you qualify for a gold watch or something by now,' Sister Pringle says. She keeps a tally of successful cardiac resuscitations in Casualty. In three months John Blake has revived eight patients from a total of twelve attempts.

'It's the on-the-spot stuff that's enhancing my record,' John tells her. Since senior nurses and doctors have started going with the ambulances to the scenes of cardiac emergencies, Anderson General's survival figures for first-time coronary sufferers have improved by more than a third. 'All the same, Sister,' John adds, 'I think my right jab's definitely getting better.'

In the view of Anderson General's medical administrators, everything about John Blake's professional performance is getting better. His competence was never doubted, but there were people who believed that a Senior Casualty Officer's appointment might overtax him. It has happened before; doctors with flair and energy have been given senior posts and have discovered they possess no talent at all for administration. Authority doesn't sit easily on them, and the strain of departmental or team management begins to show; the quality of their work declines, they become bad-tempered – one doctor at Anderson General even suffered a nervous breakdown, two months after his appointment as Senior Medical Officer in the Orthopaedic Outpatient Department.

But nothing of that order has happened to John Blake. In the year that he has been Senior Casualty Officer, his professional confidence and ability appear to have been strengthened. Sister Pringle, who admires John strongly, believes that the senior appointment boosted his morale and self-confidence. Elsewhere in the hospital, a few people have viewed John's rise to prominence with less approval, and they have criticised his promotion variously as premature, unwarranted, or as merely a symptom of the decay in old administrative standards. But John has no enemies in Casualty.

'I've a feeling,' Sister says now, as they move towards the cubicles, 'that it won't be much longer before they bring in that rape case. I'll get the clean theatre on standby.'

'And warn Glenda she'll be needed,' John says.

During the few minutes that John Blake and Sister Pringle have been attending to Terry Doyle, the rest of Casualty's medical staff have been coping with an influx of minor injuries. Sue McLean is in one of the cubicles with a teenage girl, bathing her eyes while the girl screeches vengeance on a friend who threw itching powder in her face. In the next cubicle Dr Ramsay is checking a beaten-up skinhead for signs of internal injury before he sends him to be X-rayed.

Further along Glenda Cross is dressing cuts on the arms and legs of a young woman whose husband hurled her through a glass door. A policewoman stands by and tries to get a statement as the girl howls and tries to fight Glenda off.

'I know it stings, love,' Glenda pants as she tries to bind an antiseptic pad in place. 'Try and put up with it; the stinging'll stop after a minute or two.'

'No! Don't! You're burning me!'

She is terrified, as much by the sight of her injuries as by the

34

pain, and no amount of reassurance can calm her. From what has emerged so far, it appears that the husband came home drunk and hauled her out of bed, telling her in the process that he had found out about her. The girl has no idea what he has found out, she's only aware that after being thrown the length of the hallway, she was picked up and hurled at the glass door, which smashed with the impact.

'Will I hold her down for you?' the policewoman asks, stepping forward.

Glenda, leaning halfway across the patient and struggling to get the last two adhesive strips in place, shakes her head. 'She's scared enough. Just let me battle on. I'll get the job done in the end.' She turns her head and smiles at the patient, who looks as if she might be about to scream. 'I know you don't believe it, love, but you're in great hands. Honest.'

In the waiting room there is a man with severe nausea of unknown origin, one who has torn open his arm trying to change a fan belt in his car, an old woman with a twisted ankle and a small boy with a splinter of wood wedged between two of his teeth. Claire Doughty is doing what she can to convince the patients they will be attended to as soon as possible. The man with the cut arm is being particularly abusive, and he's asserting what is daily asserted in that same room by a lot of other patients.

'The service in here's a bloody disgrace,' he tells the room at large. 'They're more interested in getting their paperwork right than they are in looking after people that want attention.'

Claire tells him snappily that the doctors and nurses are working as fast as they can. She closes her window on the man's guttural rejoinder.

It is at the times when patients are waiting and the staff are working on others that the real separateness of Casualty shows. Here, there can be no timetables or fixed routine to accommodate the needs of patients and staff. With an illness, there's a predictable pattern of development, a charted progression of events that can be medically intercepted in a way that is leisurely, compared to the pragmatic, often split-second approach that's needed when a doctor or nurse has to deal with the results of trauma, medical emergency, or despair. Even minor accidents separate Casualty from the other departments, for each one is unique and belongs to no clinical chain of events.

The point is often underlined by John Blake's consultant, Mr Hathaway, when he is addressing new Casualty Officers. Bacteria, he says, always signal their moves, so do rogue cells and slow-failing hearts. A sheared steering column in the chest of a driver, on the other hand, or a person rapidly drifting away from life because of something he's swallowed, are cases which set up desperate mysteries that have to be fathomed and cancelled in half the time it takes to diagnose bronchitis or shingles. The wards and clinics are the territory of procedural medicine. Casualty is a battlefield.

At 11.50 an ambulance driver comes in from the bay carrying a child wrapped in a red blanket. Sister Pringle points to the nearest cubicle and she and Dr Blake follow the man inside. He lays his bundle carefully on the bed and Sister switches on the overhead inspection light.

'Elizabeth Quigley,' the driver says as John carefully unwraps the blanket. 'Two years old. Scalded on lower legs and feet.'

The girl is small for her age and very thin. The fleshless little thighs look pathetically fragile, emerging from the thick dressings the ambulanceman has wrapped around her injuries.

'She's too quiet,' Sister says. She brushes her fingers through the child's matted hair and the large brown eyes watch her, but the face stays motionless.

'It's hardly surprising,' John Blake sighs.

He has opened one dressing and laid it flat. Against the white gauze, the scalding stands out bright scarlet. The superficial skin from below the knee to the top of the foot is loose and has rolled aside in places, exposing patches of the engorged tissue underneath. There are blisters on the toes, and on the sole of the foot there is a particularly large one, bulging out from the surrounding skin like a water-pouch that's been grafted on.

'She's badly into shock,' John says. 'Better get some fluid into her.' He turns to the ambulance driver. 'Where are the parents?'

'There's only the one. Her mother. She said she'd make her own way round here.' The driver pulls a face. 'Bit of a dizzy bitch, by the look of her.'

'What did she say happened?'

'She reckons she was bathing the kid, and because there's no hot water on tap at their place, she has to boil some up and add

36

it to half a bath of cold. The bucket of boiling water was standing beside the bath, she had her back turned, and before she knew it Elizabeth had climbed into the bucket.'

'Giving a two-year-old a bath,' Sister says flatly, 'at this time of night.'

John Blake goes to the telephone and puts through a call for the paediatrician, Dr Roarke. When he gets back to the cubicle Sister has removed the second dressing and uncovered a pattern of scalding nearly identical to the other leg. 'I'll get her some glucose,' Sister says. When she has gone, John stands looking at the child and she looks back at him, still expressionless, still silent. John is thankful Dr Ramsay didn't get this case.

When Dr Roarke arrives in Casualty John shows him the child. Roarke examines the injuries, smiling and chatting to Elizabeth as he does so. He straightens up after a minute and looks at John Blake.

'I thought you'd better see it,' John says. Dr Roarke is Anderson General's authority on child abuse.

'And what's the story?'

'The mother claims,' John says, 'that her daughter climbed into a bucket of boiling water.'

Roarke grunts and glances back at Elizabeth. 'I can believe a kid would put one leg in boiling water. I can't see her putting the other one in beside it.'

Sister comes back with Sue McLean, and between them they get started on Elizabeth's dressings and her shock treatment. John Blake and Dr Roarke go to the office to draft a preliminary report.

'I'll notify the police,' Roarke says, 'and I'll make the usual recommendation that the child be removed from the household for her own safety. Don't know how much good it'll do, mind you.'

In the past, Dr Roarke's views on child protection have run foul of an opposing belief, held mainly by social workers, that parents of battered and abused infants must be allowed to keep custody of those children, if any long-term adjustment – or 'child-parent imprint' as it is called – is to be accomplished. In open court, Roarke has described the theory as intellectual driftwood.

'I've seen a lot of cases like that one,' Roarke says. He folds his

37

angular body on to Sister's chair and lights up a cheroot. 'I'm sure I don't catch on to them all, though. Some of the mums and dads can be highly plausible in the aftermath of a bit of savagery.'

John Blake nods. 'Davy Powell, remember?'

The child had been brought to Casualty by his mother, a drawn, nervous woman who told John Blake she was worried about the sores on the boy's lips. She told a perfectly convincing story about the sores having appeared some weeks earlier, and how they had resisted every kind of medication she tried. The examination revealed four lesions that resembled cold sores, but something about them wasn't quite typical, so John asked the mother a lot of questions, enough in the end to make her break down. They were not sores on the child's mouth, they were cigarette burns. They had been put there to discipline the boy, 'To cleanse his mouth,' the father told the police later – each time he used a bad word. The mother had known the boy was being tortured but she was afraid of her husband, and she had only dared visit Casualty when the suppuration in the child's wounds began to scare her.

'I remember him,' Dr Roarke says. 'And Shaun Ellis, and Bobby Hamilton and all the rest of them. Timothy Mason was one of the worst. Fourteen months old and his mother threw a boiling chip pan over him.'

'Christ.'

'Not a trace of remorse, either. The kid was in dock for seven months, and at the end of it all when his system had had enough of surgery and medication and sheer bloody agony, he had a stroke and died. His mother was out of nick by that time, taking a find-yourself course with some quack in Bournemouth. She didn't want to know. She told the authorities the boy had caused too much pain in her life, she didn't want to be reminded of it. The grandparents buried him.'

'Unbelievable,' John Blake says, though he finds it perfectly believable.

'And there was the Indian kid, Kadijah something-or-other...'

Sessions like this have been precipitated before, usually when John Blake or another casualty officer has sent for Dr Roarke to look at a suspected case of abuse. Roarke is not by nature a rambler. His usual professional manner was demonstrated earlier, when he came in to help with the men who had been burned. He is calm, methodical and quietly waggish, and he always gets on with the job. His approach to the patients in his wards is exemplary; Roarke is objective and unemotional, he applies the craft of medicine with a properly detached eye. But at the times when he has to deal with the young victims of cruelty, he is always inclined to pause and run the litany of other atrocities.

The door, which is never closed for long, opens to admit Claire Doughty.

'Sorry to interrupt, Dr Blake, but the police are waiting to see you. They've brought in the girl who was raped.'

'I'll be right through.' John stretches and stands up. 'Rape,' he says to Dr Roarke. 'I'll have to go over Elizabeth Quigley's case with you later.'

'Fair enough.' Roarke stubs out his cheroot. 'What about the baby's mother? Any sign?'

'I don't think so.'

'Right. I'll get the fuzz on to it. Tell Sister the kid can be transferred over to Paediatrics.' He gets up and crosses to the door, holding it open for John Blake. 'I don't envy you your rape,' he says.

John shrugs. They walk together to the main doors, and before Dr Roarke leaves he touches John Blake's arm and says, 'At the risk of sounding melodramatic, I have to say I'm getting the feeling, more and more, that rape's what it's all about these days.'

*   *   *

At 12.05 a.m. Mrs Crumley, the rape victim, is brought straight from a police car in the ambulance bay to the clean theatre. She is walking with difficulty, and as soon as she is in the theatre Glenda Cross gets her into a chair and props her feet on a small stool.

'Just sit there for a minute,' Glenda says softly. She keeps her arm around Mrs Crumley's shoulder, making no demands on her yet. It is a critical time for the patient. Although she is dazed and disorientated for the moment, Glenda knows from experience that the woman will soon be less distracted by her

39

surroundings; a stronger awareness of herself and her predica-
ment will surface. From that point on, she will need very careful
and understanding nursing care.

'Doctor Blake will be coming to see you soon,' Glenda says.
'He's a nice man. You'll like him.' She squeezes Mrs Crumley's
shoulder, feeling the start of a tremor.

The public is about evenly split in its like and dislike of
doctors, and even among the Likes there's hefty discrimination
between one healer and another. A tradition of cynical adages
has grown up around the profession, and although few of them
are accurate they tend to be muddy, so they stick.

Considering the special nature of physicians' and surgeons'
work, it's no mystery why they can induce adoration in some
people and distrust or hatred in others. As far back as 1735, Ben
Franklin was saying things like, 'God heals, and the doctor takes
the fees'. As recently as the night before Glenda Cross read on
the stucco wall of the nurses' canteen, a terse graffito maintaining that doctors wear rubber gloves so they won't leave
fingerprints. Doctors in general take no offence: it's a tradition
after all and harmless enough, even amusing.

But the profession does have at least one persistent and
widespread shortcoming. A talent for diagnosis or a deft touch
with a scalpel doesn't grant a man or woman charm, or even
tact. Many doctors have achieved skill and expertise without
knowing the first thing about putting an old lady at her ease. In
the words of an American psychoanalyst, 'The technicalities and
status politics of medicine have put too many practitioners at a
distance from their patients. The human touch has lost ground.
There are people in their thousands who are as wary nowadays
of doctors as they are of getting sick.'

Of all the catastrophes a doctor has to deal with, rape is
perhaps the one most requiring tact, kindness and gentleness.
John Blake is an appointed police surgeon, and in his examination of rape victims he operates an enlightened code which is
backed up by a couple of unofficial tactics among Casualty
Sisters; certain clumsy doctors are steered away from rape
victims, and no junior nurses are ever in attendance. The aim is
to induce as much trust and reassurance as possible.

John Blake goes first to the sluice, where Detective Sergeant
Mick Halliday is having a cup of coffee with a uniformed

constable. Halliday is a frequent visitor to the department, a haggard, middle-aged man with patchy baldness and a pale, abnormally wrinkled face that Glenda Cross describes as scrotal.

The two policemen nod to John as he comes in and Halliday pulls his notebook from the pocket of his anorak. 'The second one on my patch in six days,' he says, flipping open the book. 'This country's obsessed with sex, Doctor.'

John Blake feels no temptation to discuss the point with Halliday, who is a man with a preference for simple philosophies. 'It's the wholemeal bread that's doing it,' John says.

Halliday finds the right page. 'Her full name's Doris Maria Crumley. She's twenty-seven, married, two children.'

John has entered the details on a case sheet. 'So what happened, Sergeant?'

'Mrs Crumley works evenings in a cinema kiosk. Selling popcorn and sweets. Her husband's on nights at a bakery. He goes off to work at ten, so there's a babysitter comes in to bridge the hour or so until Mrs Crumley gets home. The sitter's a relative of Mr Crumley's, a niece. Anyway, tonight as usual Mrs Crumley got home at about eleven, and five minutes later the sitter's boyfriend turned up to drive her home. Seems he's always been a bit on the heavy side with Mrs Crumley – you know...' Halliday makes a face that conveys nothing in particular. 'Dropping compliments and slow winks, telling her he wishes the niece was built like her, stuff like that, all jokey but not quite jokey enough.'

'And there's the phone calls,' the constable says.

Halliday nods. 'Obscene calls in a fake Irish accent. Mrs Crumley's been getting them for a couple of weeks, pretty regularly. She'd already told the niece she thought it sounded a bit like the boyfriend.'

'And he's the one who attacked her, I assume?' John says, anxious to get to the point.

'Right. He took the niece home, then went back to Mrs Crumley's place and said he'd dropped a key earlier. She lets him in and he starts laying it on really heavy. Mrs Crumley gets panicky, threatens to call the law and that does it. He hits her a couple of times and when she hits him back he starts punching in earnest. Then he rapes her.'

'Poor girl,' John murmurs. So often it's the woman's physical

41

defence of herself that triggers the rape. The innate view of many men is that sex is something they do *to* a woman, either by consent or by force – 'giving her one'· is a euphemism that betrays the underlying violence of the attitude – and sometimes an assault, to be properly justified, needs 'provocation'. By hitting back, Mrs Crumley provided it. There's a lot of controversy surrounding the point, but in John Blake's experience the passive victims suffer a lot less than the ones who put up a fight.

'She's still a bit hysterical,' Halliday says. 'It comes and goes in waves. She calmed down in the car, but she looked like she was winding up for a hairy-Mary when we brought her in.'

Claire Doughty comes to the door looking flustered. 'I wonder if the constable would give us a hand?' She waggles a thumb in the direction of the waiting room. 'A drunk's shut himself in the toilet and he won't come out.'

Halliday grins as the constable puts down his cup and shuffles off behind Claire.

'I'll go and take care of Mrs Crumley,' John says. 'I should have the bits and pieces for you in about twenty minutes.'

John goes to the clean theatre. Mrs Crumley is on the table, covered with a sheet. A policewoman is standing beside her, watching intently as Glenda Cross comforts the woman with pats on the hand and a steady stream of promises about everything being all right now, everything being sorted out.

'Hello Mrs Crumley.'

John comes to the side of the table and stands near the patient's feet, so that she can see him clearly. He introduces himself quietly, to soften the possibly disturbing impact of the word 'doctor', and tells her that he and Staff Nurse Cross are here to help her. Her teeth are clenched and she's controlling her breathing with a struggle. Her eyes dart from John to the policewoman to Glenda, and the nails of one hand scratch steadily on the back of the other. She has a pretty, soft-featured face; her skin is so pale that the cuts and bruises look as if they have been painted on.

'Would you like something to settle you a bit?' John asks her. She stares at him for a second. 'Don't worry,' he adds, 'we won't knock you out.'

Mrs Crumley nods sharply. Glenda already has the syringe of

Valium prepared. She hands it to John and he injects ten milligrams in the patient's arm. Administered in this way, Valium has a rapid action on the muscles, relaxing them and consequently making the patient feel more at ease.

'You'll be better in a minute,' John assures her. He glances at the consent form lying on a side trolley and sees that Mrs Crumley has already signed it. Her clothing is in a plastic bag alongside, ready to be transferred to the forensic laboratory for examination.

'If you'll just excuse me, Officer...'

The policewoman is a necessary witness, for John Blake will probably have to give evidence of his findings in court, and police corroboration of medical procedures in cases of rape is required by law. John motions for her to stand back to where she can still see what's going on without her presence being too obvious to the patient.

'It'll only take a few minutes to get this over and done with,' John tells his patient. 'I know it'll be upsetting, but I promise we'll do nothing to hurt you.' Glenda Cross has wheeled a trolley over beside John. On it are the instruments and containers he will need. He can see Mrs Crumley looking at them. The sight of glinting chrome is unnerving to any patient, so John leans across the table and pats the woman's hand. 'No pain, I promise.' He smiles at her. 'Feeling any more relaxed?'

'A bit,' she says throatily.

'Good.'

John begins the examination. He will make an effort to balance the inevitable distress by talking to Mrs Crumley throughout. The talking, in fact, is part of the examination; the patient's responses concerning the attack have to be put on record, together with anything she might say about how she feels physically, or about her mood or apprehensions.

With as much delicacy as the procedure permits, Glenda Cross raises Mrs Crumley's feet and positions them in the slings of the stirrups which are mounted high up on either side of the table. The patient is now in the lithotomy position, one of the least dignified in the clinical repertoire.

'Oh, please...' The cry is sudden and agonised, Mrs Crumley's reaction to a new assault on her sense of propriety.

John takes one of her hands and squeezes it momentarily. 'It's only for a very short time, Doris.' In cases where there are strong emotional overtones, there's some skill in knowing when to start using first names. John believes he has timed it well enough; the woman's hand has slackened in his grip; he has managed to impart some reassurance. In greener days, the subtleties of timing and inflection occasionally escaped him, and he would be confronted by patients who found him over-familiar or patronising.

Glenda arranges the sheet so that Mrs Crumley has at least the illusion of being properly covered. At the same time Glenda switches on the inspection lamp at the foot of the table.

'Any special pains?' John asks. He has moved to the lower end of the table, keeping his expression bland and casual as he makes a swift preliminary appraisal of the examination site. There are scratches and bruises and a slight discharge of blood. John reaches for the speculum, an instrument designed to ease the task of internal examination.

'My back hurts,' Mrs Crumley says.

'Is that because of the way we've got you hoisted?'

She shakes her head. 'I fell against the side of a chair. It hurt at the time, now it's got worse.' The Valium is starting to have a noticeable effect by now. The patient's face is much less tense and her hands are lying loosely on the sheet. In a softer voice, almost a whisper, she adds, 'I hurt a lot there, as well.'

John has inserted the speculum and already he has seen a small tear in the delicate membrane. When a woman's body is unprepared for sex, the traumatic results of enforced coitus can be harrowing. This is not the worst John Blake has seen, but it is bad enough. He takes some smears with cotton-ended sticks and puts them carefully into sterile glass tubes.

'He punched me on the ear,' Mrs Crumley says quietly. 'I don't feel anything; it's kind of gone numb.' While the Valium hasn't exactly put her at peace, it has made her objective.

'Which ear, Doris?'

'The left one.'

John has completed his internal examination and is passing a fine-toothed comb through the pubic hair. Loose hairs are being caught in a plastic envelope. They may be identified later as belonging to Mrs Crumley's attacker.

'How about your head? Any buzzing or ringing or flashing

44

pains, things like that?'

'It just aches a bit.'

'Uhuh. Eyesight all right?'

'Fine.'

In the space of seconds John has put smears from his patient's thighs on to microscope slides and sealed them in tubes. He takes one more swift, careful look at the entire site, then he stands back and nods to Glenda Cross. Glenda lifts Mrs Crumley's feet out of the stirrups and settles her legs gently on the table again.

'How bad am I hurt, Doctor?'

'Well.' John looks hard at her face, keeping his own placid. Her awareness is dulled by the Valium, but even so, the mental trauma is unmistakable. Mrs Crumley's life has been changed profoundly, and some of the deeper damage will be permanent. For the moment, John answers the woman's question with a physical prognosis. 'You've taken a lot of punishment, but there's nothing very serious. We'll keep you in the hospital for a few days, and for maybe a week after that you'll feel stiff and tender. I've got to examine the rest of you yet, but I'd say you'll mend nicely, Doris.'

The information makes no visible difference. Mrs Crumley maintains her look of dreamy preoccupation. 'I suppose that's good to know,' she says.

In the United Kingdom doctors have been slow to appreciate how devastating the long-term effects of rape can be. It's not unusual for victims to undergo radical changes of personality, or to lose the will to live. The sex drive is always impaired and often destroyed; a permanent, low-key hysteria can develop, making it impossible for the woman to lead anything like a normal life.

In America, Rape Care centres have existed for several years. There are doctors and nurses who specialise in the complex support and therapy regimes that are necessary, in practically every case, if the victim is to be brought to a state that resembles normal living. Nothing so well organised exists in Britain, but enlightenment is spreading.

John spends another ten minutes giving the patient a thorough physical examination. He finds bruises on the back, shoulders and breasts, two small cuts on the scalp, and

45

numerous bruises and small cuts on the face and neck. There appears to be a torn muscle fibre in Mrs Crumley's lower back, and her left ear is badly swollen, although the eardrum looks undamaged.

When he has finished John tells the patient what he has told her already; she's been badly knocked about, but she should heal without any complications. 'I'm going to leave you to Staff Nurse Cross's gentle ministrations for a while, but I'll be back. Just keep remembering...' John leans low over the table, smiling, reassuring. 'We really do know how bad it's been for you. You're not alone and we all want to help.'

The policewoman picks up the bag with Mrs Crumley's clothes and follows John out of the theatre. 'That's the first real one I've seen,' she says as they walk towards the sluice.

John glances down at her. 'There are a lot of real ones,' he murmurs.

'Oh, I know that. But you've got to be careful with rapes, haven't you? There's always more than meets the eye.'

He has known since he laid eyes on her that if she ever got to speak to him, she would do something unpleasant to his hackles. The girl radiates glibness.

'There's more to everything than meets the eye, Officer.'

John suspects she belongs to a school of thought which holds that all rapes, to some extent at least, are brought on by the victims themselves. He has heard nurses and doctors of both sexes express the same opinion. John finds the view shallow. On the solitary occasion he was drawn into an argument on the topic, he pointed out that to some extent boils, asthma, piles and VD are brought on by the sufferers, who are nonetheless entitled to consolation and therapy. To the policewoman, however, John says nothing more.

In the sluice John gives Detective Sergeant Halliday the envelope containing the samples and smears for the forensic lab.

'No serious injuries,' he tells Halliday, 'but it's not from any want of trying. Have you got this fellow in custody?'

'We will have, soon enough. He'll be running out of steam by now. There's a couple of bobbies waiting for him at his digs.' Halliday moves to the door. 'Maybe he's had the savvy to clean himself up, mind you.'

'I don't think it would make any difference,' John says. 'He left enough of himself behind with Mrs Crumley.'

As they are walking towards the main door Halliday says he would like to talk to the patient again. 'Soon as possible, just to get her statement sewed up.'

'We'll hang on to her for two or three days. She needs some attention from a gynaecologist. And she needs rest. If you could leave it till Monday, Sergeant...'

'That'll be fine,' Halliday says.

'And you will be careful, won't you?' John adds. 'I'm not telling you your job, but the wrong questions can do a hell of a lot of damage.' John's eyes flick for a moment to the police-woman, standing behind Halliday. 'Moral concussion can be tricky, if you follow my drift.'

Halliday promises he will be careful, and he leaves with the policewoman.

On his way to the office John sees the constable who went off earlier to help Claire Doughty with her barricaded drunk. He is leaning against the wall outside X-ray, dabbing his lip with a handkerchief.

'What happened?' John asks him. There is a red weal on the policeman's chin and his lip is split.

'That bloke in the bog. I got the door open, stuck my head through, and he nutted me.'

'Where is he now?'

'In one of your cubicles,' the constable says. 'Out cold.'

'What did you do to him?'

'Nothing.' He winces as the handkerchief touches his lip again. 'He made a run for it, right past me and out through the door. He went belting across the car park and he'd have got away, too, if he'd been less pissed and hadn't kept looking over his shoulder. Ran smack into a lamp post.' The constable laughs carefully. 'Never saw anything like it. He looked like a bendy toy when they wheeled him back in here.'

John offers to do something for the policeman's injuries, but the man declines. 'I'll just hang on here until I can have words with the clown, then I'll get on my way. It'll look better if I turn up at the nick with some blood on me. Shows I'm trying.'

Business has obviously been steady while John has been with Mrs Crumley. He sees Sister Pringle moving at speed from one cubicle to another, and Dr Ramsay, somewhere beyond, is

47

yelling at someone to lie still for his own good. Sue McLean is helping Phil Cowley to get an old woman into a wheelchair by the door to Emergency.

John picks up the top card from the half-dozen in the box by the waiting room door and reads the brief details. Jack Ridley, forty-nine, bus inspector, complaining of chest pains. John goes to the waiting room and calls out the name. A small, thin, worried-looking man comes forward. John leads him through to an empty cubicle and tells him to take off his shirt and lie on the bed. While he is doing that John steps outside to look for a sphygmomanometer, the instrument for testing blood pressure. He nearly collides with Dr Ramsay, who is racing stiff-kneed towards the office. From past experience, John knows that the funny walk is a feature of Donald Ramsay's anger.

'Bloody skinheads,' Ramsay says as he skids to a halt.

'Giving you aggro?'

'In a passive kind of way,' Ramsay sighs. 'This one got himself kicked to a smooth texture outside the Romany Tavern. Gave me all the details – how many were on to him, where they stuck the boot in, where it hurts, even how it started. But he didn't tell me he's diabetic.' Ramsay looks at his watch. 'He started to go funny when they brought him back from X-ray. It's taken me five minutes to figure it out.'

'And what's your verdict?' John asks.

'Alcohol-induced hypoglycaemia. And the punch-up didn't help. I was on my way to look for you.'

They go together to the cubicle where the young man is lying on the bed, groaning. His shaven head and deep-sunk eyes give him the appearance, John Blake observes, of a concentration camp victim. He is semi-conscious and is shifting his legs and arms restlessly.

'The X-rays are clear,' Ramsay says. 'When he started to lose consciousness I had another look at the skull plates. Zero damage. I did some quick reflex checks, got nothing there, either. Then I caught a whiff of his breath. Beery, like earlier, but with something else in it.'

John leans forward and sniffs. He looks up at Ramsay and nods. 'Acetone.' He touches the youth's arms and face and finds them damp with sweat. 'Diagnosis spot-on, Donald. Give him fifty grams of glucose intravenously.'

When the injection has been given, both doctors stand watching the patient, timing his reaction to the treatment.

'Poor, silly sod,' Ramsay mutters.

The main danger is that the patient will suffer some degree of brain damage. The nervous system is unique in that it relies almost exclusively on glucose for its energy. A diabetic who takes alcohol – especially a drink with a sugar content – often suffers an unnatural surge of insulin into his system. The insulin absorbs too much of the glucose in his blood, and the condition called hypoglycaemia sets in. The nervous system becomes sluggish and its components start to disintegrate. Brain damage follows rapidly.

'There we go,' John says as the patient opens his eyes suddenly and stares about him. The reaction to the injection of glucose has taken less than a minute.

'Feeling better now, Bert?' Ramsay asks.

The youth is confused. He blinks at the doctors and stares at the curtains and bed covering. He will be like that for several minutes, until his patterns of reaction and memory restore themselves.

'Book him into Medical,' John tells Dr Ramsay. 'They can get him balanced again, and maybe somebody'll talk some sense into him while they're at it.'

John goes back to his patient with the chest pains, taking a sphygmomanometer with him. The man is lying flat on the bed, breathing nervously through his mouth.

'Can you tell me something about your pains, Mr Ridley? Where are they exactly?'

The patient spreads the fingers of both hands and touches them to his upper chest. 'All across here,' he says.

'And do they interfere with your breathing?' A heart pain will invariably make it impossible for a person to inhale properly.

Mr Ridley thinks about it for a minute, then shakes his head. 'Not really. I can feel it aching, like, when I breathe. But it doesn't interfere.'

'Let's check your blood pressure, then.' John wraps the cuff of the instrument around Mr Ridley's arm and inflates it. The box containing the scale from which the pressure is to be read is placed at the head of the bed, level with John Blake's eyes, and the end of the stethoscope is laid lightly over the brachial artery.

In this instance, John will take account of Mr Ridley's nervousness, which will have raised his pressure slightly.

'It's just the ballooning in the cuff you're feeling,' John says. Mr Ridley is staring at the instrument as if it's capable of squeezing right through his arm. 'Try to relax, this'll be over quickly...'

The cuff has obliterated the pulse in the artery. John releases the cuff pressure slowly, and when he can hear the arterial thump he takes a reading from the mercury in the scale. He releases the pressure even more, and when the thumping gives way to a steady pulse John takes another reading. He is impressed.

'Your blood pressure's a hundred and twenty over seventy, Mr Ridley. That's a very good reading. Jumping on and off buses must be good for you.'

John removes the arm cuff and listens to the patient's heart, then his lungs. He taps the chest wall for signs of dullness and checks the nails and the margins of the eyes for signs of anaemia. Then he stands back.

'Found it, have you?'

'You're about the healthiest person we've had through here this week,' John tells him.

'I'm not imagining it, you know.' Mr Ridley sounds indignant.

'I'm sure you're not.' John asks him to point to the painful areas again, and Mr Ridley does. 'I only have to move and it hurts. It's that bad I could hardly get my sweater over my head this morning.'

'Is that when the pains started? This morning?'

'As soon as I got up.' The anxiety widens his eyes. 'You hear so much about these things. We had a chap at the depot last week, same age as me. Keeled right over, dead. He'd been complaining about pains in his chest all morning.'

'Your heart's in excellent shape,' John assures him. 'Let's just try something else.' John is pretty sure by now that he knows what's wrong. 'Put your arms up over your head, high as they'll go.' When Mr Ridley has done that, John touches his fingers to the chest, but two inches higher than the patient did a minute ago. 'Still sore there?'

Mr Ridley makes a pained face and nods.

50

'Right, you can relax now. Put your shirt on.'

Looking puzzled and still faintly indignant, Mr Ridley does as John has told him.

'I'm going to demonstrate a bit of sharp detective work,' John tells him. 'Two days ago, you did something pretty strenuous, something that involved more effort than you're used to making. Am I right?'

Mr Ridley's face goes blank. He starts to shake his head, then stops. 'Mrs York, our next-door neighbour. I carried some furniture upstairs for her.'

'And you strained your chest muscles in the process. It's like when you're a kid, you play the first game of football for months, and it's usually two days later it hits you. The stiffness and the aching. The muscles are reacting to a bit of unaccustomed stretching and tension.'

'I'd forgotten all about it.'

'That's natural,' John says. 'The pains in your chest would drive everything else out of your head. People tend to fear the worst. If it had been a pain in your back, mind you, you might have made the connection.' John goes on to explain that the site of the pain moved up when Mr Ridley raised his arms; with an ailment located inside the chest wall, the pain would have stayed put, no matter how much the muscles moved around. 'You'll be right as rain in a couple of days.'

'Good grief.' Mr Ridley shakes his head, and for the first time he smiles. 'The relief, Doctor...'

'I bet you were imagining terrible things.'

'Terrible.'

'And that's why you turned up here at this hour of night.' It's the usual time, John knows, for worry to turn into panic.

Mr Ridley is nodding, buttoning up his jacket. 'It's a damned good thing I came in,' he says. To John, he looks several years younger already. 'If I'd stopped at home I'd likely have fretted myself into a box before daylight.'

When Mr Ridley has gone home, suffused with relief and gratitude, John fills out the card and then sits for a minute, wondering how the reprieve will affect the little man, after the first flush has subsided. He has spent an entire day in a purgatory of growing fear that has been transformed, in minutes, into something that looked like the onset of joy. Maybe

51

he will get home and astonish his wife by kissing her for the first time in ages. Maybe he'll dig out a bottle and get yodelling drunk.

John stands up and goes out into the passageway, smiling to himself. These corny moments in Casualty delight him. The commoner, sombre realities will settle on him again soon enough, but for the moment it's harmless recreation to picture Mr Ridley skipping off down the drive, throwing his cap in the air and shaking a fist at the moon.

* * *

By 1.15 a.m. Michael Crosby is at the Chester Road Police Station, waiting to be questioned in connection with the rape of Doris Crumley. Crosby is twenty-two, a motor mechanic and part-time barman. He has a broad, sleepy-eyed, handsome face, a coarse replica of a certain television actor's: Michael is aware of the similarity, people have pointed it out to him, and he arranges his lank hair in a way that enhances the resemblance. He is tall and well built and it's his habit to move in a way that suggests he was designed to hand out punishment.

The room where they have put him is a stark little enclosure – three yellow walls and one green with a two-foot square window set into it. There is a table, two chairs and a rickety fan heater with an alternating buzz and hum that can be unnerving after five minutes.

A young constable is standing by the door, facing the chair where Michael is sitting. He doesn't look at Michael and Michael doesn't look at him, but their awareness of each other is enough to keep either one from relaxing a muscle. They have been like that for nearly ten minutes, and uneasiness is starting to erode the belligerence that was shoring-up Michael's hard exterior. His face is strained with the effort of looking dangerous. A confrontation is one thing, an invisible threat is another.

'Right, then!'

Detective Sergeant Halliday sends the words before him like a fanfare as he strides into the room and shoulders the door shut behind him. He drops into the chair opposite Michael Crosby and slides his elbows on to the table, giving the prisoner a swift smile that carries no warmth at all.

'Let's have your version, sonny.'

Michael's mouth is dry. When he speaks his tongue clicks on his palate. 'I want to know what I'm doing here.'

'Save me all that,' Halliday sighs.

'And I want my gear back.' When he was arrested, Michael had to change his clothes and hand over the ones he had been wearing during the evening.

'Your sweaty raiment,' Halliday tells him, 'is at the lab. I don't think they'll want to hang on to it any longer than they have to.'

'They better not damage any of it.' Michael's aggression is coming back at a gallop, now that he has a focus for it. 'And that bleeding doctor wants reporting, while I'm at it.'

'Hurt you, did he?'

'It was a dead liberty, and don't imagine I'm leaving it at that.' The medical examination of a man suspected of rape is searching in the extreme. In Michael's case it was all the more upsetting because the police surgeon had been called from his bed, and he worked with less delicacy than he might have. 'I'll be laying an official complaint.'

Halliday yawns at him. 'Your outraged modesty's been noted, we'll maybe get round to that when we've handled another official complaint. Mrs Crumley says you raped her, Michael. Now let me have your side of it.'

'Bullshit!'

'There's going to be a lot of evidence...'

'Yeah!' Michael thumps the side of his fist on the table and glares at Halliday. 'You'll get plenty of evidence that says I had it off with her. Not the same thing, mate, is it?'

'So what are you saying?'

'She laid it on, that's what I'm saying. More than once. So this time I say yes please and have a plateful, then she goes off yelling stinking fish. Beautiful.'

Halliday is shaking his head steadily. 'She was thumped about, Michael. Bad. Beaten up and raped, that's what the picture says.'

Michael leans forward, showing Halliday the edges of his teeth. 'Fuck the picture.' This kind of exchange is second nature to Michael. He has the courage of his vulgarity. 'Any bumps she's got on her, she got them by request. A lot of chicks like that kind of thing, y'know.'

'You're making this bad for yourself, son,' Halliday warns him.

'I'm making it straight! Just go out there and ask anybody about Doris Crumley. Biggest bloody pop-on in the district.'

Halliday is silent for a moment, tapping the edge of the table with one finger. 'You're saying Mrs Crumley has a reputation for being promiscuous?'

'That's what I'm saying.'

'She didn't strike me as that sort.' Halliday's tone leaves less room for uncertainty than his words do.

'What?' Michael looks astonished. 'She's had more pricks than a second-hand dartboard, for Christ's sake!'

The interview is opening new territory for Sergeant Halliday. He has questioned rapists before and they have often handed him versions of the story Michael Crosby is telling, but never with such vehement self-assurance. It's as if the young man has managed to seize and hang on to a total belief that he's being wronged. That doesn't raise any possibility of Crosby being innocent, though. He's as guilty as he's repugnant, Halliday has no doubts about that.

'It happens a bit too much, this,' Michael says, with a trace of rough indignation.

'What does?'

'This. Women making out they've been raped when they haven't been. Non-rapes. The papers are full of them.' He lowers his head, looking straight at Halliday. 'They fancy a bloke, lead him on, then can't live with themselves for doing it. So they make out it never happened the way it did. And they've got to punish the bloke for what he knows about them.' Disgust makes a sharp line of his mouth. 'It's sick.'

Halliday can almost admire this talent. Before his eyes, Crosby is turning himself into a martyr. It's the sergeant's growing conviction that a psychiatrist will figure prominently in this saga before it's ended.

'You really should get hold of a lawyer, Michael.'

'I don't need one.'

'You're up to your neck,' Halliday says patiently. 'You've got a rape charge coming at you, and another one for Grievous-Bodily that's serious enough to get promoted to attempted murder, and on top of all that you're lining-up to add slander to the catalogue.'

54

'I don't need no lawyer to prove that's all crap.'

Halliday makes a gesture of abdication with one hand. 'Suit yourself. Personally I don't give a monkey's what happens to you, as long as it's painful, but I like to see the game played straight.' He stands up. 'I'll get somebody to bring you along a cup of tea.'

'I don't want no tea. I want to get back to my drum.'

'Not possible at present,' Halliday says. He nods to the constable and opens the door. 'Have the tea, it'll give you something to do. I'll be back in ten minutes to charge you.'

Michael jumps to his feet, but sits down again when the constable takes a step towards him. 'What the hell are you talking about? How can you charge me?'

'Easy. Just sit there and rehearse your story, we'll be writing it down next time.'

Halliday closes the door and walks along the corridor to the CID office. He sits down at his desk and reads the messages that have been left, then he picks up the telephone and dials the number of Anderson General. When the switchboard answers he asks for Dr Roarke.

'Hello? Ah, I got your message, Doctor. Sorry I missed you, I was up at the hospital earlier. What's the problem?'

He listens, nodding at the mouthpiece as Roarke explains his misgivings about Elizabeth Quigley, the child who was taken to Casualty with scalded legs and feet. Roarke finishes by telling Halliday that the mother still hasn't put in an appearance at the hospital, which for both men is a familiar signal of guilt in child-abuse cases.

'I think this is one for our lady detective,' Halliday says. 'She's on duty at eight, I'll see she makes it her first call.' Before he hangs up he makes a note of Mrs Quigley's address.

A constable clerk comes in with a stolen goods list, and Halliday asks him to take a cup of tea along to the man in the interview room. 'He looks the kind who likes plenty of sugar. So don't put any in.' As the constable goes out the Desk Sergeant comes in, pantomiming havoc.

'Crumley's out there,' he says to Halliday. 'The raped woman's husband. He's kicking up buggery.'

Halliday sighs at his blotter.

'He went over to Anderson General and they wouldn't let him

see his wife. Now's he's wanting full explanations out of us. Nature of injuries, name and whereabouts of suspect, all that, and he won't be put off.'

'So you want me to have a word.'

'It might save us some damage.'

Halliday gets up. 'I'd have to talk to him some time, anyway. It might as well be sooner as later.'

As they go along the passage together, Halliday makes an observation he's made before, in casualty departments as well as police stations. 'The whole world outside this place,' he says, 'is just one bloody gigantic mental ward.'

'Definitely,' the Desk Sergeant says.

*   *   *

It's 2.00 a.m. Since midnight eleven cases have been handled by Casualty, most of them minor. The waiting room is empty again and the only patient still in the unit is Mrs Crumley.

The drunk who collided with a lamp post in the car park has been put in a surgical ward for observation. He is heavily concussed and still fairly intoxicated, so his respiration will be monitored and his blood pressure checked periodically, to make sure that the head damage doesn't join forces with the disturbed nervous system to produce brain complications. No one knows why the man was in Casualty in the first place. A thorough examination by Dr Ramsay has shown no injuries other than those he picked up in his bid for freedom. It's likely he just wandered in, as drunks occasionally do, creating havoc for the hard-pressed staff and disrupting order in the waiting room.

John Blake and Sister Pringle have gone to the canteen for a half-hour break. Claire Doughty and Phil Cowley are eating their sandwiches. Dr Ramsay is helping Nurse McLean to replace the dressings and packets of disposables that have been used during the past hour. As they move from cubicle to cubicle Donald Ramsay explains to Sue why Glenda Cross is still in the theatre with the rape victim.

'It's a triumph of compassion over bureaucracy,' he says. 'Have you heard of emergency environment therapy?'

Sue shakes her head.

'Dr Blake and Dr Lloyd set it all up, three months ago. Miss Parker and some of the others in admin tried to knock it down.'

56

Vernon Lloyd is a Consultant Psychiatrist with a keen interest in the links between physical trauma and stress illnesses. He has collaborated with John Blake on a number of papers covering the topic. 'It took ages to get the procedure accepted,' Dr Ramsay goes on. 'Old Mother Parker wouldn't believe what they were telling her. She doesn't trust much that's got psychiatric connections.'

'And what's the procedure?'

Ramsay pokes his head outside to see if there's anyone about, then sits down on a bed and lights a cigarette. 'The whole thing hinges on the difference between injuries caused by accident, and the ones brought about by human aggression. A man hit by a bus has physical injuries, and apart from the odd touch of hysterics, that's that. His wounds are all on top. But if he's been attacked by another human being, it's a whole different game of Scrabble. There's psychological wounding, and it can be desperate if the right First Aid isn't applied.' He smiles at the intense concentration on Sue's small features. 'Are you with me so far?'

'I think so.'

Ramsay moves his hands in front of him to suggest the shaping of a concept. 'Even the attempted suicides that come in here are a lot less likely to cop for mental overthrow or emotional crackup than rape victims are. Or old folk that have been mugged. For one thing, the failed suicides have passed their emotional crisis by the time they get here. The ones who've been raped and battered still have it to come. So. Doctors Blake and Lloyd proposed a special therapeutic regime. A preventive drill.'

'I can see why Miss Parker didn't like the idea,' Sue says. 'Too finicky.'

'Right. She's all for black-and-white medicine with no shades in between. And she gets a lot of backing from the philistines upstairs.'

Conversations between hospital medical staff usually carry some reference to the obstructive behaviour of the administration. Often they are dominated by it. The fundamental difficulty is that doctors and nurses are motivated by concerns that are at odds with the bureaucratic ideals of the National Health Service.

'They went rigid on Dr Blake,' Ramsay says. 'Told him there was no precedent and no space within the guidelines for anything like the scheme he was proposing. They hang on to those guidelines like security blankets.'

Healers can't work to inflexible rules of procedure; the NHS claims it must, if it is to keep the hospitals functioning. Mr Hathaway, the Consultant Surgeon, has his own way of expressing the problem. A doctor's proper concern, he says, is to improve the health of his fellows through prevention, diagnosis and treatment of sickness, whereas the NHS stands firm on three immovable rocks called Central Strategic Planning, Regional Planning and Supervision, and Area Planning and Operational Control. There is as much chance of harmony between those two groups, Hathaway concludes, as there is between a poet and a bank manager.

'How did Dr Blake and Dr Lloyd swing it, then?' Sue asks.

'Pressure. They wouldn't take no for an answer. They kept putting memos together, and they got longer all the time. Miss Parker and her crowd couldn't cope with it. They came up with the argument that special care was the province of the ward, but John Blake blew holes in that one. Rapes and muggings and the like all need an *immediate* sense of stability and support. *Then* they can face a crowd of strangers and all the hussle and faffle on the ward. There's bags of evidence to support the argument, and most of it found its way on to Miss Parker's desk. So she gave in.'

'What is it, exactly?'

'What?'

'Environment thingummy... What you called it.'

'Emergency environment therapy,' Ramsay says. 'You set up an emergency environment – it's a two-part deal. First, you put the patient in surroundings that convince her she's getting top-level treatment. That's why the raped woman's in the theatre. Looks more Hollywood in there. The second thing you do is lay on a two-person team, nurse and doctor, that the patient has time to get familiar with and trust.'

Sue holds out a throw-away gallipot for Dr Ramsay to flick his ash into. 'How long does it take? Staff's been in the theatre for ages.'

'It takes as long as it takes,' Ramsay says. He stands up, stubs out the cigarette in the pot and hands it back to Sue. 'Come on. We better get finished. I'll buy you a bun in the canteen when Sister and Dr Blake get back.'

The stillness in the department is emphasised by the rustling of packets and sheets as Dr Ramsay and Nurse McLean continue replenishing the cubicle supplies. The quietness of the place is like a period of held breath, before an expected onslaught. That's how it seems to Phil Cowley, who has finished his sandwiches and is moving around the department putting trollies in straight lines, regimenting wheelchairs and doing an eye-count of blankets and gas cylinders.

Phil is restless. He has been deeply unhappy for a long time, and although he is never prone to real despair, he finds this time of night hard to cope with. Researchers have discovered that human life is at its lowest ebb between two and three in the morning. Nobody has ever told Phil that, but he senses it well enough. As the hours pass he'll get brighter, he might even manage a joke or two with the other porters. For the time being, he is occupying himself and running a melodic old song in his head, to counter the barbs of memory that come at him during this part of the shift. If that doesn't quite work, if his misery starts showing, he'll take a brisk walk in the cold air. One circuit of the grounds is usually enough.

In the theatre, Glenda Cross has adjusted the posture-control wheels on the sides of the operating table, until the end has risen enough to put Doris Crumley in the propped position she would have in an ordinary bed. She can see more now and she's more comfortable. The overhead lights are dimmed and one bright lamp shines down on the sheet. Glenda is stripping off her rubber gloves. She drops them in a bowl on the trolley and smiles brightly at Mrs Crumley.

'Finished,' she says. 'Do you think you could cope with a cup of tea, after all that?'

Mrs Crumley shakes her head. 'I don't think I could keep it down.'

'We'll leave it a bit, then.'

The past two hours have put a serious strain on Glenda. For ten minutes after Dr Blake had completed his examination, Mrs Crumley was quiet. She appeared to have control of herself. But when Glenda started attending to her injuries the patient became hysterical again. She resisted no move that Glenda made, but her condition of panting fear, verging on terror, became so bad that Glenda had to stop what she was doing and concentrate on applying comfort and nothing else.

Glenda has had psychiatric training, and she was quick to classify Mrs Crumley's condition. The restless arms and legs, the transient look of apprehension and sudden plunges into panic are all classic signs of the Hysterical Neurotic Reaction, a classified emergency that can have devastating results for the sufferer.

The main danger, in this patient's case, is that the intensity of her reaction could produce permanent changes in her personality; she could develop a chronic, incapacitating illness. Persistent anxiety can harden into phobia and compulsion, until the patient's waking hours are dominated by bizarre rituals – touching certain objects in a precise order, avoiding contact with certain other objects, never using some words and always using others in accordance with a complex mental pattern – which the sufferer believes are essential in warding off doom. Psychotherapy provides varying degrees of relief, but rarely a cure. The most worthwhile course of treatment is preventive, and it consists of nothing more than reassurance.

For several minutes it didn't appear that Mrs Crumley was even hearing Glenda. She whimpered, bit into her lip, threw her head from side to side and clawed at the sheet. When Glenda started talking close to her ear, telling her over and over that she was safe, she was in no danger, Mrs Crumley's hysteria actually got worse.

John Blake, making one of his ten-minute checks on the patient, finally calmed her. He stood beside the table, holding tight to one of her hands as he gave her the same comforting words Glenda had, but in a deep, rhythmic monotone. The technique is derived from the medical hypnotists' procedure for inducing light anaesthesia. Mrs Crumley became less agitated after a minute of the therapy, and in two minutes she was stabilised again – tearful but in control.

'I've never had to do that before,' John admitted quietly to Glenda. 'Thank God it worked.'

To have done anything else would have been either useless or dangerous. In the past, doctors have treated patients suffering this reaction with drugs that acted on the brain to suppress the symptoms. The results often bordered on the tragic. Like a computer, the brain has to close down by ordered stages, as it does when a person is falling asleep. An abrupt removal of consciousness, especially in a hysterical patient, leaves the brain patterns suspended in disorder, and when consciousness returns the personality is splintered, left with no adequate central guide. The results of drug intervention in hysterical seizures have sometimes matched the worst symptoms of LSD poisoning.

For over an hour after that, with occasional visits and renewed reassurances from John Blake, Glenda performed a high-wire act, clinging to her professional objectivity in the face of the patient's fragile, barely-maintained composure. John told Glenda she could administer a second dose of intravenous Valium, but only if Mrs Crumley showed signs of relapsing into the dangerous hysteria.

Now, the necessary clinical measures have all been taken. Mrs Crumley has been given penicillin, a standard measure to cover her against gonorrhoea. She has told Glenda, after cautious questioning, that she takes the birth pill, so there has been no need to cause her extra distress by coaxing her to accept contraceptive measures. The cuts and scratches on her face and body have been dressed and a temporary antibiotic dressing has been put on the vaginal wounds, which will be attended to later by a gynaecologist.

Glenda is exhausted, but she's careful not to let Mrs Crumley see it. Her job isn't finished yet; now the treatment has to be focused away from the patient's body.

'You're going to have to make yourself lie back and let people pamper you,' Glenda says. She has a feeling that sounds fatuous, but it serves as a ground-breaker. 'The more you just accept things the better you'll feel later.'

It is difficult to plumb the woman's anguish, beyond knowing it's extreme. She looks directly at Glenda with a pained, tentative expression that suggests she wants to say something that refuses to surface.

'If there's anything you want to tell me, love...'

The woman breathes in sharply against a sob then swallows a couple of times. 'Trev,' she says, almost whispering.

Glenda nods and takes Mrs Crumley's hand, the way she has a dozen times since midnight. 'Your husband?'

'Yes.'

'You're not to go imagining all sorts...'

'*He* will.' More tears roll down Mrs Crumley's face. 'I know what he's like.'

'Ssh.' Glenda has both the patient's hands now, squeezing them. 'Put all that out of your mind. You're just magnifying everything. It'll be fine, don't fret.'

'He was against me working at the Regal because of the men...'

'Don't dwell on it, not tonight. Wait till there's some daylight, things'll be more manageable then.'

In truth Glenda's own expectations about the husband's conduct are a fair match for Mrs Crumley's. He has already been turned away from reception by John Blake, who told him firmly that his wife was in no condition to see him – at least, not as he was. Mr Crumley presented himself with a set jaw and an eye for justice; his approach suggested that he didn't hold his wife entirely blameless.

'There's never been a soul since Trev. I've swore it to him...'

'Please, Mrs Crumley...'

'And the kids. They were in bed, but they'll get to hear about all this...'

The future is opening like a pit in front of Mrs Crumley. In extreme cases of this kind, where the only respite lies in memories of a happier time before the trauma, patients have often taken that route with stunning completeness. It could be Doris Crumley's alternative to an anxiety illness; she could become locked in a reverie that would shut out pain and reality. Glenda has seen people inhabiting their past; it's one of the eeriest experiences in psychiatric practice.

Mrs Crumley lets out a howl so sudden and loud that it makes Glenda jump. She grabs the patient's shoulders and hangs on, keeping her from throwing herself off the table.

'Lie still! You've got to lie still!'

The table rocks violently as the patient bangs one of the levers at the side which control its angle; Glenda has to right it again and swing Mrs Crumley's legs back into the centre.

'Don't move!' Glenda pleads into the screaming face, and she reaches out to the trolley, leaning all her body weight against the struggling woman. She flips the cover off the Valium syringe and brings it across. It's enough to show it to Mrs Crumley. She goes quieter, seeing the object that she knows can make her at least accept things for an hour. Gradually she calms her own breathing, then lies back and lets Glenda put the needle into her arm.

*   *   *

It's now 6.30 a.m. In the past four hours there have been five admissions to Casualty, none of them serious. Two young drunks, who had beaten each other senseless, had their wounds dressed by Sister Pringle and Sue McLean, then they were taken away by the police to be charged with being drunk and disorderly. A girl who trapped her thumb in a car door was given a pain-killing injection and had the fracture splinted by Donald Ramsay. John Blake spent ten minutes stitching the wounds of a woman who had knocked a water glass off her bedside table, and had then got out of bed in the dark to pick up the pieces; she stepped on two jagged fragments, which broke again and inflicted four deep cuts in the sole of her foot. An old man whose dog attacked him when he disturbed it in the night was given anti-tetanus cover by Sue McLean while Sister dressed two bites on his hand.

There has been time to tidy the department. Phil Cowley has taken the plastic sack containing a three-day accumulation of used hypodermic syringes into the sluice and broken off the needles with pliers. It's always necessary to do that before the syringes are thrown away; with the introduction of disposables, drug addicts took to raiding the refuse bins in the hospital grounds.

John Blake took a few minutes away from the department to visit Cardiac Care. Terry Doyle, the man who had a coronary attack in a pub and was later resuscitated by John, was asleep on an angled bed, surrounded by breathing apparatus and monitoring equipment. His wife was by his side, a small woman looking wan and lost in the midst of the winking and humming machinery. John spoke with her for a few minutes and suggested, as the unit staff had, that she go home and get some sleep. Later, he spoke to the physician in charge of the unit, who told him that Terry's chances were fifty-fifty.

A girl of seventeen has arrived by ambulance and Donald Ramsay is examining her in a cubicle. She has three-tone hair and a leather jacket with chains attached, back and front. Her

63

jeans are made entirely of patches. It's hard to tell, because of her elaborate yellow, pink and purple make-up, if she is pale or flushed. But she sounds very ill.

Beside Sue McLean, who is loosening the girl's clothing, the patient's friend is standing, dressed much the same, though her face is less imaginatively disguised.

'Tell me what happened,' Ramsay says. He already has his hand on the patient's chest, over the heart, and he can detect a clear palpitation.

'We were walking home from this party and she just keels over . . .'

'How long ago?'

The girl blinks a couple of times. 'Dunno. Might have been an hour.'

'That long?'

'Yeah. About.'

'What kept you, then?' Ramsay is pressing on the patient's abdomen. She is groaning and mumbling something.

'I couldn't find a phone. They was all busted.'

The girl is sounding defensive suddenly and Ramsay softens his tone.

'I'm sorry, I know how hard it can be. But it's important to know how long she's been like this. Where was she, all the time you were trying to find a phone?'

'She was with me,' the girl says. 'I mean, she come round like, a bit groggy but fit enough to walk hanging on to me.'

'Had she taken anything?'

The girl looks at Sue, then at Dr Ramsay. 'Drugs, you mean?'

Ramsay nods. 'I'm not trying to land you in it. I just need to know.'

'Well, I dunno. We was at the same party, but we stayed split up most of the night.' After a pause she adds, 'She didn't look like she'd taken anything. Not drugs, anyway. Most she ever touches is a bit of grass, and there wasn't any about, far as I know.'

'What do you mean, "not drugs anyway"?' Ramsay asks her. 'Did she act like she *had* taken something? Drink?'

The girl nods. 'She likes the vodka. Had a few, I reckon, the way she was gigglin' an' that.'

Ramsay listens to the girl's heart with his stethoscope. The palpitation has subsided and the beat is practically normal. Ramsay sniffs her breath. What he smells is food.

'When did she last have something to eat?'

'Just before we left the party. The geezer's got a microwave. He heated up some of last night's leftover take-away.'

Ramsay sniffs again, then he straightens. His face is beatific. He turns to Sue McLean. 'It was the time of night that threw me. I've only seen this three times before, and always around midnight. I never even thought of it.' He cups the moaning girl's jaw. 'Hot,' he says, and now he's smiling. He runs a finger along the edges of her eyelids. To her friend he says, 'Did her eyes start streaming at any time? And was she clutching her chest?'

The girl looks impressed. 'Yeah. Said she couldn't breathe, something like that, and she was clutching at herself, just like you said. The tears were running out of her, I thought she was crying.'

'I think we'll just leave her for a while,' Ramsay says. 'She can have a big mug of black coffee when she comes round.' He puts the sheet over the girl and leads the way out of the cubicle.

'What is it she's got?' the friend asks, as Ramsay is showing her where the waiting room is. Sue McLean's intense little face is asking the same question.

'Chinese Restaurant Syndrome, it's called,' Ramsay says, 'on top of far too much booze.'

'Never heard of it,' the girl says. 'You mean she got all that through eatin' the Chinky food?'

'She got it from the stuff they use to improve the flavour. Monosodium glutamate. Some people are sort of allergic to it.'

'She's never had bother with it before. She eats plenty of Chinese.'

'She's probably never had it microwaved before,' Ramsay points out. 'A lot of the moisture would be driven out of the food, and the concentration of the chemical would get higher than usual, high enough to trigger your friend's reaction. Coupled with a lot of alcohol in her bloodstream, it must have been quite spectacular. But she'll be all right. Go and take a seat and we'll call you when she's feeling more like herself again.'

Casualty is the best place for a doctor to gain speed and accuracy in medical detective work. There is no time for laboratory tests when a patient is distressed or unconscious; the doctor has to rely on experience and an alertness to small clues in the patients' appearance or behaviour.

A month ago, Donald Ramsay treated a case which was just as misleading as The Chinese Restaurant Syndrome. An old man was brought to Casualty suffering an apparent coronary attack. His face was blue, he was semi-conscious, and his breathing was laboured. Sister had made preparations to administer the usual cardiac emergency treatment, but there was one sign that made Ramsay doubt this was a heart case; the patient was silent. Always, the patient with a cardiac emergency groans or cries out continuously.

With his finger and thumb, Ramsay reached into the old man's throat and located a half-chewed lump of meat. In less than a minute after the obstruction had been removed, the patient was returning to normal. The so-called Café Coronary has probably gone undetected many times, although casualty officers are more alert to it nowadays. The patients are usually old, they nearly always have false teeth, and they don't chew their food properly. Their silence is the only clue to what is really wrong.

Sue McLean goes off to keep an eye on the girl in the cubicle and Ramsay opens the office door and peers in. Sister Pringle is at her paperwork. In the chair opposite the desk, Glenda Cross is lying back, fast asleep. Ramsay opens the door wider.

'She looks almost innocent like that,' he says.

Sister smiles through a screen of cigarette smoke. 'She's had a lousy night. I told her to relax for a while.'

Ramsay closes the door and goes out to the ambulance bay, where John Blake is standing, hands in pockets, sniffing the air. He turns as Ramsay comes through the door.

'Donald, my son. Join me. I'm checking the lead level.'

They stand together and watch the faint light in the sky. It has been raining and the growing traffic noises beyond the grounds have a sibilant edge that rises and falls like distant, lapping waves.

'Home time soon,' John says. 'I'm ready for my bed.'

'I was ready for mine an hour ago.'

Blake and Ramsay have a natural harmony. They have never felt any awkwardness in each other's company, nor have there been any major disagreements in the time they have been working together. Donald Ramsay joined the Casualty team three weeks after John's promotion to Senior Casualty Officer, and over the period since then they have become friends socially as well as professionally. Though John Blake has never spoken about it, he believes that what they have most strongly in common is an even temperament, plus a sense of proportion – and they never take themselves too seriously.

'What's the latest on your patient?' Ramsay has no need to say which one.

'Not good.' John waves a hand in the direction of the gynaecology block. 'She's over there now. They're getting Vernon Lloyd to look in on her later. I don't think it'll do much good, though. There's nothing to take a grip of and encourage her with.' He sighs. 'It'll be a long haul, prognosis so-so.' He shows no inclination to discuss the matter any further.

Lights are going on all over the hospital. A breeze from the kitchens brings the scent of hundreds of breakfasts that are being transferred to the mobile heated containers. John groans as an ambulance comes speeding up the drive, but it turns right and disappears round the other side of the block.

'One hour,' Ramsay yawns, looking at his watch.

'The longest one.'

They gaze at the edge of the sky turning silver for another couple of minutes.

'Sometimes,' Ramsay says, 'I get paralysed by the variety.'

John Blake looks at him. 'Paralysed by the variety of what?'

'Accidents. Emergencies. Trauma. Maybe not paralysed, but I go a bit lame, mentally.'

'You can be very opaque at this time of day, Donald.'

Ramsay shrugs. 'I just looked at a kid with MSG syndrome. It struck me then, the conspiracy angle ... the way I used to feel about bacteria – millions of them out there, waiting to pounce. I feel that way about accidents now. I mean, you can't even eat a mouthful of chow mein without one landing on you.'

John Blake stares across at the blue light streaming from the side door of the laundry. 'I sometimes wonder about you,' he says softly.

The rain is starting up again. Large spots strike the doctors' shoes and put dark ovals on their white coats. Dr Ramsay pushes open the glass door and they go back into the warm.

Saturday

On what is always the busiest day in Casualty, the day-shift staff usually have plenty of time to organise the department before the cases start coming in. But not today. At 7.40 a.m., ten minutes after the last members of the night team have gone home, three ambulances pull up in the bay and the attendants start wheeling in the passengers, six injured football fans whose coach crashed after travelling overnight from the north of England.

The day team's Senior Casualty Officer, Alan Smedley, hasn't arrived yet. He called earlier to tell Sister Harper that his car wouldn't start. Student Nurse Lunt appears to have 'flu and Desmond Owen, the Junior Casualty Officer, has hurt his back playing squash.

'I'm going to be in a rotten temper today,' Rose Harper tells Dr Owen as they approach the first trolley. 'You see if I'm not.'

They stand on either side of the trolley. Dr Owen is tall, over six feet, and he bends awkwardly to make his examination, trying to keep the strain off his back. Sister, seeing his difficulty, briskly lifts the blanket off the patient and starts undoing the young man's clothing. She is a short squarish woman in her forties who can't avoid making all her movements look angular.

The patient is conscious but confused. He has a four-inch laceration running diagonally across his forehead and a smaller one on the point of his chin. Blood has spread into his hair and dried in places, making the injury look much worse than it is. Dr Owen feels the patient's ribcage carefully, then flexes his arms and legs.

'Mildly concussed, that's about all,' Owen says. 'Will you get him to a cubicle and check his BP please, Sister?' He moves off to look at the next patient.

69

Sister Harper signals to Nurse Lunt, who comes forward and starts pushing the trolley to the cubicle area. Staff Nurse Iris Cole, who has been helping the ambulancemen get the trolleys through the doors, goes across to Sister. She points to Nurse Lunt and murmurs, 'I think we'll have to send her back to the home. She looks terrible.'

'I know, I know,' Sister groans. 'Let's just wait till the flap's over. We need all the hands we can get.'

Iris nods. 'I'll keep an eye on her. She said she was feeling dizzy earlier.'

Sister taps the glass of her fob watch. 'We're supposed to have two extra nurses here this morning. Where are they?' She looks round suddenly, scanning the department and craning her neck to see into the waiting room. 'And where's Miles? He's never about when he's needed, that one.' She's referring to Miles Campbell, the early-shift porter. He is a young, permanently-smiling Jamaican with a leisurely workstyle that's come under fire from Sister Harper, almost daily, since he got the job two months ago.

'He's outside somewhere.'

'Well, if you see him before I do, send him to me.' Sister's warning about her temper is moving towards fulfilment. 'Look at this place. It's not eight o'clock yet and it's a shambles.'

The floor, spotless five minutes ago, is marked with muddy bootprints and damp tyre tracks from the trolleys. An intermittent breeze, blowing through the doors while the ambulancemen have been bringing in the patients, has detached several sheets of paper from the bulletin board and they're scattered across the space between the office and the bay. Five trolleys are in an untidy line from the outer doors to the entrance to X-ray.

'Don't worry,' Iris Cole says soothingly, 'we'll get it cleaned up.' To her husband, Iris has privately confided that she spends nearly as much on-duty time comforting Sister Harper as reassuring the patients. Sister has a peptic ulcer, and when it is troubling her – which is often – she's inclined to feel oppressed.

As Sister goes off to take the blood pressure of the man in the cubicle, Dr Owen beckons Iris Cole to the case he is examining. The patient is middle-aged and grossly overweight. He is making no sound but his fleshy cheeks are wobbling steadily, as if an electric current is being passed through him.

70

'He's haemorrhaging badly,' Owen says. 'I don't know where yet, but we better get some Dextran into him.'

They wheel the patient into the Emergency room and Iris starts setting up a drip feed. The Dextran she's going to use is a chemical compound called a polysaccharide, a complex collection of sugar molecules which makes a powerful substitute for blood. In an emergency it can be used until a patient's blood group is determined and whole blood can be administered.

Dr Owen is feeling the man's abdomen carefully with flattened hands, checking the liver first for signs of haemorrhage. When it's normal, the liver is felt as a clear, regular border that moves under the pressure of the advancing fingertips. In this case, because the man is so fat, Owen is having difficulty detecting the liver at all.

'He's getting bluish,' Owen mutters, and switches his searching hands to the patient's chest. 'Get the Dextran into him the fast way, Nurse. And use the blood warmer.'

It is common enough for injured people to bleed to death without a drop of blood ever showing. This patient is already dangerously near death, so to counter the decline the replacement solution will be put into his veins much faster than a normal transfusion, with the aid of a machine called a pressure infuser. With this technique, there is always a danger that the heart will stop, because of the sudden drop in blood temperature, so the Dextran will pass through a machine which raises its temperature before it reaches the body.

'Got it!' Owen lifts his hands from the patient's chest. 'Haemopneumothorax. You carry on getting the Dextran into him, I'll alert the boss.'

The indication is that the patient has a torn lung, so his jeopardy is twofold. He is losing a lot of blood, and the combined leakage of air and blood is collecting in the cavity of the chest and putting the heart under pressure.

On his way to the telephone Dr Owen is intercepted by Sister Harper. She tells him the young man with the lacerated face has normal blood pressure. 'But there's something else wrong. He has trouble opening his mouth.'

'Hang on to him. We've got an emergency in there.' Dr Owen goes off to the office at a gallop, then brakes as pain jolts through

71

his back. Sister sighs and begins examining the four remaining cases.

During the daytime the Consultant Surgeon, Mr Hathaway, is on call to Casualty in the event of any serious chest injuries being brought in. If major surgery is urgent, it will be performed in Casualty's own big theatre, which is always on standby.

When Dr Owen has contacted Mr Hathaway, he outlines the case and waits while the consultant considers his course of action. In this instance it takes only a few seconds.

'It's more likely he's got torn vessels in the thoracic cage,' Mr Hathaway tells Dr Owen. 'Get a tap into the chest and I'll organise a theatre team. Are you setting up Dextran?'

'Right this minute, sir.'

'Push it to the limit,' Mr Hathaway says. 'Give him 500 mils in five minutes, and keep giving it to him until the theatre's ready. And get a sample for grouping. I'll be with you in about ten minutes.'

Alan Smedley, the Senior Casualty Officer, comes into the department as Dr Owen is hobbling back to Emergency. He stands by the door for a minute, catching his breath.

'The late Dr Smedley,' Sister says, coming across from the trolleys. 'How's your car?'

'Terminal rust,' he tells her, 'thrombosed fuel feed and something like atheroma on the plugs.' He is a short, thickset man in his late thirties with a highly mobile face that's mimicking tragedy. 'It's had it. Trouble is, I'm fond of the beast, having it put down will be hell.' He buttons his coat and straightens his tie, gazing at the trolleys as he does so. 'What've we got, Sister?'

'A coach accident. Six passengers were on their feet when it happened and they're all here. There's one emergency, one mysterious jaw complaint, and the others are the usual collection of cuts and bruises.' Sister points to the nearest trolley. 'He's got a dislocated shoulder.'

The two extra nurses Sister has been expecting come in through the ambulance bay doors. Sister goes across to them and starts giving them orders before they have their cloaks off.

Alan Smedley goes to the Emergency room where Dr Owen fills him in on what's happening. 'I'm glad you're here,' Owen says. 'I'm not too hot at putting taps in chests.'

Smedley takes over. First, he puts on sterile gloves and has Iris Cole clean an area of the patient's right lower chest. The area is then surrounded with sterile towels. Next, Dr Smedley injects lidocaine, a local anaesthetic, into the area he will operate on, which is the sixth inter-rib space. As he is doing this, Dr Owen has taken over the administration of the Dextran, giving regular squeezes to the bulb on the pressure infuser and checking the gauge all the time.

'Right,' Smedley says, when he is content the anaesthetic has taken effect, 'let's have a nice sharp knife, Staff.'

Iris hands him a scalpel from the emergency trolley and Smedley holds it carefully, in a penholder grip, over the operation site. With the other hand, he traces the point he wants to penetrate, then he makes a one-inch incision. It goes deep, right through the skin and into the chest wall. Smedley pushes the knife a little deeper, then withdraws it. With one straight finger he probes the opening he has made, while Iris swabs away the blood from the incision.

'Give me the tube. Quick.' Dr Smedley has completed the opening into the chest cavity with his finger, and he has satisfied himself that the lung is not adhering to the chest at that point. Now he is plugging the completed opening with his finger until the air and blood can be properly channelled.

The drainage tube is handed to him, clamped by a pair of forceps. Smedley removes his finger from the hole and pushes the tube in swiftly; the first few inches of the tube are perforated around the circumference, to eliminate the danger of blockage that would occur if there were only one opening. All of these holes have to be within the chest wall before the clamp is removed.

'Needle and heavy nylon suture, Staff.'

As Dr Smedley is advancing the tube into the patient's chest, Iris threads a curved needle with strong gut and hands it to him when he's ready. Smedley makes a rapid stitch between the skin and the tube, anchoring the drain in place.

'Make sure the hole in the bag's clear,' Smedley says to Iris.

The drainage tube ends in a transparent collecting bag with a measuring scale on its side. Because a lot of air will be coming out of the patient's chest when the clamp is taken off the tube, it has to be given an escape route, or the bag will inflate like a balloon. Iris checks the hole and nods to Dr Smedley.

'Stand by for blasting.' Smedley takes the forceps off the tube and blood surges through it, sputtering at first as the escaping air cuts a turbulent path to the hole in the bag. After a few seconds the flow settles to a steady stream.

The patient's colour has improved already. The combined effects of reduced pressure in the chest and the blood substitute have put him in a position of containment, until he can be operated on by Mr Hathaway.

'Can I leave you to it now?' Dr Smedley asks Dr Owen.

'Certainly,' Dr Owen says. 'And thanks.'

As with a lot of junior surgeons, Owen still finds the immediacy of casualty work unnerving at times. The leisurely approach of his theatre training has given him meticulous habits that he now has to adapt to the needs of the battlefield. He has been in Casualty for two months, and although there are still situations that can overthrow his judgement and ability, Mr Hathaway and Dr Smedley are satisfied with his progress.

'If there's any panic, I'll be outside,' Smedley says. 'By the way, Desmond, have you done your back in again?'

'I'm afraid so, yes.'

'Serves you right. Sport's a vice, you know. You should learn to overcome it.'

All of the remaining cases have been transferred from the trolleys to cubicles. Smedley goes to the first cubicle and looks inside. Nurse Lunt is fixing a dressing on the forehead of the young man with the unspecified jaw trouble.

'Are you all right, Nurse?' Smedley has noticed straight away the girl's unnatural pallor and the stoop of her shoulders.

She turns her eyes to him and they have the sparkle of fever. 'Touch of 'flu I think, Doctor.'

'A touch?' Smedley goes forward and puts his fingertips on the skin of her cheek. It is dry and hot. 'A shade more than a touch, I think.'

'I'll have a couple of aspirin when I've finished here.'

'If you're determined to stay on duty, you'll have more than that. I'll make you up a cocktail when I get a minute.'

Nurse Lunt moves aside and Dr Smedley looks at the patient's injuries. After a swift reading of Sister Harper's notes on the case card, he feels the sides of the jaw. The young man is more alert now, and he is blinking his eyes rapidly, the way people do when they are experiencing sharp, recurring pain.

'Can you speak at all?' Dr Smedley asks.

The patient moves his jaw a fraction, then closes his eyes tight with pain.

'Try to relax.'

Smedley touches the bony area in front of the youth's left ear, then the right. The patient groans loudly and Dr Smedley pats his shoulder several times, calming him.

'I won't do that to you again. I want you to lie still and try not to move your jaw. We'll give you something for the pain in a couple of minutes.'

Outside, Dr Smedley speaks to Sister. He tells her that the boy's jaw is going to need surgery.

'It's broken, then?' Sister looks puzzled. 'I couldn't find a break anywhere.'

'It's an interesting kind of break. The laceration on his chin was the signal. He must have hit the deck jaw first, and the impact snapped off his right condyle.'

Sister winces in sympathy. The condyle is the rounded lug of bone that forms the hinge of the jaw with the cheek bone. Every time the young man has tried to open his mouth, sharp-edged bone fragments have raked across the tissue surrounding his ear.

'Get him to X-ray as soon as possible, then have him admitted to Men's Surgical,' Dr Smedley says. 'Give him ten milligrams of morphine when he's been X-rayed.' Smedley rubs his hands. 'Now. Do we still have some brandy in the hidey-hole?'

Sister's got her puzzled look again. 'About half a bottle.' She takes a key from her pocket and hands it over. 'Leave us some for Christmas, won't you.'

'I'm on an errand of mercy. I'll deal with the dislocated shoulder in five minutes.'

A theatre team is preparing the large theatre and Mr Hathaway is scrubbing up in the room adjacent to the sterile zone, at the rear of the theatre. Trays of instruments have been put in position beside the operating table and the mobile anaesthetic machine is being set up. Ellen Mackie, the Theatre Sister, is in Emergency, preparing the patient for surgery.

Hathaway is a stout, white-haired man of fifty, a thoracic surgeon with twenty-three years' experience of emergency chest

75

operations. He is the co-author of a widely-praised book on heart surgery, and he makes annual lecture tours in Europe and the United States, explaining his advanced methods of dealing with certain heart and lung injuries which, until a few years ago, were invariably fatal. A colleague has described Terence Hathaway as having ultra-modern skill and an Edwardian social style. He is popular with everyone, including the administrators.

Hathaway is the man who, more than anyone else, has campaigned hard to give Casualty Surgeons a specialist status at Anderson General. Unlike America, which has an abundance of casualty specialists, British medical practice has never had a distinct category for the men and women whose daily work is the treatment of accidents and emergencies. Casualty has traditionally been the Cinderella department, often run on a day-to-day basis and manned by whoever was available. All that is changing fast; there are senior men like Alan Smedley and John Blake who make Casualty their full-time job, and nurses who do the same; they have the active support and encouragement of Mr Hathaway, who has set up a recruitment and training scheme which is being used as a model by other London and regional hospital boards.

This morning, Mr Hathaway has asked Dr Owen to assist him in theatre. Owen has worked with the consultant before, and although the prospect makes him nervous, he knows he'll learn something.

When both men are scrubbed-up, gowned, masked and gloved, they go into the theatre. The patient is already on the table, and Sister Mackie, the senior nurse on the theatre team, has set up a support drip of matched whole blood.

'These radiographs,' Hathaway says as he examines the X-ray plate attached to the light box, 'can be desperately misleading.' The picture of the patient's chest cavity looks almost normal. 'I can see where the trouble is, but I've been a damnably long time learning the knack.' He encircles an area with his finger. 'See it?'

Owen looks hard. 'I'm afraid not, sir.'

'Never mind. The fault's not yours, Doctor. It's technology's.' He goes across to look at the patient.

The anaesthetist, Dr Wolfe, is manipulating his wheeled apparatus at the head of the table. He has chosen to feed the patient nitrous oxide, which acts faster than most other anaes-

76

thetics. A cardiac monitor is giving a continuous picture of the patient's heart rhythm, and Wolfe uses the display to modify his gas and air mixture as the injured man's level of consciousness drops.

'He's had a close shave, by the look of him,' Hathaway says. 'Have we reached the mysterious third stage, Dr Wolfe?'

'A minute or so,' Wolfe mutters, keeping his eyes on the monitor.

The patient is lying half on his back and half on his right side. The site of the operation has been disinfected and surrounded with green towels. Mr Hathaway moves close, altering the angle of the operating lamp.

'A very neat drain, Dr Owen,' he says.

'Dr Smedley did it, sir.'

'I'm sure yours would have been just as elegant.' Hathaway glances across at Sister Mackie, who is checking the instrument layout with one of her nurses. 'Sister, I know it must seem callously irrelevant at the moment, but can I take it we'll have some black coffee when we've finished?'

'The percolator's on, sir.'

Hathaway waggles one bushy eyebrow appreciatively. 'Thank the Lord.' He turns to Owen. 'We celebrated my father's eightieth birthday last night,' he murmurs. 'There was a lot of claret. If this poor man had any idea how much I absorbed, he wouldn't let me anywhere near him with a knife.'

'Ready now,' Dr Wolfe says. The third stage of unconsciousness, called surgical anaesthesia, has been reached. The patient's breathing is shallow and regular and his muscles are totally relaxed.

'Off we go, then.' Mr Hathaway takes up a knife, ready to lay open the patient's chest. 'Stand by with suction, Sister. Dr Owen, you should stand as close to me as you can. You'll see something interesting, I fancy.'

* * *

8.50 a.m. The young fan is lying face down on a trolley that has been jacked up until he is five feet above the floor. His right arm is hanging over the side, and he's holding a bucket of water. His fingers have been taped around the bucket handle, so he can't drop it.

'I feel daft like this,' he tells Nurse Lunt.

'It's for your own good.'

'It's embarrassing.'

Dr Smedley decided on the treatment after he examined the young man's dislocated shoulder. X-rays confirmed there were no fractures of the collarbone or the upper part of the arm, so it was safe to go ahead with the unorthodox-looking procedure, which in fact is the best way to treat this particular dislocation.

The bucket is empty when it is first taped into the patient's hand. It is carefully filled with water, and its weight exerts a steady traction on the arm. The patient is given a five-milligram injection of Valium to help his muscles relax, and after a short time the dislocated shoulder usually corrects itself.

'Just lie still and be grateful it wasn't something more serious,' Nurse Lunt tells the patient. 'Or more embarrassing.'

She steps out of the cubicle and sees Staff Nurse Iris Cole lugging a pile of case folders that's so high it nearly obscures her line of vision.

'Let me help you, Staff.'

'No, it's all right.' Iris dumps the folders on a table by the sluice and blows a quiff of red hair out of her eyes. 'Our absentee porter, Laughing Boy, can shift them for me when Sister's finished with him.' Iris peers close at Nurse Lunt's eyes. 'You still look a bit down, Maggie. Sure you're coping?'

'I'm a lot better, honestly. Dr Smedley's concoction's helped.'

'He's got a few of those,' Iris says darkly. 'One too many and you're hooked.'

'It's brandy and something...'

'Something.' Iris shakes her head. 'Spanish fly, for all you know.'

Dr Smedley comes across from the office, swinging his stethoscope. 'Everything under control, ladies?'

'I was just explaining to Nurse Lunt,' Iris says, 'that your cocktails tend to be addictive.'

'Only some of them. I'll let you try out a new one I've cooked up for Christmas. It's called Death in the Afternoon. A real belter.' He winks slyly at Maggie Lunt and goes into the cubicle to see the boy with the dislocation.

Iris looks around her. 'All square now, I think. Time for a cuppa.' She goes into the sluice and Nurse Lunt follows her.

Departmental harmony, disturbed by the bad start to the morning, has gradually been restored. The patient with the jaw injury is in a surgical ward and the man with the injured chest is being dealt with in theatre. When the youth with the dislocated shoulder has been strapped and bound he'll be released, as the other three have been. The only matter outstanding is the reprimanding of the porter, Miles Campbell, and Sister Harper is taking care of that in the plaster room.

'Your attitude to the job's all wrong,' she tells Miles. He makes this kind of thing difficult for Sister; Miles is a foot taller than her and the gentle smile on his face is uncannily fixed. 'We expect a bit of speed and efficiency in this department. You knew that when you took the job. Now this is, what, the third time I've had to speak to you about going missing...'

'But ah told you, Sista...' Miles's voice is another barrier to sustained attack. It's melodious and soothing, as likeable as the rest of the man.

'You told me,' Sister cuts in, 'that you went round to help out at the laundry. It's no excuse at all, Miles.'

'But they asked me.'

'Because they know you don't argue. Next time anybody from another department asks you to do something, refer them to me.'

'Right you are.'

Sister stares at his big, pitiful eyes and decides to cut the interview short. 'I'll say this once more, and if you don't take it seriously this time, you'll be reported to the Secretary.' She puts up a warning finger and Miles stares at it, as if it might go off. 'You'll remain in the department at all times unless I or members of my staff require you to leave for some good reason. And when you're asked to do something, you'll do it as fast as you can.'

'Right, Sista,' Miles says quietly.

'On you go, then.'

When he has gone Sister sits down and draws her hand slowly over her stomach. The pain has become steadily worse since she came on duty. At times it reaches the proportions of a separate object, something big and heavy invading her tissues, burning as it spreads. She knows nowadays why laymen with stomach ulcers often think they're ten or twenty times the size they actually are.

In the large theatre, Mr Hathaway is halfway through the chest operation. He began by having the patient turned carefully on his right side; his right arm was moved up over his face, out of the way. Mr Hathaway then made a long cut into the bed of the sixth rib. The shoulder blade was raised and the skin and ribs were held apart with a clamp called a rib-spreader. While Dr Owen tied off some bleeding points and put clamps on others, Mr Hathaway steadily widened and deepened the opening into the patient's chest. Finally, he stepped aside and asked Dr Owen what he made of it.

When Owen looked, he barely recognised anything he saw. The normal contours and colouring of the vessels in the chest were transformed to engorged, pulsing masses with a uniform dark scarlet tint. In spite of steady suction from Sister's probe, there was a pool of blood that appeared to be deepening as Owen looked, obscuring the bottom of the chest cavity and complicating the picture even more.

'It's a bit confusing, sir...'

'You can imagine how I felt when I first saw one,' Mr Hathaway said. 'It scared the wits out of me. Nothing I recognised. Nothing I could hold without it sliding out of my fingers. And all that blood. Ghastly.'

Without yet telling Dr Owen what's wrong with the patient, Mr Hathaway has cleared the operation site considerably. Additional suction has kept pace with the bleeding, and heavier organs have been moved aside to facilitate further cutting. Even so, Mr Hathaway is working with his hands in a puddle of blood, moving his fine scalpel an inch at a time behind the guiding fingers of his left hand.

'Any ideas yet, Dr Owen?'

'I can't quite see what your knife's doing, sir...'

'Neither can I.'

'Well...' Owen is reluctant to commit himself to an opinion, but Mr Hathaway is expecting one. 'A tear somewhere on the aorta, perhaps?'

Hathaway nods. 'Close enough, Doctor. It's a nick, really, a very small puncture. Hence the squirting nature of the blood leak. And of course, there's an associated tear in the left lung. That's pretty small too, but in combination the pumping and blowing swept this unfortunate soul pretty close to his maker's front door.'

80

'Can you stitch it, sir?'

'It's to be hoped so. If not, I'll have to put in a bypass, and really, I'm long overdue for that coffee.'

The surgery Mr Hathaway is performing is extremely difficult. To reach the curve of the aorta, he has to cut along the left subclavian artery, which is a tributary of the aorta and join it at a point where it dips down behind the heart. When he finally has his fingers around the aortic curve he asks Sister Mackie for a tape, which he loops around the aorta to help him hold it.

'Now. Let's have a look.' Hathaway raises the ends of the tape and the thick, snaking length of the aorta rises out of the blood. 'There's the blighter.' He points with his scalpel to what looks like a small clot. When he draws a finger across it however, the hole is clearly visible, still pushing out blood in a thin, pulsating stream. 'Thank goodness it's a round one,' Hathaway murmurs. 'Square holes are the very devil to stitch.'

While Sister Mackie threads a very fine needle with catgut, Mr Hathaway plugs the hole in the aorta with a piece of gauze. He leaves the gauze in place to soak up the excess blood as he starts to surround the hole with catgut, pushing the needle carefully through the soft tissue until the tear is completely encircled. He then takes out the gauze plug and tightens the ends of the catgut. The special stitch he has made is called a purse-string suture, and as he pulls firmly the hole closes in a tight pucker, which Mr Hathaway pushes inwards before he tightens the stitch fully and ties it.

'There.'

Dr Owen's admiration is limitless. He has felt himself edge close to panic at times, as he tried to get a stitch into an organ that was relatively simple to handle, such as the stomach. He has known the day-long depression that has followed a fumbling, protracted appendicectomy where the need for accurate cutting and suturing has been thwarted, maddeningly, by the sheer slipperiness of the organs as they slithered on the lubricating blood covering his gloves. Yet Mr Hathaway has made a murderously difficult operation look like a straightforward, routine piece of surgery.

'That was magnificent, sir.'

'No,' Mr Hathaway replies softly, as he feels for and finds the

81

small hole in the patient's lung. 'That was competent. Magnificent's when I achieve the impossible, which is usually on Fridays.' He looks at Dr Owen for a moment, and the wrinkling of his eyes above the mask indicates that he's smiling.

The lung has the ability to heal itself rapidly and needs only a little help from the surgeon. Mr Hathaway puts two fine catgut stitches across the wound, and after he has satisfied himself that the hole is properly closed, he stands away from the table.

'If you and your ladies would care to mop up in there now, Sister, I think we can re-assemble the gentleman.' To Owen he says, 'You won't see too many cases like this. Usually the internal damage is more dramatic, so it's easier to locate and rectify, though you've got less time.'

'How do you think it happened, sir?'

'He was most likely coughing when the vehicle crashed. Lots of pressure in the chest. Pop. Something had to give. If he'd had less fat cushioning him, and less elastic organs, he would probably have died on the spot.'

It takes another twenty minutes to complete the operation. The patient is removed to a surgical ward and Dr Owen gets ready to go back to Casualty.

In the changing room, Mr Hathaway takes Owen aside for a moment.

'Do you think you're going to survive in Casualty, Doctor?'

'I think so, sir. I like the work.'

'That's good to know. It puts pressure on all your resources, as I told you at the start, but it's very rewarding.' Mr Hathaway eases off his rubber shoes and sits down. 'What you have to watch out for, as time passes, is a falling-off in your enthusiasm. You can get away with half-power devotion in other fields, but not in Casualty.'

Owen nods. 'I'll bear it in mind.'

'There's a knack to it,' Hathaway says. 'It's simple, too. Think of your work as play, make yourself feel positively self-indulgent, as if there's something *else* called duty that you should be attending to. It might sound odd, but it works.' He smiles. 'I've been doing it for my entire professional life.'

When Dr Owen returns to Casualty, a man is being wheeled into Emergency.

'Overdose,' Dr Smedley says. He is on his way to Emergency with his stethoscope already in his ears. 'How's your back feeling?'

'It's killing me.'

'Go and sit down for a bit, then. There's nobody waiting.'

In Emergency Iris Cole has opened the patient's shirt and is pushing up his vest, clearing the chest. The man is in his twenties and has a pale, acne-pitted face that reminds Iris of one she's seen on a poster in the waiting room, warning people about the perils of glue sniffing. Part of the similarity comes from the vague, characterless eyes.

Nurse Lunt comes in behind Dr Smedley and stands to one side, waiting to carry out her part in the proceedings.

Alan Smedley has read the brief case details brought in by the ambulancemen, and he comes across to the trolley. 'Can you hear me all right, Mr Mulraine?'

The patient nods.

'What were the tablets you took? What were they called?'

The man moistens his lips. 'Codis.'

'Your mother says you told her you'd taken them about an hour ago. Now is that right? Was it as long ago as that?'

The patient tries to think, but finally he shakes his head. 'I don't know. Seems a long time.'

'How many did you swallow?'

'Two packets.'

'How many tablets in each packet?'

'Twenty.'

Dr Smedley puts his stethoscope on the man's chest and listens. The heart is beating strongly, but it is slower than normal. The patient's skin is clammy and his pupils are dilated.

'We'll get out what we can, Staff.' Iris goes to get the gastric lavage equipment and Dr Smedley leans close to the patient. 'We're going to wash your stomach out, Mr Mulraine. We have to take away as many of the tablets as we can.'

The patient rallies. He lifts himself on his elbows, shaking his head at Dr Smedley. 'I don't want the stomach pump.'

'It isn't a pump. It's nothing that scary. And it's essential we do it.'

Mulraine is still shaking his head. 'Nah. Don't need it.'

Smedley isn't prepared to waste time. 'You told your mother about the tablets because you got frightened afterwards, right? Well you've got even more cause to be frightened now. You're ill and from here on it starts to gallop. Unless we get the stuff out of your stomach.'

Mulraine lies down again. He looks troubled, but he's passive now, enough to let them get started, which is all that's needed.

Iris has the equipment on a wheeled table at the top of the trolley, where the patient won't see it. A stomach washout is a procedure that always distresses the patient, and a sight of the daunting-looking tools would only make things worse. On the table Iris has a bucket, two large jugs full of warm water, a lab specimen bottle, a large bowl, a funnel, and a long, red rubber stomach tube. There is also some auxiliary equipment – a tube of KY jelly to lubricate the tube, paper towels, a plastic airway, and a gag, consisting of a large wooden spatula with one padded end, to keep the patient's mouth open.

Mr Mulraine is turned on his right side and a plastic cape is put around his neck and shoulders. A waterproof sheet is slipped under his head, and as Iris is doing this Dr Smedley does what he can to reassure the patient.

'Remember you won't come to any harm. We're doing all this to help you.'

Iris winds up the bottom end of the trolley until the patient's feet are several inches higher than his head.

'Relax now,' Alan Smedley says, patting the patient's shoulder, moving gradually around to the other side of the trolley. He has never once seen any conscious patient able to relax during a washout, but the less tense Mr Mulraine is when they begin, the better it will go.

Iris has lubricated the tube and she lays it within Dr Smedley's reach. Standing behind the patient, Smedley asks him to open his mouth. He checks that there are no false teeth, then he inserts the gag at the side of the mouth, positioning it carefully between the teeth.

'You're doing fine, Mr Mulraine. Just fine.'

Dr Smedley nods to Iris and she steps forward and firmly grasps the patient's wrists. Mulraine tenses instantly.

'There, there. Nothing to worry about.'

Smedley brings forward the stomach tube, which has a

rounded end to assist its travel; drainage takes place through two holes in the tube's wall, close to the tip. Maintaining his grip on the gag with his left hand, he slides the tube across the patient's tongue until it's touching the back of his throat. Mr Mulraine's breathing is getting faster.

'Just swallow now. I know it's hard with your mouth open, but you can do it.'

As soon as the patient's neck muscles start jerking Smedley pushes the tube down into his throat. Mulraine starts gagging and squirming violently, and Iris has to throw one knee across his legs while she leans forward on his chest, still hanging on tightly to his wrists. Nurse Lunt moves forward to help, but Iris shakes her head. If the patient thinks too many people are suppressing him, he could develop the kind of panic that would tighten his throat around the tube.

'Marvellous, marvellous, you're doing great...' Dr Smedley steadies the patient's head with the heel of his left hand, then he tells him to swallow again. Mr Mulraine tries and the tube is pushed another ten inches down his oesophagus. He lurches so violently that Iris nearly falls.

'Right, that's just about it,' Smedley says, close to the ear of his grunting patient. 'You've nearly done it. I know you think you're going to choke, but you won't. Believe me, you won't choke. Now one more time, once only, swallow for me.' Smedley pushes the tube in another few inches, then looks up at Iris, who is red in the face with the effort of holding the patient down. 'Coping?' he asks her. She nods, and he beckons for Nurse Lunt to come over. 'Specimen first,' he tells her.

Maggie Lunt opens the lab bottle and puts it in the bowl, then she places them both on the floor, as Dr Smedley brings over the free end of the tube and lowers it. Stomach contents start to trickle from the end of the tube into the bottle.

When it is full Maggie closes it, and she directs the remainder of the flow into the bowl. The bottle contains the first concentrated drainage from the stomach, and it's important that it be examined in the lab so that any subsequent therapy can be guided by the biochemical picture the analysis produces.

'Let's have a look.' Alan Smedley is still holding on to the gag and the tube, and he is using his left forearm now to stabilise Mr Mulraine's head. He peers at the bottle as Nurse Lunt holds it against the light. 'Promising,' he murmurs. There is evidence, in the form of a distinct sediment and particles of tablets, that a substantial amount of the drug hasn't yet been absorbed by the patient's system.

Nurse Lunt has now attached the funnel to the end of the stomach tube and she raises it and pours in a few ounces of the warm water, while Dr Smedley steadies the patient's head with both hands now.

After a few seconds the funnel is turned down over the bucket, and the water siphons out. It is muddy and flecked with particles of food and more of the part-dissolved tablets. The process of pouring the water into the stomach and siphoning it out again will continue until the siphoned water runs clear, indicating that the stomach is clean.

'Just a few more minutes, Mr Mulraine,' Dr Smedley says.

In fact they will probably be washing him out for another ten minutes. Throughout that time Iris Cole will have to go on restraining him, and Alan Smedley will need to keep the jaw jammed open, for the distress of a washout doesn't lessen with the passing of time. Mulraine will still feel that he's going to choke any second, and the fluttering nausea running between his throat and stomach will make him feel worse than any amount of vomiting would.

Gastric lavage is an invaluable procedure, for all its drawbacks. It has saved countless lives. But it has an unusual feature that medical statisticians have known about for some time: it is a deterrent to suicide. A Swedish report puts it succinctly.

'Few men or women who have attempted to kill themselves with drugs, and who have subsequently been saved by gastric washout, ever make the attempt again. Even in those instances where a person has overdosed on several previous occasions, the introduction of the washout procedure causes an abrupt change of behaviour: fewer than five per cent will ever try again.'

Alan Smedley is aware of those facts, but he has his own observations on the topic, and they tend to modify the deterrent theory. Looking down now at poor, shuddering Mulraine, Alan is convinced *he* won't try again. Mulraine is no true death-seeker. But there have been others – three in Alan Smedley's experience – who have attempted suicide again, quite shortly after being saved by gastric lavage, and all three succeeded on that attempt.

86

They succeeded because they made sure they would, by taking truly massive overdoses. The conclusion needs research to substantiate it, but even so it has a seductive likelihood: a stomach washout will deter some people from suicide, but it will make others fiercely determined to get it right next time.

Out in the waiting room Connie Lewis, the day receptionist, is helping a small, terrified-looking woman to get her husband through the door to the treatment area. He is a man of around fifty, pale and disorientated, and there is a thread of saliva dripping from the corner of his half-open mouth. He is dressed for the fireside in shirtsleeves and carpet slippers.

'Can somebody help us, please!' Connie cries out.

The man's feet slide aimlessly as the two women push him ahead of them. He is mumbling feebly and the fingers of both hands flex and unflex all the time.

'OK now, I've got him.' Miles, the porter, has come across and taken the man under the arms. He half-carries him to a trolley and rolls him on to it.

Sister comes out of the office. 'What's happened here?' she asks the woman.

'I don't know.' She is at that pitch where anxiety makes her stare, searching faces for an answer to the conundrum. To Sister Harper she says, 'He was in the bathroom. I heard him coughing.' Then her frightened eyes dart to Miles's soft-smiling face and she tells him, 'He came out, staggering, still coughing a bit, then he started wheezing.' She looks at her husband lying on the trolley, still mumbling and drooling. 'He sort of slid down into a chair. I couldn't get any sense out of him. It was a terrible job getting him here. He kept falling over in the car.'

Sister calls Dr Owen, and when he comes he makes an immediate check of the man's level of consciousness. He shines his torch into the patient's eyes, presses his thumb hard on his chest, pinches the skin of his arms and face and squeezes the Achilles' tendon at his ankle.

'What's his first name?' he asks the woman.

'Denis.'

Dr Owen calls the name sharply, first in one ear and then the other. To this stimulus, as to all the others, the man makes no response.

Sister Harper takes the woman aside and asks her for some

details. Her husband is Denis Wyatt, he is fifty-one, an electrician, and he has no record of any serious illness. He drinks very little and gave up smoking ten years ago.

'Is it his heart?' Mrs Wyatt asks.

'I don't think so,' Sister tells her. 'Now can you tell me everything that's happened this morning, right from the time your husband got out of bed?'

Mrs Wyatt is turning pale. The delayed shock of an event that's wildly out of the ordinary is settling on her now. Sister abandons her questioning and leads the woman to a chair and tells one of the auxiliary nurses to bring her a cup of tea. Mrs Wyatt sits motionless, watching the increase of activity around the trolley.

Dr Owen has decided that Denis Wyatt is sinking into coma, though of what kind he can't be sure. The first thing to do, since the man's breathing has become shallow, is to get him on to a ventilation machine. Miles Campbell is already wheeling it across to the trolley. An auxiliary nurse is helping Dr Owen to put the patient in a position where the air will travel to his lungs in as straight a line as possible.

Owen stops what he is doing suddenly. Watching him, Sister thinks for a second that he's hurt his back. Then she sees he's staring at the patient, and his fingers are on the carotid artery, trying to locate the pulse.

'He's arrested!' Owen hisses to the nurse. 'Quick!'

Between them they rush the trolley across to the clean theatre. Miles Campbell leaves the ventilator standing and goes after them.

'What is it?' Mrs Wyatt's voice is a scared squeak.

Sister Harper sits down beside her immediately and puts an arm along the back of her chair. It's a rule in the handling of relatives that the nurse will never try to offer comfort or reassurance from a distance. 'Just sit tight, love. They're doing everything they can.'

As soon as they are inside the theatre Dr Owen, Miles and the nurse lift Mr Wyatt off the trolley and put him on the floor. Miles brings over the defibrillator and plugs it in, while Dr Owen thumps the patient's chest and the nurse checks for a pulse.

Outside, Mrs Wyatt has been given her cup of tea, but she is so agitated now she can't hold it. 'What is it they're doing?' Her voice is shaky and tears are coming. 'What's wrong with my husband?' The tone demands an answer that will make everything right again.

In the theatre the emergency procedure for cardiac resuscitation is carried out and completed in less than two minutes, and Dr Owen goes on trying for another two after that, in spite of the pain that tears through his back every time he exerts pressure on Mr Wyatt's chest. But none of it works. Mr Wyatt is dead.

When she is told, Mrs Wyatt rejects the news utterly.

'He can't be! Denis has never been ill!'

Dr Owen says nothing. The phase of rejection has to be allowed to run its short course. Some people experience it for only seconds, others rant for minutes before their minds will accommodate the sombre truth.

'How can a big strong man...? He's only fifty-one!'

Sister Harper puts her arm round the woman's shoulders and in an instant she buckles. The first racking sob distorts her mouth and she begins rocking back and forward, holding herself, letting the pain whine in her throat while tears slide along her face.

'Come on, love, come on.' Sister leads Mrs Wyatt away to the office. Dr Owen and the nurse watch them until the door closes.

Owen sighs. 'Better get the body over to the mortuary.'

'Any idea what it was?' the nurse asks him.

'I haven't a clue. One second he was there, the next he wasn't.' Owen flexes his back stiffly. 'There'll have to be an autopsy.'

The nurse smiles up at him. He's gritting his teeth as both hands tentatively massage the injured region at the base of his spine. 'You've had a rotten Saturday morning so far, haven't you?'

'Terrible,' Owen says. 'The pits, as they say. But a sense of proportion eases the misery.' He points at the office door. 'However you look at it, my Saturday morning hasn't been a patch on little Mrs Wyatt's, has it?'

*   *   *

By 1.15 p.m. – apart from the six early cases from the coach crash – the number of admissions has been average for a

89

Saturday. Two fractures were treated between 10 o'clock and midday; there were three minor motoring accidents and a false-alarm miscarriage during the next hour.

At 12.30 p.m. the overlap shift came on duty. There should be six personnel – the part-timer, Dr Morrisey, a Senior Registrar called Jack Lester, Sister Jean Boyd, Staff Nurse Elsie Pitt and two second-year nurses, Sarah Bloom and Isobel Tait. But Dr Morrisey won't be attending today; his wife called to say he has 'flu. The others are content enough to face the prospect of coping without him.

The overlap team will work until nine o'clock. From four o'clock they will be on their own.

Alan Smedley is in a cubicle with another attempted suicide, a 23-year-old actress called Sophie Patterson. Her life is not in danger. Even so, she has lately made a discovery very much like the one made by would-be suicides who have their stomachs washed out: Sophie tried to slash her wrists, but she would never have used that method if she had known how much it was going to hurt.

Only one wrist is injured. There is a razor cut two inches long and not very deep, although it did go into a vein and caused a lot of bleeding. It was the copious blood, plus the searing pain of superficial nerves being sliced, that made Sophie scream so loud that the neighbours called the police, who in turn called an ambulance.

Sophie is sitting up on the examination bed, watching Dr Smedley putting four Steristrips on the cleaned wound. The dressings are similar in appearance to strips of Sellotape, and when they are used to close suitable wounds they give a very satisfactory healing scar, as good as stitching and less uncomfortable to the patient.

'Is that it, then?' Sophie is attractive, in a steely way, with long auburn hair and expressive green eyes. Her mouth has a natural pout that's emphasised by her small, rounded chin. Dr Smedley has noticed that, when she speaks, only the lower lip moves, showing neat, expertly capped teeth.

'Just a bandage to stop you waggling it about too much,' Smedley says, 'and a tetanus jab, if you haven't had one recently.'

'Haven't had one in my life.' She sighs elaborately. 'It's such

an anti-climax, all this.' She is giving Smedley a tough-girl look –
straight, challenging, ready to issue a putdown. 'Don't you have
to moralise or something? Bring me to tears, tell me what a silly
bitch I've been?'

'No, nothing like that.' Smedley smiles at her. Hostility from
attempted suicides is nothing new.

'But aren't you curious?' Sophie shifts her weight, making her
jeans creak. 'Don't you wonder why I did it?' There is less self-
assurance in her than she tries to project. It shows in the way she
makes her eyes too big and holds her neck too stiffly. 'Or perhaps
curiosity about people is something you lose when you're in a
profession that thinks it's one stage removed from being God.'

Alan goes to the door and calls Iris Cole. When she comes, he
asks her to put a bandage on the patient's wrist and then give her
an anti-tetanus injection. He turns to Sophie. 'If you come back
in a couple of days, we'll have a look at the dressing and make
any necessary adjustments.' He smiles at her again and leaves.

Iris tears the wrapping off a rolled bandage and starts to put it
on Sophie's wrist. She asks the patient, in a friendly way, how
she's feeling.

'Oh, you know,' Sophie says, 'just about the way *you'd* feel if
you'd a hole in your wrist and had just fucked-up your suicide.'

Iris doesn't respond. She puts on the bandage and straps it in
place with a length of surgical tape. She is aware that Sophie is
glaring at her, almost willing her into some kind of combat.

'I suppose I should have been a nurse myself.'

Iris looks at her, keeping her expression neutral. 'Fancy the
job, do you?'

'I fancy the easy shortcuts it gives you. Automatic authority
over people, the power of fear...'

'Oh, it's nothing like that,' Iris says pleasantly. 'You're
confusing us with tax inspectors.'

Sophie groans through an overdone sneer. 'God! How devas-
tatingly droll.'

Iris goes to the lock-up cabinet outside the cubicle and comes
back with a pre-packed syringe of tetanus vaccine. Sophie is
sitting fully upright on the bed now, grasping the sides.

'Suppose I say I'm not having that?'

She is showing anger, real and focused, without knowing her
behaviour is the opposite of what she believes it to be; it is

91

conformist, almost a commonplace among young people of her temperament who have failed an attempt to get out of the world.

'I'm supposed to convince you you should.'

Iris deliberately contributes to the impasse. She stands in front of the patient with the syringe poised at an angle that could be called aggressive, and she is no longer looking calm and bland. She looks confidently combative.

'Well you can shove it!' Sophie screeches at her.

'Oh, I'll shove it, all right.'

Iris glares hard at Sophie and takes the cover off the needle. Although it might not seem like it to a layman, and it certainly doesn't to Sophie, Iris's behaviour is entirely professional. She is obeying the rules established by experience.

Sophie jerks herself round and kneels up on the bed. 'Make one fucking move, just one!' She is trying to rush a showdown. She needs to.

Iris reaches out with her free hand and closes her fingers firmly round Sophie's upper arm. 'In my own opinion, love,' she says, 'it'd be a good thing if you didn't have the jab.' She pauses, watching Sophie's eyes start to waver. 'Without it, there's a risk you'll get lockjaw.'

Sophie's mouth opens, closes again, and then she starts to whimper. She sits back on her heels and puts both hands over her face and cries into them.

Iris moves swiftly and smoothly. She straightens the girl out on the bed and rolls a blanket over her. Sophie doesn't resist, and when the blanket is on her she buries her head beneath it and goes on sobbing against her hands.

Iris leaves the cubicle, taking the syringe with her. She goes to the office, where Dr Eva Price has been waiting. She is a Registrar in psychiatry, and she was called by Dr Smedley before he started treatment on Sophie Patterson.

'I think you're needed,' Iris says.

It's customary for attempted suicides admitted to the wards to be seen by a psychiatrist. With cases brought to Casualty, where there is no medical reason to have the patient kept in hospital, the approach is to have a psychiatrist standing by, just in case. Often a patient will seem calm and balanced at first, and then begin to disintegrate as treatment proceeds. Others, like Sophie, show strong signs from the start that they need help, but the psychiatrist will only intervene if matters come to a head.

'How is she?' Dr Price asks.

'Crying her eyes out.'

'Sounds like a good time to pop in and see her.' Dr Price stands up and smooths her white coat. She is tall and carefully groomed, and looks more like a mature model than a doctor. 'What did she do, Staff? Threaten to do you in?'

Iris explains what happened, and as she talks the psychiatrist nods steadily, listening to a familiar tale.

'And one little bit of sustained resistance brought her tumbling down,' Dr Price says, when Iris has finished. 'That's probably the story of her life.'

They leave the office and start walking towards the cubicle.

'What is it with people like her, anyway?' Iris asks.

Dr Price stops. 'I'd guess she's failed a lot of attempts to handle, rather than be handled. She's wanted to prevail in life, but she hasn't got the psychological build for it.'

'Why does she want to be like that?'

'Maybe she felt it was expected of her,' Dr Price says. 'She moves in a brittle society. And there's a lot of pressure on women to be winners these days. The big catch is, the impressionable ones take it most to heart, and they're usually the ones least equipped to carry it off.'

'So it got too much for her.'

'It's likely,' Dr Price says. 'From what you and Dr Smedley told me, it seems she's well into the old aggressive cynicism, and that's usually the last resort before the fuse blows.' Dr Price realigns loose strands of hair on either side of her head. She is as self-aware as someone with a mirror permanently in front of her. 'The way she tried to despatch herself, that backs up the speculation. It's a psychiatric rule of thumb – the more socially impotent an attempted suicide is, the more violent the method of suicide.' She starts to move away. 'End of lecture. Give me ten minutes with her, then come in.'

The waiting room is filling up. Dr Jack Lester has just called in one of the patients, an elderly priest called Father Aston. He is a frail man, and as they walk to a cubicle Dr Lester notices that the priest's right hand continually makes the same finger and thumb movement, as if he were rolling a cigarette. It's a symptom of Parkinson's disease, and so is the shuffling way he walks.

93

Dr Lester is a newcomer to Anderson General. He is a 33-year-old bachelor and he has worked in Casualty Departments in Lancashire and Warwickshire. In the month he has been with his present team he's provoked mixed reactions.

Sister Boyd thinks he is a good doctor – in fact a superb one – but she's confessed she'd like to take him outside and hoover him. The doctor's passive approach to dandruff, his shabby clothes, and his habit of shaving only on Saturday nights have brought on some rumblings among the older administrators, too. And there have been other complaints. For a senior doctor, he is considered by some people to be too dismissive of his own authority, and he's far too familiar with the junior nurses. Senior Nursing Officer Parker thinks he's uncouth.

'In here, Father. Sit down and let's have a look at you.'

The priest has an improvised rag-and-sticky-tape dressing on his cheek and a crude, blood-soaked bandage on his left hand. Ordinarily, a nurse would take care of a case like this one. But the police have spoken to Dr Lester, and he has decided to attend to the job himself.

'Who did the fancy first-aid on you, Father?'

'My housekeeper.' Father Aston smiles wanly. 'She doesn't have much of a clue, I'm afraid.'

'What's her cooking like?' Lester puts a plastic sheet across the old man's knees, then he eases the pad off his cheek and examines the wound underneath. It is a jagged-edged cut, seeping blood. When he removes the hand bandage, which is tied very tightly at the wrist, blood surges out on to the sheet, even though the wound on the palm is only superficial. 'Tourniquets,' he murmurs. 'Why has everybody got this thing about tourniquets?' It's clear that Dr Lester is talking to himself, so Father Aston says nothing.

It takes ten minutes to clean the wounds and give anti-tetanus cover. When he has finished, Jack Lester pulls up a chair for himself and sits down facing the priest.

'Your cuts'll heal up nicely,' he says. 'But how about yourself? What are you feeling like inside?'

Father Aston takes a long time to answer. The police have told Dr Lester that the old man was attacked by two youths when he caught them stealing ornamental plates and candlesticks from the church. The assault lasted only a couple of seconds – one sharp blow from a candlestick on Father Aston's cheek and one on his hand when he tried to grab the weapon – but it was his first experience of violence since childhood. Given his age and poor health, he could be traumatised to an extent that might shorten his life dramatically.

'It's difficult to describe,' Father Aston says finally. 'But I feel changed, I have to admit.'

Lester watches the sad, confused old face. Lester's Law, which is a mental ragbag of notions and certainties put together during seven years of casualty practice, says that the best therapy goes deep, far beyond the physical damage. Jack will always be prepared to spend time talking people down from their terrors.

'Part of it's shock, Father. Medical shock, the kind that throws the system off balance. That part will correct itself, it's doing it already. But fright's another thing, and so's the broken rhythm, if you see what I mean, Father...'

Father Aston smiles lopsidedly, showing teeth like old ivory.

Jack smiles back. 'Did I say something funny?'

'No. Just a coincidence. A week or two before I stopped giving sermons, I delivered one on the importance of life having a rhythm. Is that what you mean?'

'Yes, and a life like yours has a very distinct rhythm, I imagine. It comes to be as important to your health as good food or warm clothes. You're not young, so you're not all that flexible, either. This, ah, disruption you've had, it could scramble a lot of your wires for good if something isn't done to prevent that.'

'Oh, I've seen it,' Father Aston says. 'Old folk, parishioners, turned into recluses and living with the curtains closed. I think if the youngsters could experience the terrible disruption as you call it, they'd not be so cruel.' He shakes his head. 'They *are* cruel, nowadays. Thoughtless.'

'And I daresay you've got a theory or two about that, Father.' Jack Lester says it with expectation in his voice, for he wants the priest to go on talking. As with rape cases, the vital first measure, after medical attention has been given, is to have the patient distanced from the event before there's time for any dangerous brooding.

While Dr Lester is talking to the old priest, Dr Owen is taking a telephone call from a pathologist, Dr Murray. Like a lot of men in his profession, Murray is constantly making jokes. He also smokes too much, and his conversation with Dr Owen is steadily punctuated with harsh coughing.

'I keep getting the feeling you're cooking these things up for me,' Murray is saying. 'I've had four really weird ones from Casualty this month, and you've been on duty every time. What are you doing? Dragging them in off the street and murdering them every ingenious way you can think of?'

'Not guilty,' Owen says. 'What have you found, anyway?'

'Come over and have a look, if you've a minute. I've got something else I want to show you, while you're at it.'

'OK. But I won't stop for tea, if it's all the same to you.' Owen puts down the telephone and tells Sister Harper he'll be back in ten minutes. 'I'll be in the charnel house if anybody wants me.'

Dr Owen doesn't like mortuaries. He believes he is as rational as the next man, and he is properly aware that death is a negative thing, an absence. His unshakeable reaction to it, however, is just the opposite. He feels that death is a presence, and a pretty disquieting one at that.

Dr Murray is in the post mortem room when Owen arrives.

'Come on through, Desmond,' he calls. Although Dr Murray is a consultant, he treats most other doctors as equals. In the past, he has told people he's always slightly awed by men who get to lay their hands on living patients.

Owen makes his way past two trolleys with sheeted figures on them. There are refrigerated chambers on either side with neat labels on the doors, listing the occupants. On the door by the post mortem room there is a sticker, and Dr Owen pauses to read it. It says: MANY ARE CHILLED BUT FEW ARE FROZEN.

Dr Murray is standing by the dissection table, smiling, beckoning Dr Owen to come in. He is a tall, broad-chested Irishman with a wiry red beard. He is wearing a green plastic apron, theatre trousers, a polo-necked sweater and moccasins, typical autopsy-room attire that has earned him the soubriquet of the Pox-Doctor's Clerk.

'You've hurt your back again,' he says cheerfully. 'You want to put yourself in the hands of a competent therapist.'

'Do a bit of that in your spare time, do you?' Owen makes a sour face at the corpse on the table. It is Mr Wyatt, the man who died earlier in Casualty. His body has been cut open from throat to pubis, and most of the abdominal contents are lying beside him on the table and in steel collecting vessels. 'What was it then?'

Dr Murray has a flair for drama. He comes forward with a small glass dish cupped preciously between both hands. 'Three guesses.'

'I haven't a clue.'

Dr Murray extends the dish and Owen looks into it. There is a piece of lung tissue on the bottom. Owen looks closer. 'What's the white stuff?'

'They're going to have a look at it in the lab. Just to confirm. But I know what it is. So should you, if you examine it carefully.'

Owen takes the dish and with one finger he probes the granular substance that is spread across the dark blue tissue.

'Well?' Dr Murray says.

Dr Owen shakes his head. 'Don't know.'

'Aspirin,' Dr Murray says. 'One tablet, half dissolved.'

'Bloody hell.'

'Desperately unfortunate way to go.' Dr Murray takes back the dish and puts it on the table. 'I've seen it twice before. One of them was a patient on a medical ward. Nipped into the loo for a quick bit of self-medication, inhaled while the tablet was on his tongue, and that was that. Extensive brain damage within thirty minutes, dead in forty-five.' He taps Mr Wyatt's head. 'I'm going to have the brain out in a minute to take a look, but I know what it'll be like.'

'I've only ever read about it,' Dr Owen says. The action of aspirin, if it ever comes into direct contact with the lung, is devastating. It doesn't always kill, but the results are invariably tragic, ranging from mild brain damage to blindness, total deafness and paralysis.

'Well,' Owen says, 'thanks for letting me see. I wouldn't have missed it for the world.' He turns to leave, but Murray detains him.

'Hang on, there's something else I want to show you.' He grins. 'Have you read this week's *Lancet*?'

'I don't take it.' The *Lancet* is a shade too learned for most doctors, but it's the last word in authoritative medical journals.

'You'll never believe this. Wait there a moment.'

Dr Murray goes out of the room, leaving Dr Owen alone with the body. He looks at it, struck as he often is by the oddness of life. Hours before, the thing on the table was a warm, breathing, intelligent human being. Now it's nothing, yet that sense of a presence persists.

'Here we are.' Dr Murray comes back in, carrying a folded-open copy of the *Lancet*. 'There is now a clinical condition with the official name of – wait for it . . .' His finger stabs the page and Dr Owen reads aloud: 'The Gay Compromise Syndrome.' He stares at Dr Murray. 'I *don't* believe it.'

'Does the *Lancet* lie?'

'What is it?' Dr Owen asks.

'An epidemic chest ailment that's mowing down a lot of New York homosexuals. As yet, nobody's got much of a clue what's causing it.' Dr Murray is shaking his head gently, as if he has witnessed something deeply sad. 'Before you can whistle, that name'll be in the text books. Imagine. There'll be a whole flock of them after that.' He frowns for a minute, concentrating, then he smiles. 'Nancy Necrosis,' he says. 'Bull Dyke Fever.'

The two of them turn to the table again and look at Mr Wyatt's stiff, sombre face. 'It's a real tragedy, isn't it?' Dr Owen says.

Dr Murray nods. 'His wife'll be saying "if only" for the rest of her days.'

'A bloody aspirin.' Dr Owen moves away from the table. 'People who want to die can take fifty of them and survive. All that poor bloke wanted to do was get rid of a headache.'

Dr Murray leans across the table and picks up a bistoury, a broad-bladed knife used for cutting skin and muscle. He starts making an incision across Mr Wyatt's scalp, from ear to ear. 'Don't come in here and start spouting paradoxes at me,' he says. 'This is the temple of paradox.'

'And you're the man who knows everything . . .'

'A day late,' Dr Murray says, finishing the quotation for Dr Owen. 'Do you want to stay for the opening ceremony?' He is folding Mr Wyatt's scalp down over his face.

'No, I won't, if it's all the same to you,' Dr Owen says. 'I'll go back to Casualty and look at something more pleasant. Like a weeping leg ulcer.'

On his way out Dr Owen hears loud, cheerful whistling

coming from an ante room. He looks inside and sees Mr Logan, a local undertaker. He is warbling as he ties a shroud on to the body of an old woman. On a second trolley, a younger female corpse is having its hair brushed by the assistant. Logan looks up and nods to Dr Owen.

'You're a real reverential lot,' Owen says, shaking his head as he regards the mute bodies and the two men working with the casualness of window dressers.

'It's all a matter of approach,' Mr Logan tells him. 'Attitude, you see.' He waves his arm over the two bodies. 'To keep yourself level-headed in this job, you have to keep remembering that these are empties.'

In Casualty, Dr Lester is still in the cubicle with Father Aston. The old man is visibly calmer now, after several minutes of talking. Jack Lester is a good listener, and a number of times he has questioned some of the priest's remarks, directing the flow in ways he hopes will be productive.

They are back on the topic of cruelty and general indifference among local young people. Father Aston has already aired the opinion that youth has a damaging tendency to explore only the things that are within easy reach. As he talks, one trembling hand carefully strokes the dressing on the other.

'There's an old saying that cruelty ever proceeds from a vile mind. There's a great deal about these days to make a child vile-minded, isn't there? Television and films, books and music, packed with the tawdry and negative things in life. And the youngsters have their own brand new cultures, don't they? The history books have plenty to say about how vile most cultures are in their early days.' Father Aston shrugs, one shoulder rising higher than the other. 'They've no fragility. A touch of that would soften their hearts, I think.'

'And what about your own fragility, Father?' Dr Lester asks. 'Do you think you can rationalise what's been done to you, keep it in proportion?'

'I know I should try.'

'Yes, you must,' Jack says. 'And one of the best ways I know is an old one. Go over the attack in your mind again and again, and don't skip any of it. It's like picking up spiders – terrible for some people to contemplate, but if they make themselves do it often enough, it's nothing. That technique will take the harm out of your experience better than any fancy medication.'

'I'm grateful for your advice.' Father Aston points to the clock on the wall. 'If that's the correct time, I'll have to be getting back. I'm marrying a couple this afternoon.'

'Are you up to that?'

'I'll make myself up to it. The wiser course, don't you think?'

'Well, if you can cope . . .'

Father Aston stands up. 'This creeping affliction of mine,' he holds up his wavering hand, 'has taught me the value of always doing a little more than I feel like doing. I'll cope, Doctor, because if I don't, I'll have time to feel sorry for myself.' He moves to the door, smiling. 'Self-pity's a sin, you know.'

They walk out together to the car park, where a police car is waiting to take Father Aston home. The driver helps the priest into the back seat and Jack Lester has a parting word through the window.

'Remember,' he says, 'What you *mustn't* do is avoid the memory. That turns it into a phobia, and then the door's open for more neuroses than you can shake a stick at.'

'You've been very kind, Doctor, and I won't forget what you've said.'

Jack watches the car drive off, then he goes back to Casualty.

Everyone is working at full stretch. In the past twenty minutes the stack of case cards by the waiting room door has doubled in thickness. Jack Lester is picking one up as an ambulance driver goes past, loosening his tie. Lester nods to him.

'Bloody bedlam,' the man says, and carries on out through the ambulance bay doors.

The clean theatre, the plaster room and all the cubicles but one are in use, and the waiting room is still nearly full. Alan Smedley is removing a fish hook from a boy's eyelid. Staff Nurses Iris Cole and Elsie Pitt are splinting the broken arms and legs of a motorcyclist. Sister Boyd is in the Emergency room with Nurses Bloom and Tait, setting up a stomach washout for a girl who has overdosed on Mogadon. In cubicles, waiting to be treated, are a man with a one-inch splinter of wood under his fingernail, a girl who believes she is miscarrying, a woman with recurring stomach cramps, a half-drunk soldier who has fallen in the street and cut his head open, and two cases of suspected food poisoning.

Dr Owen has just examined a patient with a hand injury and

has sent him for X-rays. While he is waiting for the results he goes into the office to massage his ailing back, and finds Sister Harper standing by the desk, one hand pressed to her stomach. She is very pale.

'Bad, eh?' Owen says.

'Murder. It was the bad start that did it.' She looks up at Owen. 'How's your back?'

'Murder. But it'll get better. Your prognosis isn't that straightforward. You're going to have to let somebody treat you properly, Sister.'

She shakes her hand dismissively. 'The diet's fine. Usually I can keep the thing under control, even when we're busy. But I've got to work from a slow, steady start.'

'Dieting's not the answer...'

'It worked before,' Sister says firmly. 'I don't hold with all these stomach drugs.'

'One drug. Cimetidine. It's a marvellous treatment. It's replacing surgery for hundreds of people. And you'd get sustained relief from the damned pain right from the third or fourth day after you start the course.'

She sighs. 'I'll have to read up on it first.'

'I'll bring you the literature.'

'Hmm.' Sister opens the door. 'I'll get back to the front, then. The last I saw of them, my troops were under heavy fire.'

'Sister,' Dr Owen says.

'What?'

'Take it easy.'

When she has gone Dr Owen unbuttons his coat and starts rubbing the spot on his back that seems to be radiating pain in pulsed doses. He has been standing there massaging for about a minute when Staff Nurse Elsie Pitt comes into the office, looking for a stethoscope. She is a strikingly attractive girl, a blue-eyed blonde who has more trouble from male patients than all the other Casualty nurses put together.

'Did you happen to see Sister Harper?' she asks Owen.

'Yes, I saw her. She looked shocking.'

'I don't think she should be working.'

'Hah.' Dr Owen stops massaging himself and buttons his coat again. 'You try telling her; and let her know she should take some proper medication, while you're at it.'

Elsie finds her stethoscope under the day ledger and goes to the door with it.

'Nurses amaze me,' Owen says to her. 'They spend their lives handing out help to the suffering, but they won't lift a finger to help themselves. It's not just Sister Harper, you're all a bit that way.'

'True,' Elsie says. 'And what have you been taking for your back?'

Owen stares at her for several seconds. 'That's different.'

'Uhuh.' She is expressionless as she stares at him. 'Excuse me, Doctor. Got to run.'

He stares at the door for a while after it closes, still seeing Elsie's face clearly. If she'd only stayed a minute longer, he thinks, he could have come up with a smarter answer.

*   *   *

At 5.30 p.m., after the waiting room has been empty for an hour and there has been time to tidy the department, a young woman brings in an infant boy who appears, at first sight, to be in shock. Dr Lester carries the child into a cubicle and lays him on the bed.

'He's been worrying us since last night,' the woman says, frowning at the expressionless child.

'Last night?' Lester stares at her. 'Why didn't you bring him in sooner, or call your family doctor?'

Concentration tightens the woman's face. 'Well...' She is not articulate and she is obviously struggling to put an adequate answer together. 'Last night, he wasn't like this. He was quiet. But it's not like him, usually he cries a lot.'

Dr Lester slides a chair forward and tells the woman to sit down. He glances at the brief details on the case card and says, 'I see your son's ten months old. How long would you say he's been that way, crying and so forth?'

'Oh, I'm not his mother. He's my sister's kid. The crying – well, it's gone on a while, I suppose. He's just a sort of grumpy kid, I reckon.'

'Couldn't his mother come in?'

Concentration again, then she says, 'No. Well, we've no idea where she is.'

Jack Lester looks at the child again. He is small and thin; his big blue eyes seem to be dwelling on something between himself

102

and the ceiling. There are no visible signs of ill-treatment and his woollen clothes are clean and neat. He presents a solemn picture, as solemn as the name on his case card – Samuel Dobson.

'Does he live with you?'

'Oh yes. Been with me and my hubby for four weeks.'

Lester waits for the explanation to continue, but the woman is expecting to be asked another question.

'I think I'd better get some facts down.' He takes out his pen. 'What's your name, first of all?'

'Mrs Walker. Tracey Walker.'

'And Samuel's been living with you lately. Tell me about his mother. Did she run off, or what?'

'Went up north – Newcastle – to see about a job. She does hotel work, see, chambermaid – that's what she was when she got pregnant with Sam. She wrote us a week after she left, said she was getting took on up there, and would we hang on to Sam two more weeks till she could come down for him. No address on the letter, and that was the last we heard.'

Concern is dawning in Dr Lester. 'There's no father?'

'Got to be one somewhere,' Mrs Walker says, and she flashes an unsteady smile. 'My sister said she was never sure who it was.'

Jack Lester hooks his stethoscope around his neck. 'Had the baby been living with her all the time before he came to you?'

'That's right. They stayed in a little bedsit she had.'

'Any other relatives around during that time – grandmother, yourself?'

Mrs Walker shakes her head. 'Mum wouldn't have nothing to do with her and I only saw Sam two or three times before we got landed with him. There's no other family.' She sighs and shakes her head again. 'She's a bit odd, my sister. Stayed in all the time, clinging to the baby, then she ups and pushes off like that.'

Lester examines the child. Physically, he is perfectly normal, except that he doesn't respond to speech or touch.

Turning to Mrs Walker again, he says, 'So last night he went quiet. Did he sleep well?'

'Great. Best night we've had with him. Then this morning he wouldn't take no food. Didn't cry or nothing, just wouldn't eat. Lunch time my hubby tried him with some chopped-up chicken.

103

Sam usually likes that, but not today. Then later, about an hour ago, I noticed he'd gone like that. Numb looking, gazing into space.'

'He doesn't respond at all when you speak to him?'

'No. Not a flicker.'

'Stay with the baby a minute, will you, Mrs Walker?'

Dr Lester goes to the telephone by the Emergency room door and calls Paediatrics. He speaks to Dr Greene, a Senior Registrar. Greene listens to the case outline Lester gives him and then says he'll come down right away.

Sister Boyd is by the office door as Dr Lester is on his way back to the cubicle.

'Trouble?' she says.

'Looks like it.'

'Not another battering...'

'No. But it could be something as bad, in it's way. We'll see what Dr Greene makes of it.'

Back in the cubicle, Lester asks Mrs Walker how much time, on average, she spends with the child. 'I mean actually making contact with him. Talking, playing, things like that.'

'Well, playing with him...' She is picturing the concept of play. 'He's not really a baby that plays. I mean, I'm with him most of the time, doing things, the housework and such.'

'Do you talk to him?'

'I s'pose so.' Defensiveness is in the woman's eyes now. She is about to say something else when Dr Greene comes into the cubicle. He is a short man with thick, pebble-lens spectacles. When he turns his head aside, his eyes seem to disappear. He nods curtly to Dr Lester, then leans over the bed and draws down the child's lower eyelids.

'This came on suddenly, did it?' he asks Mrs Walker.

'That's right. Pretty suddenly.'

Dr Greene feels little Samuel's pulse and lifts each of his legs in turn, letting them flop back on to the bed. The child remains impassive, still looking towards the ceiling, breathing gently through his mouth.

Turning to Dr Lester, Dr Greene says, 'I think it's what you suspected. We'll get him into the ward and have Dr Roarke look at him tonight.' He turns to Mrs Walker. 'I'd like to talk to you about the boy,' he says. 'Perhaps you'd come up to the ward with him. I'll get you a cup of tea and we can have a chat in my office.'

'Serious is it, Doctor?' Throughout the time she has been in Casualty Mrs Walker has shown nothing that could be called concern. Even now she looks no more than curious.

'I believe it is,' Dr Greene tells her.

When the child has been taken away to the paediatric ward, Dr Lester goes to the sluice, where Sister Boyd and Staff Nurse Pitt are having coffee.

'Can I scrounge a cup, Sister?'

'You've got the authority to demand one,' Sister says. She opens the cupboard and takes out the Snoopy mug Dr Lester always uses. 'What's the score with the baby?'

'It's marasmus.'

Sister pauses with the coffee jug tilted at the rim of the mug. 'Marasmus? I haven't heard of a case of that in years. The poor little beggar.'

'What is it?' Elsie Pitt asks.

'Sounds like a Dutch theologian, doesn't it?' Lester says. 'It's the final phase of a condition called hospitalism. It used to be fairly common in kids who got separated from their mothers for long periods.'

'What are the symptoms?'

'Tearfulness at first, weepy all the time, then the kid starts to look dazed. That phase can last for a while, and it's when the diagnosis has got to be made.' Lester takes the coffee mug from Sister and sips from it. 'The condition's reversible up to that point.'

'How?' Elsie Pitt asks.

'Re-establish contact with the mother, or find an adequate substitute parent. If you don't do that, the condition proceeds to the marasmus phase, and that's fatal.'

Elsie Pitt looks sceptical. She will rarely accept any explanation at the first telling. 'There's *nothing* that can be done?'

'Nothing at all,' Lester assures her. 'The baby just fades away. Subcutaneous fat disappears and the entire system seems to exhaust itself. Feeding doesn't work because the digestive tract goes out of action. The only response you can get, with a lot of effort, is a scream. The life-drive drops to nil and the patient dies quite quickly. You can think of it as terminal sadness.'

'But how did the kid get that way?' Elsie asks. 'He's got his mother, hasn't he?'

'Had his mother,' Lester corrects her. 'Now he's got an aunt. A witless mare of an aunt who hasn't a clue what neglect's about. The boy had a strong pattern of contact with his mother, then suddenly he had nothing, beyond food and shelter.'

There is always uneasiness among medical people when they discuss the hopeless cases; they know, better than anyone, how vast a chasm of ignorance there is between what is understood and what is mystery. In spite of years and fortunes spent investigating the components of human personality and will, there is no adequate explanation – or cure – for a person who contracts a death wish.

'It makes you want to take your short change out of God,' Dr Lester murmurs, breaking a small silence.

'So the treatment's TLC,' Elsie Pitt says.

Lester nods. 'TLC, for as long as it takes.'

In hospital parlance TLC – tender loving care – has become the general codeword for a variety of passive therapies.

'What I'd really like to do now,' Jack Lester says, after draining his coffee cup and putting it down, 'is go out there and shake Auntie till her teeth rattle.' He turns and opens the door.

'Let me know if you decide to,' Elsie Pitt says. 'I'd like a go at her, too.'

In the waiting room the part-time evening receptionist, Mrs Lumsden, is trying to explain reception procedure to a young female patient.

'It's the ruling, dear,' Mrs Lumsden says patiently. She feels that the girl is not so much reticent as cagey. 'I've got to put down on this card your name, date of birth, address, occupation, and the nature of your accident or illness. It's all confidential, love.'

The girl is sullenly clicking one fingernail against another. She has given her name as Rita Podmore, even though the initial necklace she's wearing is a large gold B. She has said she is eighteen but, in spite of her heavy makeup, she looks much younger. The address was delivered haltingly, which in Mrs Lumsden's experience means it's false and hasn't been adequately rehearsed. The girl refuses to say what's wrong with her.

106

'I'll tell the doctor,' she mumbles. 'I'd like to see a lady one.'

'We don't have a female doctor on duty at present,' the receptionist tells her. 'Maybe a nurse will be able to cope with you.' There are shadows of truculence in the girl's expression, so Mrs Lumsden has decided not to push the matter of her complaint. 'If you'll take a seat, somebody will call you.'

There are no other patients waiting and after only a couple of minutes Staff Nurse Pitt comes for the girl and leads her through to a cubicle.

'Well now, what's the trouble?' Elsie Pitt's striking good looks are always counter-balanced by a brisk, no-nonsense approach to patients. Young females tend to dislike her, but Elsie lives with that. After several seconds, when the girl hasn't replied, Elsie says, 'We have to be told *something*, Miss Podmore. We're not vets.'

The girl sniffs and meets Elsie's eyes for a second. 'It's kind of embarrassing.'

'Don't worry,' Elsie says, 'there's very little we haven't come across before. And we never get embarrassed, so there's no need for you to be.'

The girl sighs. 'It's my Tampax,' she says hoarsely. 'It's got stuck.'

'And how did that happen?'

'I was going to take it out, and the string came off.'

Elsie nods. 'Take off your pants and your skirt and lie down on the bed. There's a blanket there you can put over yourself. I'll fetch the doctor.'

Jack Lester is in the office, trying to finish a letter to his mother, when Elsie Pitt comes in and tells him about the girl in the cubicle. He listens, then shakes his head slowly.

'There's not a lot of ingenuity about these days, is there?'

'None at all,' Elsie says. 'What annoys me is the way they hand out that patter, as if we're really dumb enough to swallow it.'

'I was,' Lester says. 'The first two or three times, anyway.' He stands up and goes to the door. 'Come on, let's dig it out.'

Most casualty departments in the larger hospitals have regular experience of girls showing up with Miss Podmore's complaint. In practically every case the tampon has been deliberately inserted high in the vagina, as close around the neck of the womb as possible. To get it out or at least, according to the mythology of the clubs, pubs, discos and wine bars, a casualty officer will have to poke around so hard with his instruments that he will produce a much-wanted abortion.

The girl is on the bed when Jack Lester and Elsie Pitt enter the cubicle. She has the blanket drawn up tight around her neck.

'Hello,' Lester says, and he smiles warmly at the girl. 'Staff Nurse has told me about your problem. We'll soon sort it out.'

It takes less than two minutes with a speculum and forceps to remove the tampon. When he has it out, Dr Lester holds it up on the forceps for the patient to see.

'All done,' he says. 'And I'll bet you didn't feel a thing, right?'

The red-faced girl nods at him.

'That was because we worked *very*, very carefully, Miss Podmore. We didn't want to disturb anything delicate.'

The annoyance that creases the girl's eyes is as clear as a confession. 'Yeah. Thanks.'

'Don't mention it.' Lester drops the tampon into a dish Elsie Pitt is holding, then he suddenly peers down into it. 'Very odd that, Staff,' he says, and Elsie has to work at keeping her face straight. 'Not a drop of blood on the thing. Not a trace.'

Later, when the girl has gone off in what Dr Lester referred to as moderate dudgeon, Sister Boyd leads through a young coloured woman who has a striped hand-towel wrapped around her face. She is sobbing into the folds of the towel, and when Elsie Pitt takes her shoulders to comfort her she finds that there is blood seeping through the girl's sweater.

'One of her neighbours brought her in,' Sister tells Jack Lester. 'It's a "domestic". I've got Mrs Lumsden to call the police.' Sister goes off to the plaster room to check on Nurses Bloom and Tait, who are putting a cast on a child's broken arm, while Jack Lester and Elsie Pitt lead the crying girl to a cubicle.

Nurse Bloom is talking to the child, a boy of eight, who is sitting on the edge of the table in the plaster room. He is not crying but he is apprehensive, trying to see past Sarah Bloom to the wet bench, where Isobel Tait is preparing the plaster. The boy's mother is standing at the end of the long table, looking as uneasy as her son. On the side benches there are grotesque-looking metal splints, shears of various sizes, bandage scissors and electric plaster saws. The saws, in particular, appear to draw the mother's attention.

'Don't worry yourself,' Sister says to her as she enters the plaster room. 'The worst thing about this place is its appearance. The job'll be done in a jiffy.' She walks over to the child and puts her hand on his head. 'Tell me how you did it, Brian.'

The mental effort of getting his tale together distracts the child for a moment as Sarah Bloom slips a tube of heavy gauze over the injured arm. The fracture is simple, little more than a crack in the radius bone of the left forearm. There is no misalignment of the bone, and immobilisation is all that is necessary. As she works, Sarah is careful to keep the limb in the same position, pointing upward with the elbow supported on a padded block of wood.

'I fell off my bike,' Brian says. He winces as Sarah puts his thumb through a hole near the end of the gauze, but Sister is staring at him intently, requiring him to go on with his story. 'I put out my hand . . .'

'That's just what I did,' Sister says. 'I was twelve. It hurts a bit, doesn't it?'

Nurse Bloom has put a plastic sheet across Brian's knees to protect his clothes. She turns and nods to Nurse Tait, who brings across the bowl of plaster with the bandages soaking in it.

Brian is distracted now. He doesn't like the look of the bowl.

'This is the funny bit,' Sister tells him. 'Just watch Nurse trying not to splash her apron. She gets in a terrible mess, sometimes.'

Isobel Tait makes some show of clumsiness as she wobbles towards the table with the bowl.

'She got it all up her arms yesterday,' Sister goes on, and Brian makes a brave smile. His mother is smiling too, but she's frowning at the same time.

Nurse Tait takes the first bandage out of the wet plaster and squeezes the excess moisture from it. In the process, her hands get covered in the thick white liquid, and she makes a wry face at Brian. His smile isn't holding.

'Nurse is just going to wrap it round the stocking you've got on your arm,' Sister says softly; she takes Brian's hand and holds it as Isobel Tait starts applying the first bandage. She begins at the hand and works towards the elbow. Sarah Bloom is supporting the arm to minimise it's movement as the bandage is wound into place.

Sister Boyd is simultaneously reassuring young Brian and watching that the bandage is put on correctly. It doesn't have to be applied to a regular pattern, but the thickness should be uniform along the entire length of the cast. If it is not, the dried cast will be inclined to crack at the junctions of thick and thin plaster.

'Just look at the mess she's made of her apron, Brian!'

The texture of the plaster has to be kept uniform, too. Isobel smooths it along the coils of bandage as she works, at the same time making sure there are no wrinkles forming. A wrinkle would make the inside of the cast irregular; to be properly effective, it must dry smooth and snug, moulded to the contours of the arm.

'There,' Sister says. 'That's the first one on. Just one more, Brian, then it'll be time for a sweet.'

Brian looks at Sister and smiles. His mother looks deeply relieved.

'I told you the sight of this place was the worst part,' Sister says to her. Turning to Brian, she says, 'Your Mummy's been very brave. I think we should give her a sweetie, too.'

In the cubicle nearest to the waiting room door, Dr Lester and Staff Nurse Pitt have finally coaxed the coloured girl to let them take the towel away from her face. She has lain on the bed for several minutes, moaning and sobbing, keeping her hands clamped against the towel. Since this is a case with strong emotional overtones, Jack Lester and Elsie Pitt have been patient and gentle in their persuasion.

Lester lifts the towel away slowly.

'Jesus wept.' Lester didn't mean to say that aloud. It was an inadvertent, shocked response to the girl's injuries. He turns her head carefully, counting twelve small, deep flesh wounds, like scarlet-edged craters on her cheeks, forehead and chin. The sight is bizarre, for although this is obviously a human face, the injuries create an unreal and deeply repellent appearance.

'How did it happen, love?'

The girl says something indistinct, then she clears her throat and repeats it. 'He bit me.'

'Your husband *bit* you? All those times?'

'Yeah.'

110

Dr Lester steps away from the bed for a moment and raises his eyebrows at Elsie Pitt.

'He must have had a mouthful of her face by the time he'd finished,' Elsie whispers.

Lester nods. 'Let's have a look at the rest of her.'

With great care they remove the girl's sweater and skirt. She has stopped crying now, but her eyes are wide with fear. As the garments come off Jack Lester keeps reassuring her, telling her she's safe, she's fine, she'll be all right.

There are more wounds on the shoulders and arms, and the patient's knees are grazed.

'Did he bite your arms too?' Lester asks.

'No. He had his knife...' The girl speaks with stiffened lips to avoid moving the muscles in her face. 'He's got this penknife, it's not sharp...'

'Sharp enough, love.'

With careful movements, watching the patient's face all the time, Dr Lester examines her abdomen. In cases of domestic violence there is often internal injury from punching and kicking, and often the distressing appearance of facial wounds can blind an inexperienced doctor to the possibility of life-threatening damage elsewhere. In particular, the liver can be split when a body jacknifes violently, and the spleen can be torn just as easily. Lester probes these areas, but he finds no indication of damage.

'I know your face hurts a lot, but can you feel any pain at all in your tummy or your chest?'

The girl thinks about it, then shakes her head.

'Fine.' Lester pats her arm. 'I'm going to cover you with a blanket for the moment. Just lie still, we'll get you taken care of in no time.'

Outside the cubicle with Elsie Pitt, Dr Lester assesses the situation.

'It's the face we've got to concentrate on. She's had chunks bitten out of her and there's lots of deep tissue missing.'

Elsie is ahead of him. 'I'll tell the girls to get the clean theatre ready.'

'Right. I'll get on to Mr Bryant. While I'm talking to him, I'd like you to give the patient an anti-tetanus jab, then clean and dress the wounds on the shoulders and arms and start bathing

111

out the ones on the face. Saline only. I'll put Sister in the picture.'

To make sure the girl won't be permanently disfigured, it is necessary to resort to plastic surgery. While Dr Lester is alerting the surgeon, Elsie Pitt will be improving the chances of a successful operation by cleaning the wounds thoroughly with saline. Although there are a number of new and highly acclaimed skin cleansers available to the medical profession, none of them seems to offer any significant advantage over saline, which is a solution made by adding nine grams of salt to one litre of sterile water. One of the greatest factors in saline's favour is that it is an isotonic – a substance that can be mixed with human body fluids without causing any physical or chemical disturbance. In the case of the girl with the bites, it's vitally important that the cleaning should be deep and thorough, to remove all traces of her husband's saliva. Among its less useful properties, saliva contains enzymes that can kill human tissue.

Dr Lester is telling Sister what's happening to the coloured girl when they are interrupted by a crash from the waiting room. A second later Mrs Lumsden can be heard screaming and yelling and there's the sound of a man's voice overlaid on hers, grunting something, as if he's exerting himself.

'Get a porter!' Jack Lester tells Sister. He runs from the office to the waiting room and finds the floor littered with bits of glass. Mrs Lumsden is shut in her room with the communicating window closed. A big, mauve-cheeked young man is leaning on the ledge, bawling at her through the glass. He's wearing a donkey jacket, a woolly football supporter's hat and a matching scarf. He looks murderously angry.

'What's going on here?' Dr Lester surprises himself with the firmness of his own voice. He feels anything but firm.

The man's head jerks round, glaring. He starts moving towards Jack Lester.

Mrs Lumsden jerks open the window and puts her flustered face in the opening. 'He threw a beer bottle at me!' she screeches.

'Back now!' Lester shouts at the man. It's all he can think of. The man keeps coming. 'I'm warning you!'

'Get stuffed, you!' The belligerence is as harsh as a punch. For one instant the man looks terrifyingly dangerous, broad, lumbering, swinging his arms and exuding lethal malice as he strides across the waiting room floor at Dr Lester. Then his foot slips on a bevelled fragment of glass and he goes down, clutching a flimsy chair that skids and makes his descent faster.

Lester wastes no time. He dives forward and stands spread-footed beside the grunting, cursing drunk. As soon as his target is in line, he kicks out once with his right foot and once with his left, cracking the man's shins. In the process of learning how to alleviate pain, doctors learn a good deal about causing it.

'Aah! Jesus!' The man is roaring and clasping his legs. He tries to get up but the pain forces him down again. 'Bastard!' He gets on hands and knees and snarls up at Dr Lester. 'You're dead, fucking hear that? Dead!'

A porter comes running through the swing door.

'Grab his arm!' Lester yells, and between them they drag the spluttering hulk as far as the door. 'Phone for the police!' Lester tells Mrs Lumsden, who is watching them twitchily. 'And hurry!'

There's a sudden heightening of the emergency as the prisoner manages to get one foot flat on the floor and push himself up. The top of his head collides sharply with the porter's chin, making his teeth crack shut. The porter howls and lets go the arm he's been clasping.

'Watch it!'

Lester's warning is too late and the porter takes a punch square on the mouth. He hits the wall, tries to correct himself, then slides sideways, looking glass-eyed and astonished. He hits the floor elbow-first and rolls on to his face.

Mrs Lumsden is screaming into the phone and Jack Lester is hanging on to the intruder's left arm with both hands, trying to swing him off his feet again.

'I'll show you! Bloody shit!' The man is dishearteningly strong. Even though his legs must be well below capacity from the booting Jack Lester gave them, he is using them to brace himself in the angle of the walls by the swing door, and all the time his free arm is chopping the air in front of Dr Lester's nose. 'One punch,' he's grunting, 'one pigging punch...'

Lester realises he has no chance of overbalancing his opponent. He also realises that if something drastic isn't done, the man will maim him.

113

The pattern alters abruptly. The man is coming away from the wall, he has strength and balance again in his spread legs, and there's something like triumph glittering through his malice. He opens his mouth wide, as if to yell, when Jack Lester's foot leaves the floor at speed and the man has the sudden conviction that his scrotum has caught fire.

As he sinks to his knees, moaning and clutching his groin with his free hand, Jack Lester drags him forward sharply and his chin strikes the seat of a chair. He calls Lester something through clenched teeth, then rolls over on his side on the floor and stays there.

Dr Lester drops the man's arm and looks across at the porter, who is sitting up, rubbing his jaw. Beyond him, Mrs Lumsden is coming forward tentatively, chewing her lip, staring at the man on the floor.

'I don't believe any of this,' Lester says breathlessly. He looks down at the fallen warrior, who is still having a lot of pain from his outraged testicles. Lester is still wondering what to do with him next when the police arrive.

'Had a bit of bother, I see,' one of the constables says.

Jack Lester blinks at him. 'You could say that, I suppose.' He pulls up a plastic chair and sinks on to it, waving his hand at the man on the floor. 'We get stuff like this practically every weekend. We call it Saturday-night fever.'

A sergeant crosses over and bends down by the man. 'Is he going to need treatment, Doctor?'

'A bit of bed rest, if he didn't come in with something else.' Dr Lester looks at Mrs Lumsden. 'What was he doing here, anyway?'

'He just came in and asked me if we had a toilet.'

'And?'

Mrs Lumsden clasps the clipboard to her chest. 'I told him he couldn't use it.'

'And that's when he threw the bottle?'

'After a bit of arguing, yes.'

Lester shrugs. 'What's the drill, Sergeant?'

'We take your statements, Doctor, then we haul this one in and do him for D and D.'

'Right.' Lester stands up and runs his fingers through his spiky hair. 'Could you take my statement first? I'm a bit pressed

114

for time,' he sighs. 'There's more to this job than kicking people in the goolies, you know.'

*   *   *

By 7.30 p.m. the girl who was bitten – her name is Teresa – is in the small theatre. The plastic surgeon, Mr Bryant, is about to begin the operation on her face.

From the surgeon's point of view he will really be performing several operations. Because of the scattered pattern of the wounds, and because each one lies at a different angle to the tension lines of the skin, each has to be treated as a separate problem with an individual solution. The colour of Teresa's skin presents an extra hurdle for Mr Bryant; if the closures aren't made with absolute precision, lighter-coloured scars will form when the wounds eventually heal.

Teresa is on a standard operating table with the head end raised, so that there's a minimum of tension on her face. Forty minutes ago, she was given a forty milligram tablet of Valium, to calm her and assist in the relaxation of her muscles. When she arrived in theatre five minutes ago she was given a Valium injection, to maintain the relaxed state.

'You'll stay awake,' Mr Bryant tells her from behind his mask, 'but I promise you there'll be no pain at all. Are you nice and comfy?'

Teresa nods; she even attempts a smile. In the time that's passed since she arrived in Casualty, the wounds have settled and now they look like a dozen small mouths.

'Don't let all these people milling around worry you,' Mr Bryant adds. 'They're here to help me. I'm the only one who'll touch your face.' He winks at Teresa. 'I'm really awfully good.'

Wounds such as bites should be closed as soon as possible, in order to prevent the tissue around the edges dying and increasing the danger of ugly scars. The bacteria in a wound, even when it is being well managed, double every six to eight hours. If the concentration gets beyond a certain level there may be clinical infection later, which would mean the wounds would have to be opened and drained and a good cosmetic effect would then be out of the question. After six hours there is really no hope of making a closure that will present a good appearance after healing, so it was fortunate that Teresa was brought in promptly.

115

Because he has to use scalpels and needles to repair the wounds, Mr Bryant will have to inject a strong local anaesthetic – in this case Xylocaine. In a patient who is wide awake, this is a very painful procedure, but there's been a recent discovery that gets round the problem.

'You'll feel the tiniest prick in your arm,' Mr Bryant says, and he nods to his Sister. She puts the tip of a hypodermic into a previously located vein in Teresa's left arm and injects a small dose of a drug called Ketamine.

'In just a few seconds, Teresa, you'll find something quite pleasant happening. You'll still see me and hear me, but you won't feel anything.'

Ketamine is a synthetic compound with very unusual anaesthetic and analgesic properties. Anaesthetists describe its effect as being 'dissociatively anaesthetic', which is an ungainly way of saying what Mr Bryant just said – the patient remains alert and can obey commands, but there is absolutely no sensitivity to pain.

The effect of Ketamine lasts only five or six minutes, so Mr Bryant has to work fast. Using a fine-bore needle, he injects the local anaesthetic into the margins of each of the wounds. Teresa remains calm, and later she won't remember having the injections, for Ketamine also acts as an obliterator of memory.

As he waits for the facial anaesthetic to take effect, Mr Bryant checks the instruments on the tray beside him. Plastic surgery requires the finest of workmanship, so the instruments are invariably small and delicate. On the tray there are slim, double pronged hooks for grasping and raising skin and underlying tissues; miniature forceps for tissue retraction; clamps of various shapes, designed to shut off individual blood vessels; tiny scissors for cutting away precisely shaped wedges of skin and tissue; splinter-fine needles and catgut that is no more than a filament, and No. 15 and No. 11 knife blades, which are short, slender and extremely sharp.

There is a wound on Teresa's forehead. When the anaesthetic has taken effect, Mr Bryant starts on that one. As with any injury that occurs over a bony part, the smallest trauma can go as deep as the periosteum – the membrane that covers and nourishes the bone. That's the case with Teresa's forehead injury and Mr Bryant first uses a small torch to check that the membrane hasn't been broken. He finds it intact, so he can

116

proceed with the closing of the wound.

The skin edges are crushed, meaning that the tissue there is probably dead. With a No. 15 blade in his scalpel, Mr Bryant carefully cuts off thin strips of the tissue, being careful to hold it away from the underlying muscle with a hook. When he is satisfied that there is only fresh, blood-bearing tissue around the wound, he holds out his hand to Sister and she passes him a threaded needle.

The frontalis muscle of the forehead has to be closed separately, otherwise it would be misaligned and cause a facial distortion rather like a permanent, one-sided frown. It takes ten minutes to insert the soluble stitches, and when the job is complete Mr Bryant steps away from the table.

'I'm taking a breather,' he tells Teresa. 'It's going fine, don't worry about a thing.'

Plastic surgeons are always alert to the chance of blunders caused by simple fatigue. There is great strain on the back, arms and wrists and except in those cases where a surgeon can stand straight and work with his hands supported on a patient's limbs or abdomen, he will take a five-minute break every half hour.

Teresa is perfectly calm. She is lying with her hands clasped on the green sheet, watching the movement of the surgical team around the table. Even when the Staff Nurse held her head firmly against the rest when the muscle was being stitched, she didn't look alarmed or even anxious. It's been observed that people who have stressful daily lives are the most relaxed under the influence of Valium.

When Mr Bryant goes back to the table, he looks at the wound carefully, touching the edges to determine the natural lines of skin tension. These have to be married correctly and they are judged by sliding the opposite sides of the wound against each other and noting the movement of nearby surface marks such as the hairline and the eyebrows.

'An advancement flap, I think, Sister.'

The secret of good wound closure in plastic surgery is an absence of tension on the edges. Too much tension turns the edges inward, exposing the patient to infection and certain scarring. With this wound, the edges can't be drawn together without tension. Adjustments have to be made to the underlying tissue, in order to provide extra free skin for a closure where the

117

sides of the wound are kept no more than touching.

The so-called advancement flap is made by first undermining the edges of the wound, separating the skin from the tissue beneath it. Two things now become possible: the skin has much more 'give' once it is free of the underlying connections, so it can be stitched without having to be stretched, and the exposed periosteum can be covered with the loosened tissue which is also much more elastic when it is separated from the skin.

Mr Bryant performs the undermining with scissors and a scalpel, then he uses two hooks to draw loose tissue over the stitched area of muscle. Next, he carefully inserts four stitches which go through both the skin and the separated tissue, marrying them again.

When he is finished he stands back and looks at his handiwork.

'Not bad,' he murmurs. 'I think this is one of my *especially* good days, Teresa.'

The closure of the forehead wound presented the most difficult task, because of the tautness of the skin and the muscle involvement. It has taken forty-five minutes to perform.

While one of the nurses swabs the remaining wounds with saline, Mr Bryant and the Sister go into the changing room for a quick cup of coffee from Sister's flask.

'That went rather nicely, didn't it?' Bryant says as he unhooks his mask from his ears. He is a soft-voiced, sandy-haired Scot in his early fifties. When he talks he uses his hands a great deal, waving them before him to illustrate what he is saying. If he had taken to acting, he would have been permanently cast in kind-uncle roles. He even looks kind, with soft brown eyes and a wide mouth that smiles from habit.

'It went beautifully,' Sister says, pouring the coffee. She has worked with Mr Bryant for six years, and they have grown comfortably used to each other. 'I thought you were going to have trouble with the muscle. Her skin's very taut.'

'Ah, but it's *young*, that makes the difference. Taut-skinned old ladies have muscle that shreds. Even if I'd only stitched young Teresa's to half depth, it would have held.' He talks with the intensity of an enthusiast. 'If we do as well with the other wounds, I fancy she'll come out of it with no visible scarring at all. After a year or two, anyway.'

'Lord, yes,' Sister sighs, 'the other ones. It's a pity her husband couldn't have controlled his cannibal urges a bit. One bite would satisfy most people.'

'The others will be quicker,' Mr Bryant says reassuringly.

Sister gives him a bleak stare. 'I know, but there are *eleven* of them, don't forget.' She has the tone of a colleague, not a subordinate.

'Aye, that's true,' Mr Bryant says, and he drains his coffee cup. 'But in a wee while there'll only be ten.'

Out in Casualty, resources are being stretched again.

Nurse Tait, who is a quiet, rather timid girl, is in the sluice, crying. Nurse Bloom has been instructed to comfort her and get her back on duty as fast as possible.

'That pig!' Isobel Tait moans into her handkerchief. 'I was trying to help him!'

'Never mind,' Sarah Bloom soothes her, 'it's happened to me a couple of times. You'll get used to it. Just keep reminding yourself they're common and pukey and brain-damaged and anything else you can think of that's nasty.'

Ten minutes before, while Nurse Tait was helping a male patient with a sprained ankle to hobble to a cubicle, he suddenly slid his hand down over her shoulder and grabbed her breast. Worse, he held on to it and muttered something beerily in her ear that she will never be able to bring herself to repeat. Nurse Tait's screams unnerved a number of the patients in the cubicles and in the waiting room, and brought Dr Lester running to what could have been his second battle of the shift. Fortunately, when Nurse Tait broke free from the impromptu act of lust, the weight went on the patient's ankle again and he fell over. It took no more than the threat of a punch in the ear to control him.

'Blow your nose and pull yourself together, love,' Nurse Bloom counsels. 'We'll be off duty soon.'

'Pig,' Nurse Tait mumbles, and she blows into the hankie as she's been told. 'What's really sickening is he thought he could get away with something like that.'

Sarah Bloom raises her eyebrows in counterfeit dismay. 'What, you mean you haven't heard? We're all sluts in this business. You can ask anybody.' She squeezes Isobel's shoulder. 'What that kind thinks doesn't matter a damn. You can hardly expect them to have any decent instincts, can you?'

119

'I suppose not.' Isobel says grudgingly.

'Come on, then. Let's get back to it. I'll buy you a Babycham down at the Appleyard when we've finished.'

Sister Boyd is in a cubicle with a young mother and her baby. The child is only a few months old: she has a scalded right arm and hand. As with any injured child, Sister has to be searching with her questions. The mother in this case is slovenly, a lank-haired girl with dandruff and acne who has been on the defensive from the moment she was brought in.

'I can't be expected to have eyes in the back of my head,' she tells Sister.

'I have to ask how it happened,' Sister says. 'I'm not accusing you of anything, Mrs Hyde.' Sister has the baby on her lap, examining the reddened skin of the thin little arm. The scald doesn't look serious, but the baby is obviously in pain.

'It was like I said,' the woman mumbles. 'The cup of coffee was on the side of the table. She was over my arm and I looked away for a second. Next thing I knew she'd grabbed the cup and spilt it over herself.'

Sister has already checked the files and there's no record of a previous admission for this child. It's highly probable that the accident occurred just as the mother has said; the patterns of violence are usually more dramatic and severe.

'I'll take her into a clean room and get a dressing on this,' Sister says. 'If you'd like to go back to the waiting room, I'll bring the baby back to you when I've finished.'

As Sister is going into the room that is set aside for minor burns treatment, Staff Nurse Pitt is helping a middle-aged police constable to a cubicle. The man is very pale and his breath is rasping. He leans on Elsie Pitt's arm and takes small, painful steps.

'Only a couple more yards,' Elsie says. 'You can lie down then.'

Behind them, a younger constable is carrying his colleague's helmet and great coat. He looks as pale as the injured man.

When they are inside the cubicle Elsie helps the patient on to the bed, then tells his companion to sit down. 'What happened to him?'

The young constable swallows hard before he speaks. He gives the impression of being scared. 'It was quick,' he says, and he draws his hand across his mouth. 'Two kids walked right up to us, calm as you like, and one of them asked Bob here if he's Constable Clarke. He told them that was right. And that was it. The bigger one of the two pushes me over, right over on the pavement and the two of them put Bob down and stick the boot in. By the time I was back on my feet they were off. I went after them, but there was no sign.'

Elsie Pitt has opened Constable Clarke's tunic and undone his shirt. There is massive dark bruising on his chest and down across his stomach.

'Did they kick him anywhere else?'

The young constable nods. 'The usual.'

'It's a wonder he's still conscious,' Elsie murmurs. She touches the patient's hand, then squeezes it gently. 'Doctor's coming in a minute,' she says. 'How bad's the pain?'

Constable Clarke says nothing. Instead, he turns his head from side to side with slow, stiff movements; his slitted eyes are imploring help.

'He's a very tough man,' the young constable says. 'Said he didn't need the ambulance. Christ.'

Dr Lester comes into the cubicle, looking a trifle more unkempt and flustered than usual.

'Sorry,' he says. 'Pandemonium out there.' He crosses to the bed and smiles down at Constable Clarke. 'You've had a tussle with the local gentry, I hear.' He looks at the bruising and shakes his head. 'Bastards.'

There are enormous difficulties involved in the assessment of abdominal injuries. X-rays don't tell a doctor very much about soft-tissue damage and even the patient's description of his pain can be misleading, since there is no clear way for him to distinguish between muscle pain and the pain caused by irritation in the abdominal organs. It has even been Jack Lester's experience that certain tears and punctures will give rise to no pain at all until three or four days after the injury when inflammation sets in.

'Tell me how he's been since this happened,' Lester says to the young constable. 'Has he got paler, started feeling dizzy, anything like that?'

'Not really. In fact he's rallied a bit. At first he was dazed, out of breath, kind of stunned looking. He didn't seem to know how bad he was hurt until about two or three minutes after.'

Jack nods. The signs are encouraging. If there is any internal bleeding of life-threatening proportions, the patient gradually goes into shock and becomes vague and semi-conscious. Constable Clarke's behaviour has been just the opposite.

'And how about you, while we're about it?'

The constable looks surprised that the doctor should even ask. 'I'm OK, they just knocked me down. Didn't lay into me or anything...'

'You look terrible,' Dr Lester says. 'Was it the suddenness?'

The constable's face relaxes a fraction. He is starting to look like a man in the presence of a very understanding confessor. 'That was it, yes. Never saw anything like it. One minute we were talking about television, the next Bob's lying in the road with half the shit kicked out of him.' He glances apologetically at Elsie Pitt. 'I couldn't...' He waves his hand in a circle, trying to express the degree of turmoil and shock he experienced. 'Couldn't cope with it, if you follow me.'

'It's not uncommon,' Jack Lester tells him. 'Speak nicely to Staff Nurse and she'll rustle you up a cup of something hot and sweet. You've got a touch of shock.'

The Onlooker Reaction, as Jack Lester has sometimes called it, is very common. It has even killed people. The violent disruption of expectation, routine or even a mood, can produce deep emotional shock waves that jolt the body's centres of chemical support. A man seeing another man knocked down by a car can suffer damage at least half as bad as the accident victim's. Policemen, for all their experience of violence, are as prone to the reaction as anyone else if the disruption is sudden enough.

Turning back to the patient, Lester says, 'I'm going to give you something for your pain and then I'm going to examine you very carefully. If I don't find anything too seriously wrong, you should be in a ward within the half hour. If I find anything you might be making a stop at theatre before the ward.'

With difficulty, Constable Clarke says that he doesn't think there's anything serious about his injuries. 'Bruises,' he croaks, 'and they're worse because I tensed myself.'

Jack Lester nods. An old hand, he thinks. Seasoned policemen have a reactive way of stiffening their muscular defences at the first whiff of trouble.

As Elsie Pitt leaves to get tea for the young constable, Nurse Tait comes in and asks if she can help.

'Yes, you can,' Jack Lester says. 'You can help me to get the clothes off this gentleman.' He raises a warning finger. 'Handle him with the greatest of care, Nurse. He must be feeling like a house fell on him.'

They have Constable Clarke half undressed when Sister Boyd puts her head into the cubicle. 'Do you have a minute, Doctor?'

Lester nods to the nurse to finish undressing the patient and steps outside with Sister.

'It's a baby I've got in the burns cubicle,' Sister murmurs. 'Came in with a scalded arm. Nothing serious there. I dressed the wound, then I went out and asked the mother if the child had had all its vaccinations.' Sister clamps her mouth for a second looking truly aggrieved. 'Not one. The kid hasn't had *one* vaccination.'

Lester sniffs. 'Not too terribly unusual, I'm afraid . . .'

'Yes, I know, but anyway, I decided I'd better give the child tetanus cover in the circumstances. Just as well I did. Come and look at this.'

Dr Lester follows Sister to the burns cubicle. The baby is on the wide bed, lying on her stomach with her head turned on one side. She has stopped crying and there is a large, comfortable-looking dressing on her injured arm.

'What a niff,' Lester says, wrinkling his nose. There's a strong smell of ammonia.

'It's her nappy,' Sister says, and points to a bag on the floor where she has deposited the offending napkin. 'Lord knows when it was changed last. She'd rubber pants on over it, so I didn't notice anything at first.' Sister goes to the bed and lifts the small towel she's used to cover the baby's back. 'If I hadn't wanted to put that injection in her hip, I'd never have found this. Look.'

The child has a nappy rash, the worst Jack Lester has ever seen. Both buttocks are deep scarlet and pitted with septic ulcers.

'That's the equivalent of a full-depth burn,' Lester says.

'How long would it take to get that bad?' Sister asks him.

'Weeks.' Lester bends forward and looks closer at the lesions.

'The kid must have been in agony.'

'She stopped crying when I bathed her and put on some antiseptic cream. Isn't it terrible!'

There is still room for shock in this woman, particularly where children are concerned. Jean Boyd returned to nursing four years ago after she and her husband had been told, after years of trying, that they could have no children of their own.

'They're heartless, some of these mothers,' Jean says.

It was her husband who suggested she go back to the profession. When all hopes of having a family were finally removed Jean became depressed and marginally neurotic. After six months she knew something had to be done to stop the trend, but she lacked motivation. Her husband provided it, and within a year of returning to work Jean was back to normal, or almost; nowadays she knows that she will always be over-sensitive where children are concerned.

Dr Lester sighs and steps away from the bed. 'Get the baby admitted, Sister. And see if you can get somebody from Paediatrics to give the mother a roasting.'

Sister covers the baby again. 'She should be put away for it,' she mumbles.

'Not a chance,' Lester pulls aside the curtain and steps out into the passage. 'That doesn't constitute neglect. Not by today's enlightened standards.'

Jack Lester carries a mental impression of an arc where Casualty weekends are concerned, and as the shift is ending the arc is re-asserting its shape. It starts on Friday night and grows more or less steadily to its high point late on Saturday, then performs its dying fall through Sunday. The crest is fast approaching now.

The work pressure is aggravated by frustration. Casualty Officers and Sisters have to make their requests for supplies of drugs, dressings, instruments and most other materials through the office of the Hospital Secretary. The Secretary, in common with the other administrators, values order above speed, and the processing of requisitions is so meticulous and slow that Casualty frequently runs out of some necessary items – disposable drug packs in particular – and staff who are already busy have to leave the department and go round the wards, scrounging supplies. Tonight, there has been a run on tetanus vaccine and penicillin; someone will have to go out and find some. Sister Boyd has warned that the department's stocks of saline packs and sterile catgut are also getting worryingly low.

There are other frustrations – in addition to the standard ones of cramped working conditions, unco-operative patients and equipment that keeps breaking down – such as the practice among some Ward Sisters of sending their least experienced nurses to Casualty when a call goes out for assistance. Occasionally a male nurse will be sent to help, but even if he is efficient the rules ensure that his value as an extra team member is virtually cancelled; he has to be chaperoned by a female nurse whenever he treats a female patient.

It is also very frustrating for a Casualty doctor or nurse to walk 200 yards to the nearest staff lavatories; there have been promises that this planning oversight will be rectified, but there's no sign that anything is being done. Sister Boyd has already suggested acidly to Senior Nursing Officer Parker that the problem might be solved if the staff were to be catheterised at two-hourly intervals.

In the waiting room there are nine people waiting for attention, and there are a further seven receiving treatment or being prepared for admission. There has been a warning call from the police about a major disturbance outside a discotheque, with several people badly injured. Two ward Housemen are assisting in Casualty already, and more will probably be needed in addition to the four extra nurses Sister Boyd has appealed for.

Constable Clarke has been admitted to a ward, where further examinations and tests will be made. Jack Lester is convinced there isn't anything seriously wrong, but nevertheless the constable will be in great pain for days to come and he will be out of action, in Lester's estimation, for a couple of months. The young constable who was with him has been sent home with orders to stay off work for at least the remainder of the weekend.

In the small theatre, Mr Bryant is still working on Teresa's face wounds. He has had to give her more anaesthetic and now she is looking rather sleepy. Mr Bryant tries to keep her alert as he works. Her co-operation may be needed later as her facial tension increases with the stitching. By simply opening her mouth halfway, she could save the team an hour of preparation work on the face tissue, and by holding her chin at a given angle she could facilitate an otherwise hazardous piece of reconstruction.

'The big snag I can see here, Teresa, is that you'll be so downright beautiful after I've finished there'll be no putting up with you.' Inch by laborious inch, Bryant has closed half of the wounds, adopting a zig-zag pattern of working that keeps the overall tension as near equal as possible. 'You've been a very good patient,' he murmurs, taking a sight line behind his knife blade before he makes the slightest cut. 'An excellent patient, Teresa. I could do with more like you.' There is no end to the reassurance and Mr Bryant will only suspend it if he thinks it's helping to send the patient off to sleep.

A few minutes before he is due to go off duty, Jack Lester comes in from the ambulance bay grinning widely. Elsie Pitt, who has been helping to hold down a crazed drunk while a Houseman and a nurse gave him a stomach washout, is leaning on the wall by the doors to the bay, catching her breath.

'Serendipity,' Jack Lester says to her.

'What's that?'

'It's what's just happened.' He points at the ambulance outside. 'We've got Constable Clarke's principal attacker, no less.'

They watch as the ambulancemen bring in a stretcher, bearing a frightened youth who is pitifully trying to radiate menace. Two policemen are with him, and they're looking as pleased as Jack Lester.

'What happened to him?' Elsie asks.

'Oh, it's pure magic,' Lester beams. 'The police were out looking for him and a couple of constables spotted him over on Rutland Road. He made a run for it and jumped a garden wall – right into a cold frame. Both feet. Crash. That was bad enough, but the silly bugger tried to kick his way out. His legs are in tatters.'

Still grinning, Jack Lester goes off behind the procession that's heading for the Emergency room. Elsie straightens her apron and goes to the office where Sister Boyd is clearing the desk for the graveyard shift.

'They've just brought in the character who beat up that policeman,' Elsie says, and she tells Sister what happened. 'Isn't that great?'

Sister nods.

'Restores your faith in natural justice, doesn't it?'

Again Sister nods. 'Some things do,' she says, but decides not to say anything about the baby with the third-degree nappy rash. She has a feeling she is over-reacting there.

'The news should help Constable Clarke to have a better night than he might have,' Elsie remarks.

'It certainly will,' Sister says. 'The Lord does have a tendency to look after his own, from time to time. I think He could get around to doing it more often, though.'

She also thinks her own capacity for forgiveness is shallower these days, because she can't deny she would rather hear about something horrendous happening to that poor kid's slag of a mother.

*   *   *

'Time to repair nature with comforting repose,' John Blake says, and he pats Jack Lester on the shoulder. 'You've had a hectic day. Take a couple of Scotches and turn in early.'

It's 10.00 p.m. and they are in the car park outside Casualty. A sharp wind is creasing the puddles and putting more furrows into Jack Lester's scarecrow hair. He turns up his overcoat collar and nods towards his car.

'Thanks for the use of the foot pump.'

'A pleasure to be of assistance,' John says. During the evening, someone has let down all Dr Lester's tyres. It happens with depressing regularity and he believes there is a porter about the place with a grudge against him. 'We'll catch the swine one of these nights,' John adds.

'Right. And I'll toss you for who sticks the catheter up him.' Lester opens the car door and climbs in. 'Casualty's all yours now. I hope you have a quieter time than we've had.' He inserts the ignition key. 'I think I've left things pretty straight,' he says, 'but I'd look behind the bins and lockers if I were you, in case I've forgotten anybody.' He starts the engine, then pauses as he's closing the door. 'One thing I forgot to mention. Mrs Reilly.'

John groans quietly. 'Not her again . . .'

'The place wouldn't be the same without her,' Lester says. 'She came in just after nine. Overdose as usual.' He laughs. 'She's the only woman I know that gets her jollies having her

127

guts washed out. We didn't have to do anything this time. She threw up all over Elsie Pitt.'

'What had she taken?'

'A whole box of indigestion tablets. It was all she had in the house.'

Mrs Reilly is one of the regular overdosers, a lonely middle-aged widow who routinely swallows patent medicines in huge amounts and then presents herself at Casualty.

'What did you do with her?' John Blake asks.

'Well, we were too busy to have a chat, so I told her she needed rest and could bed down in a cubicle for a few hours. That seemed to brighten her. Maybe if somebody gets a chance later on they could talk to her for a while.'

'Right. I'll bear it in mind.' John shivers and starts moving back towards the department. 'Better get going. I'll see you some time next week.'

'Oh, one more thing,' Jack Lester calls through the car window. 'That detective was in looking for you...'

'Halliday?'

'That's the one. He said he'd come back later.'

John Blake waves as Jack Lester drives off. He goes back to the department through the waiting room, which is full of people, most of them looking at him expectantly. John tries not to meet anyone's eyes. He pushes through the swing doors and goes to the office where Sister Mary Pringle is standing behind the desk with the telephone receiver jammed against her ear. John signals that he'll come back later, but Sister beckons for him to wait.

'I can't really concern myself with the politics of it,' she says sharply to the phone, and simultaneously makes a despairing face at John Blake. 'We're developing an overload, that's the problem I'm facing.' She listens for a few more seconds, then says. 'Very well. Thank you.' and puts down the receiver.

'Hassle?' John asks cautiously.

'It's SNO Parker's speciality.' Sister picks up the burning remains of a cigarette from the ashtray, takes a couple of puffs and stubs it out. 'She was trying to tell me I couldn't have any nurses from Medical because I'd called out their spare girls twice this month already. It would look, she said, as if we were regarding Medical as a ready-made pool. We're supposed to

128

spread it round.' She sighs and shakes her head. 'Medical's the only section that *ever* has any staff to spare. I told Parker that and she told me it wasn't the point.'

'So what's she going to do?' John asks.

'She's sending me three nurses from Medical, like I asked. The position will have to be reviewed, of course. She wouldn't let me off the wire without throwing out *that* line again.'

Locating adequate numbers of temporary nursing staff – quite apart from the difficulty of finding competent personnel – is an eternal headache in Casualty. Because the flow of patients can fluctuate wildly, even during one shift, no general staffing principle has ever been adopted by the administration. Pragmatism rules, and a Casualty Sister has to do battle with the Ward Regulations every time she needs extra nurses.

'I hope the girls get here soon,' John says. 'The two wagons from the disco won't be long. In fact I'm surprised they're not here already.' He looks at his watch. 'It's a bad sign. They've had trouble.'

'They always do at those places.' Sister goes to the door and looks out into the department. 'It's building up to the Christmas rush,' she says glumly. 'I'd better get out there and do my stuff.'

'Me too.' John takes out his stethoscope and hangs it around his neck. 'I only popped in to warn you that Mrs Reilly's occupying a cubicle. An act of charity on Dr Lester's part.'

Sister nods. 'We'll leave her till it's quiet.' She goes out to the department and John Blake follows her.

The pressure on Casualty has been building since eight o'clock. The overlap personnel should have gone off duty at nine, but there were so many cases waiting to be dealt with that it was 9.45 p.m. before the last member of the team left the building. In one hour the department has handled three fractures, two overdoses, three head injuries, a scalding, a chest wound and two hand injuries. Now they are treating a further two overdose cases, a wrist fracture, a drunk who nearly suffocated on his own vomit, a poisoning, a man with multiple injuries from a road accident, and a patient with a ruptured ectopic pregnancy, who is being prepared for emergency transfer to a gynaecology theatre.

In the Emergency room, a priest has just administered the last rites to the man from the motoring accident. Staff Nurse Glenda

Cross and Dr Ramsay have been working at speed to bring the patient to a level of stability where he can perhaps be operated on, but neither one holds out much hope.

'You've a heartbreaking job,' the priest observes quietly as he folds his ribbon and puts it away.

'Some of the time,' Glenda says.

She has just checked the heart monitor and now she's attending to the de-gloving injury on the patient's right leg. Friction with the vehicle that struck him has stripped all the skin from his leg in one piece, and there has been a lot of bleeding. To control it Glenda is applying large, thick dressings and binding them in position with adhesive tape. The skin is a wrinkled tube now, gathered around the patient's ankle like a grotesque sock.

The man's other injuries are no less hideous. He walked into the side of a heavy van and was bounced from it right under the wheels of a moving car. In the process he suffered a fractured skull, broken ribs, a punctured lung and a complete amputation of one ear. Donald Ramsay has inserted a drain in the patient's chest, linked him to a ventilator and set up a rapid drip-feed of Dextran, but the heart picture still indicates that the man's life is failing.

'How long would they be working on him, if he were able to go into the theatre?' the priest asks. He is a young man, half-intrigued, half repelled by what is going on around him. 'There seems to be so much to attend to.'

Dr Ramsay says nothing. He is staring at the monitor. The signal could be interpreted in a number of ways, but experience narrows the field. Ramsay believes the patient's blood is losing its alkali reserves, probably because his metabolism has been disrupted. From the array of hypodermics in the pack in front of him, Ramsay takes out one loaded with bicarbonate of soda. He injects it in the man's arm and stands back, watching the monitor again. For a few seconds the pattern improves; baking soda is powerfully effective when it is introduced directly into the bloodstream and can often push the alkali-handling mechanisms back to something like normal. In this patient, however, the breakdown in his chemistry is too severe. The picture starts to deteriorate again after ten seconds.

Dr Ramsay turns to the priest. 'I'm sorry, Father.' He waves his hand over the patient. 'To answer your question, I'd think it

130

would take six or seven hours in theatre to patch this man up. He'd need three surgeons working on him simultaneously.'

'But you don't think there's much hope of him getting there?'

'No. That's why you were sent for as soon as we discovered the man's a Catholic. But we'll keep trying for him. It's what we're here for.'

Glenda Cross goes outside to fetch more packs of Dextran. She meets John Blake leading an attractive and stylishly-dressed young woman by the arm. John does a Groucho Marx eyebrow waggle as he passes. He takes the girl into a cubicle then, seconds later, he comes back out.

'I can't trust myself alone with her,' he murmurs to Glenda, who is ripping open the seal on a Dextran bulk container. 'She's down on the card as a photographic model. I don't think I've ever been close to one of those before.'

'What's her trouble?'

'A boil on her rump. Big one, from the way she's walking.'

Glenda laughs. 'That would disillusion a few of them, wouldn't it? A centrefold girl with a boil on her bum.'

'I'm giving her to young Dr Brent,' John says. 'He always looks to me as if he could use something to boost his libido.'

Dr Brent and Dr Cassidy are Housemen who have been assigned to Casualty until midnight. Cassidy has shown some flair for the work on previous Saturday-night stints, but Dr Brent is a humourless, plodding, heavy-handed practitioner whose big wary eyes and spotty complexion tend to alienate his patients.

John Blake finds Dr Brent sifting through the pile of case cards by the waiting room door.

'Looking for one you can handle?' John asks him.

Brent immediately looks offended.

'I was joking, Doctor.' John points to the cubicle where he took the girl. 'There's a patient for you in there. Here's the card. Take one of the nurses with you.'

Brent is staring at the card as if it might contain bad news. 'Shouldn't she be in the dirty theatre?' he asks.

'Only if you decide it's necessary to drain the boil. No need to confront the patient with all that butcher-shop paraphernalia until you're sure you have to.'

In cases where a boil or abscess is clearly filled with pus and the surface is very tense, the casualty officer will insert the tip of

131

a scalpel blade in order to drain it and relieve the painful pressure. If the infection is still in the growing phase, however, there is no point in opening the boil, since it will only go on growing afterwards and the cut skin will add to the discomfort – and possibly the infection. The proper course of action in that case is to give the patient an antibiotic injection.

As Dr Brent is going off to the cubicle with Nurse McLean, the two ambulances from the disco disturbance arrive in the bay. Sister Pringle stands by with her three requisitioned nurses as the driver of the first ambulance gives John Blake the details.

'Two girls, three men,' he says. 'As far as we can gather one of the men drew a razor. The intended victim grabbed the blade, the silly tit. His hand looks pretty bad. The girlfriends waded in after that and the geezer with the razor looks as if he's got a blow-out fracture. One of the girls has a face wound and the other one ended up with half her hair torn out and a tail comb stuck in her ear.'

'Who's the third man?'

'The bouncer from the disco. He went outside to sort it out and it looks as if everybody went for him.' The driver straightens his tie. 'Sorry we took so long. Razor Harry was still trying to have a go when we got there.'

The injured are brought in on trolleys and lined up for John Blake to make his initial assessment.

The man with the cut hand is making a lot of noise. He keeps threatening to do impossible things to the man who wounded him and when Sister tries to restrain him by holding his shoulders down on the trolley he arches his neck and spits in her face.

As Sister jumps back, mopping at her chin, John Blake steps forward, one hand extended. He calmly twines his fingers in the man's hair and twists his wrist at the same time putting a wrenching force on the hair roots. The man roars and drops back on the trolley.

'Just lie still and be good,' John tells him as he takes his hand away. 'If you don't, I'll see to it you get stitched with a blunt needle and no anaesthetic.'

It takes less than five minutes to assess the patients' conditions and decide on treatment.

The man with the injured hand will have to go to a surgical

ward for detailed examination and subsequent operation; he has been cut to the bone in one diagonal slash across his palm; muscle, nerve and tendon have all been severed. He will be given a temporary dressing and transferred as soon as possible.

The girl with the face wound is a small, skinny creature who looks disorientated and frightened. John eases off the dressing the ambulanceman has put on her and finds that a disc of flesh has been cut away from her cheek, leaving a circular wound that is oozing blood. It looks bad but isn't really serious. The wound will be carefully cleaned and dressed, after which the girl will be allowed to go home.

The other three patients are very badly injured. The girl has a raw, bleeding patch at the front of her scalp where the hair has been torn out, but it is the damage to her ear that offers real cause for concern. The comb she was attacked with must have been metal. There is tearing on the outer ear, the ear canal is slit and the eardrum has probably been punctured. It takes a good deal of stabbing force to inflict an injury like that. The girl is in obvious pain, but she defiantly keeps her teeth gritted, glaring a warning at anyone who comes near her.

'Give her morphine for the pain,' John Blake murmurs to Sister. 'It must be hellish. Then put a dressing on the scalp and get her transferred to ENT as fast as you can.'

The man who started it all has a blow-out fracture as the ambulanceman guessed. He must have received a violent punch or kick on his eye and the pressure inside the socket has been raised so suddenly and drastically that it has burst through the thin bony wall. He can't move the eye, which indicates to John Blake that an ocular muscle has been trapped in the fracture.

'Don't try to move it,' John tells the patient. 'Breathe through your mouth and don't, whatever you do, try to blow your nose.' Nose-blowing always complicates blow-out fractures; pressure from the nostrils shifts the damaged bone and tissue from beneath, increasing the damage and causing a painful swelling called surgical emphysema. 'Lie absolutely still. Sister will put a cool pad over your eye and you'll be taken to a ward where a specialist can have a look at you.'

The bouncer is the most seriously injured of all. His face and hands are cut and covered with bruises. He is conscious but very quiet and his breathing is shallow. The ambulanceman has very sensibly inserted an artificial airway into the patient's mouth and throat, since there is evidence of a head injury. Medical men were slow to discover that people can die, even from trivial injuries to the head, simply because the air passage to the lungs, and thence to the brain, is obstructed.

Three of the policemen who attended the scene of the battle have arrived, looking cold and dishevelled. One of them, a sergeant, comes over and stands beside John while he is examining the bouncer.

'He shouldn't have got himself mixed up in it,' the sergeant says. 'You should have seen them. Animals. Apes. There were about ten of them getting laid into him when we showed up. How bad is he?'

John is examining the man's eyes with a torch. One pupil responds normally to the light, but the other is gradually getting larger.

'There could be a haemorrhage around his brain,' John says.

'Doesn't surprise me. He was flat on the deck and the feet were swinging from all sides. One glue-sniffing little bag of shit kept yelling "Get him in the neck, get him in the neck".' The sergeant looks along the row of trolleys and sighs. 'They ought to bring back flogging, straight they should.'

John Blake looks up momentarily. 'I'd have argued with you on that point a couple of years ago.'

'And what do you think now, Doctor?'

'I wouldn't even argue with you if you advocated public hanging.'

An examination of the man's chest reveals three cracked ribs and extensive bruising. Two fingers on his right hand are broken and his left ankle is fractured.

John picks up an X-ray request form and fills it in. He asks for skull, chest, hand and foot radiographs, and when he has done that he beckons to Phil Cowley, the porter, and asks him to take the patient to X-ray. While Phil is wheeling away the trolley, John speaks to Sister, who has finished padding the eye injury and binding the hand wound. He asks her to get ready to strap and plaster the bouncer when he is brought back from X-ray, and to begin charting his consciousness at five-minute intervals.

'Another couple of minutes of that treatment and he'd have been dead,' John says to the sergeant.

134

'What do you think his chances are?'

'It's hard to say. We'll bind him and splint him and we'll monitor his level of consciousness. It looks to me as if he's only barely conscious now. If that gets worse, we'll have to call in the neurosurgeon.'

'What'll he do?'

John Blake finds the sergeant's curiosity oddly boyish. 'He might drill a hole in the patient's skull to relieve the pressure on his brain,' he explains. 'Or he might decide that the condition will stabilise itself. He knows best, that's why we send for him.' John looks around the department, rubbing his hands. 'That's it for the moment, Sergeant. We've got them contained. It could have been worse, from our point of view. It looks as if the wards are going to get the real headaches.'

'We only came in to make sure that shower didn't give you any bother,' the sergeant says. He makes the foot-shuffling movements of departure, which John Blake interprets precisely.

'Thanks, I appreciate that, but you can't go away without something to warm you.' He points to the door of the sluice. 'There's tackle in there to make tea and coffee, if you don't mind helping yourselves.' In a lower voice he adds, 'There's a drop of some decent stuff in a bottle below the big sink, if you prefer some of that. Be my guest.'

The smiling sergeant and his minions go off to the sluice and John winks at Sister, who has been standing a few feet away watching the last of the disco brawlers being wheeled out of the department.

'One good turn, if it's the right good turn, can generate several others where the police are concerned,' John says.

Sister nods. 'I'll write that down.'

Dr Brent goes past and John calls after him. 'How did you get on with the lady with the boil?'

Brent walks back slowly. 'Not terribly well, sir.'

'Why? What happened?'

'She kept insisting that I lance the thing, but it wasn't ready for that. She took a lot of convincing.' Brent's big eyes close for a second, as if he is trying to eliminate a painful memory. 'Then I had to argue with her before she'd let me give her the penicillin. And when I had given it to her, she complained about me hurting her with the needle. Said she'd a good mind to report me.'

'Deary me,' John says, 'I'm sorry about that, Doctor. She seemed pretty reasonable to me. If I'd thought she was going to be trouble I would have handled her myself.'

'If you had handled her, sir, I don't think she'd have been any trouble at all.'

John shoots a puzzled glance across to Sister. 'How come?' he asks Brent.

'Oh, it was something she whispered to Nurse McLean as soon as I went into the cubicle. I heard it quite clearly. She said, "Why can't the good-looking one deal with me?".'

Deeply embarrassed, John Blake stands straight-faced and tries to think of something to say. There is no need. Dr Brent excuses himself and walks away.

John turns to Sister and raises a finger. 'Don't say a word,' he warns her and has to smile at the way she's suppressing her laughter.

Dr Cassidy, short and wiry and perpetually in a hurry, comes across to John and asks his advice on a case that has been brought through to him by Claire Doughty.

'He's an elderly man, sir, and his symptoms are kind of contradictory. I mean, they don't marry up. He's got cyclic palpitation, and he's haemorrhaging from both ears. That combination's weird enough, but there's no sign of skull damage and his pupils are fine.'

'How severe is the haemorrhage?'

'It comes and goes. A trickle, but quite strong.'

John smiles. 'Does it get worse while you're actually examining the ears?'

Dr Cassidy nods. 'That's right.'

'And is the patient a bit scruffy, a dosser perhaps?'

'Well, yes.' Dr Cassidy looks puzzled. 'Is that significant?'

'It certainly is,' John tells him. 'The condition is known as the Freiwohnung Syndrome.'

'Sorry?' Cassidy's puzzlement is deepening. 'The what syndrome?'

'Freiwohnung, Doctor. It's German for free lodgings. Your patient's looking for a bed for the night.'

'I don't think I'm with you, sir.'

Sister is swallowing more laughter as John Blake explains. 'You see it a lot in Casualty. It takes several forms, but the bleeding ears and palpitating heart are about the commonest. Your patient can make his ears bleed whenever he wants to. However bizarre it may seem, a lot of people can. They hold their breath and strain, like you do when you're suppressing a cough – ' John glances at Sister '– or a laugh. The pressure opens a blood vessel near the eardrum. Your crafty malingerer steps up the pressure while you're looking at his ears, just to increase the flow and impress you.'

Dr Cassidy is looking uncomfortable now, as any young doctor does when he discovers his ignorance has wider margins than he thought. 'But what about the palpitations?'

'He swallowed a slice of laundry soap. A urine check'll confirm that.'

After a silent few moments absorbing how he's been conned, Cassidy says, 'What should I do with him?'

'Tell him there's nothing wrong with him. If he argues, say you'll have to make extensive blood tests and apologise for how painful it's going to be. He'll find his own way out.'

Cassidy goes away and Sister Pringle steps close to John Blake. 'You should have told him about the uneven pulses while you were about it,' she says. She is referring to another common trick with malingerers. They strip down a golf ball and remove the hard rubber ball at its core, then turn up at Casualty with the ball lodged out of sight in one armpit. By pressing the upper arm close to the chest, they can cause the ball to lower the rate of the pulse in one arm.

'I'll wait until it fools him, *then* I'll tell him,' John says. 'A touch of humiliation never goes wrong in the early stages.'

Sister goes off to answer the telephone. John Blake looks in on Emergency, and sees Donald Ramsay and the young priest walking towards him. Glenda Cross is dismantling the cardiac monitor beside the sheet-covered figure on the bed.

'Lost him,' Ramsay says to John.

'Nobody could have tried harder for the poor man.' The priest is looking very dispirited. To John he says, 'I couldn't do a job like this. I'm not clever enough anyway, but even if I were, I couldn't take the disappointments.'

'There's plenty to offset them,' John says. 'Though not on a Saturday, mind you.'

Donald Ramsay sees the priest to the door. When he comes

back he finds John standing with his head on one side, listening.

'What is it?'

John straightens his head. 'That waiting room,' he says, 'is beginning to sound like a four-ale bar.'

Overall containment at this hour on a Saturday is difficult, and often it depends on the majority of the waiting patients believing that Casualty is immune to disruption. The ordered, confident behaviour of the staff imposes a strong semblance of control. The antiseptic odours and the awesome machinery of the department play their part too, suppressing natural unruliness as much as illness and injury do. But there is always some kind of trouble and it has to be eradicated quickly, before it becomes clear that the place could be thrown into chaos by a handful of determined vandals.

Claire Doughty has been coping well with the pressure up to now. She has skilfully parried demands for immediate treatment from an Irish bricklayer and a fist-waving news vendor. She has calmed the hysteria of a woman who thought she had been lethally wounded by a jagged salmon tin, and three times she's coaxed patience from people whose pain didn't have serious enough cause to permit them to jump the queue.

But now matters in the waiting room are becoming, in the words of Glenda Cross, ultra hairy. The usual assortment of bruised and cut drunks are there, old hands on whom subtlety makes no impression. They worry and frighten the sober, respectable patients, but not nearly so much as the younger troublemakers – in this case four youths who appear to be drunk *and* under the influence of drugs. Only one of them is injured; he tripped on a paving stone and may have cracked a bone in his wrist. The others are his friends, and they're obviously finding the visit to Casualty a diverting variation on the usual Saturday-night routine. Even the injured one is enjoying himself, taunting the older drunks, passing barely audible comments about the two young women who are there and making periodic farting sounds that put his pals into hysterics.

One outraged-looking old gentleman has had enough. He stands up to interrupt a slanging match between one of the youths and an old grizzled drunk with a crutch.

'Would you kindly make less noise, and mind your language while you're about it!'

'Bollocks!'

138

The old man stiffens and scans the four grinning faces by the rear wall. He's not keen to engage in any exchange that might involve more of the kind of invective that's put sudden scarlet in his cheeks. But neither his pride nor his outrage are going to let him back down.

'Scum!' he glares at each face in turn.

'That's right, you tell the little turds!' the drunk with the crutch yells and blearily he tries to wink at the old man, who immediately sits down, shaking his head at his neighbour.

Now everybody seems to be shouting. Claire Doughty sticks her head through her window and tells them to be quiet. There's a fanfare of simulated farts and she withdraws.

'Stupid old cow!'

'Get back in your fucking fish tank!'

'Bollocks to you too, missus!'

A girl has started to cry, and as she bolts for the swinging doors Claire comes running out after her.

'You can't go through there! Come back!'

They both disappear into the treatment area and the waiting room erupts. The noise and the unexpected appearance of a patient being chased by Claire Doughty sends John Blake and Donald Ramsay to the sluice to fetch the police.

They get to the waiting room within seconds. Three of the youths are standing on chairs, hurling abuse and the contents of a waste bin at the other patients. One of the older drunks has fallen on the floor, after attempting to climb on his own chair, and his flailing legs have already hit a woman and another inebriate who tried to pick him up. The innocents are gathering in a knot by the doors, looking terrified as the embryonic mob picks up impetus from their timidity.

'Right!' the sergeant roars. He strides across the room and grabs the nearest youth by the leg. 'Down off there, *now!*' He lifts his elbow sharply and the youth goes clattering down, banging his head on the wall as he goes. With one smooth movement of the arm, the sergeant catches another lad before he's had time to think about obeying and he goes down too, howling, right on top of his mate.

'Don't touch me!' the third boy shouts. 'I've got a bad arm! Don't touch me!'

'You'll have two bad arms and a fractured arse if you don't get yourself down and over to that wall right now!'

The two constables are herding the older drunks and grunting dark warnings at them. Relief is visibly spreading among the other patients.

The sergeant has the youths lined up against the wall, waving his truncheon at them as he delivers an admonitory address.

'We've got enough on you lot to charge you with a breach, assault, disorderly behaviour and a half-dozen other things that'll keep you down at the nick for the rest of the weekend.' He has the face and delivery of a drill sergeant. Even so, one of the youths finds the courage to complain.

'You bloody assaulted me,' he says as he rubs the back of his head.

'So? You want to lay a complaint?' The sergeant's eyes are wide, an open invitation to special misery. 'Well, do you?'

The youth looks at the floor and says nothing.

'Very well then.' The sergeant stands back, hands on hips. 'Two options. You all bugger off except the one that's here for treatment, or you come down the nick for some of our hospitality.'

There is no conferring. Three of them break away and make for the door, leaving their injured companion staring bleakly after them.

'Straight home,' the sergeant warns them as they go. 'I'll be on the blower to the mobiles to keep an eye out for you.' He turns to the one by the wall. 'You sit here and wait your turn. If there's even a hint you're going to give trouble, you'll wind up getting your first aid from our desk sergeant. He's lousy at first aid.'

With order restored, the police go back to the sluice to finish their drinks. John Blake and Donald Ramsay equip themselves with a case card each and stand for a moment behind the waiting room door watching Claire Doughty and a couple of the patients straightening the chairs and putting the rubbish back in the waste bin.

'Do you know what my old man used to say?' John Blake murmurs.

'What?'

'Saturday night's a time apart. It's for young people to enjoy themselves.'

*   *   *

By 12.15 a.m. Mrs Reilly has been asleep in the end cubicle for over three hours. Waking her gently now, Sister Pringle watches the old woman open her eyes and stare about the small room, lost and confused during the seconds before her memory tells her where she is.

'I thought you'd like some tea,' Sister says, and she puts the cup and saucer on the locker. 'How are you feeling now?'

'Better, I think.' Mrs Reilly pushes herself up on the pillows, tucking her worn green cardigan around her. 'It's good of you to put up with me.'

Sister would be perfectly happy to let the woman stay the night. But there have been stern warnings in the past from Senior Nursing Officer Parker. The cubicles are for treatment, nobody is to be permitted to sleep in them, particularly old women who come into the department with no complaint other than chronic loneliness.

'Drink up your tea, now. It'll warm you inside.'

Sister sits on the edge of the bed and watches Mrs Reilly sip from the cup. She has spent time with this woman on four previous occasions, and always there has been the same pattern to the way she behaves during the aftermath of her pseudo-suicide attempts. She is calmed by another human presence, but after a few minutes of simple closeness, Mrs Reilly has an urge to use the other person as a hand-hold on reality. As Dr Blake has put it, Mrs Reilly needs other people's sanity and order, because she can't generate enough of her own. She has no wish to die, but she can barely withstand things the way they are.

The moment of need comes, heralded by a tightening of the lined face – something like the suppressed wince a person makes before a hypodermic is inserted.

'I got so . . .' Mrs Reilly pauses and looks into her cup. 'It was just so heavy, everything. Like a weight. I'd been trying to stop myself crying for hours. Then I'd done it before I knew. Took mouthfuls of the pills and washed them down.'

Although Mrs Reilly is able to confess before doctors and nurses, she is a shy woman – which accounts for much of her loneliness – and she can't simply walk into the hospital to ask for help. It takes an act of self-injury to get her into the presence of the people who soothe and sustain her. She always begins by making an excuse for that.

141

'I understand,' Sister says. What she understands is that the overdosing is a cause for worry only because one day Mrs Reilly might accidentally kill herself. There's no point in trying to deter her, it's her key to some peace. Even a reminder of how savage a washout can be is useless – the washout is a strong touch of reality, and it makes her feel cared-for. 'Did you do what we suggested to you before? Go out more, meet some of the people you used to know?'

'I've tried to; but it frightens me a bit.' Being out of her husband's shadow is at the bottom of her anxiety. She was dominated – in a kindly way – by Dermot Reilly for forty years; on her own she is incomplete and painfully exposed, a stranger to the business of running her own life. 'I don't think people are all that keen to know me, anyway.'

'That's nonsense. You're a nice woman, you're intelligent and you've got plenty to contribute. I'm sure there are lots of people wanting to be in your company.'

Mrs Reilly puts down her cup. 'It's nice of you to say that...'

'I mean it.' Sister leans forward and pats her hand. 'There's a lot of good life ahead of you, if you'll make the little bit of effort to have it.'

They will talk on like this for another ten or fifteen minutes, and perhaps this will be the time when Sister can convince Mrs Reilly that there's no undoing the catastrophe of her husband dying, but that she's capable of undoing the effect it's had on her. Like others in the department, Sister Pringle looks on the old lady as an amputee. She has to learn to walk with a limb missing.

Three cubicles away John Blake is examining a young man who has come in complaining of severe pain in his back. John has known from the second he saw the patient that he is lying, but in this instance John is sympathetic. He's working towards a gradual uncovering of the truth, rather than hitting the man with a direct accusation.

'Well, Mr Shearer, I can't detect anything unusual,' John says, stepping back from the bed. 'The kind of pain you've described would show some sort of outward sign.' That isn't true, but it is necessary to say it in order to get at the facts.

The patient rolls over and sits up, forgetting to clutch at his spine as he was doing when he came in. 'But it's agony, Doctor.

I've had it before, but not this bad.' His eyes are red-rimmed and unsteady and his whole body is trembling. 'I'm not asking you to put it right, but if you could just give me something for the pain...'

'I think some X-rays might give us an idea...'

'But could you give me something for the pain, first...'

'I'm afraid not,' John says. 'With pain as bad as you say yours is, ordinary pain-killers would have no effect. I can't administer anything stronger without knowing exactly what the trouble is.'

It takes no more than a simple refusal and the promise of more delay to make the patient break down. He starts to blink rapidly and then he puts his trembling hands to his face and starts crying.

'Lie down,' John tells him quietly, and he helps the patient to get the blanket over himself. The trembling is violent now, the precarious control Mr Shearer has been maintaining over himself is escaping fast. 'Try to tell me about it, will you?'

The man attempts to talk, but his sobbing and his chattering teeth make it impossible.

'Are you registered?' John asks him quietly.

Shearer shakes his head.

'Well I think you should be. It takes no time at all, I can get the wheels rolling for you.' John watches the agonising process of decision-making – a monumental undertaking when a man is into the throes of drug withdrawal.

'Don't want to,' Shearer grunts through clenched teeth.

'It's better than cold turkey,' John insists. 'What are you on? Heroin?'

'Dip...' Shearer stammers. 'Dipip...'

'Dipipanone? Is that what it is?' Dipipanone is a powerful analgesic, and it exerts as strong a hold over its addicts as heroin does.

The patient nods. He's breathing deeply through his mouth and bringing the sobbing under control. For an addict, he appears to have a lot of stamina. He is still shaking violently and John believes it may have been a day or two since he last had his drug. The fact that he was desperate enough to try to get a fix in hospital supports that estimate.

'They won't give you that stuff at a clinic,' John says. 'But at least you'll get *something*. Methadone, most likely.'

143

John has no intention of leaving Shearer in his present condition; but if the patient is to have anything to relieve his condition over the long term, then the Home Office must be notified that he's a drug addict. The patient would then attend a drug clinic where he would be given regular prescriptions in addition to psychological therapy aimed at weaning him gradually away from his habit.

'They won't put you away or anything like that. You'll be properly looked after.'

Mr Shearer is thinking about it. There's a lot to consider. At a clinic, he would be given oral drugs only. The usual one is Methadone, a heroin substitute. Many addicts shy away from the clinics because they prefer injectible drugs, which have a more powerful effect, but also because their registration as addicts at public clinics puts them under the kind of social restrictions and scrutiny they would rather avoid.

'Do you get your drug from somebody who's registered privately?' John asks.

Again Shearer nods.

'That's all right until you run out of money. There's no charity in that kind of arrangement. A clinic will always help you – one way or another.'

National Health Service general practitioners won't normally deal with addicts' requests for drugs, but there are independent, private doctors who will. They first of all notify the Home Office, and then issue the addicts with prescriptions for whatever drugs they want, apart from the ones with special restrictions such as heroin and cocaine. The excuse offered by these doctors is that they're saving the addict from the black market with its inflated prices and dangerously contaminated merchandise. To pay for the private consultations, the majority of addicts have to sell a proportion of their prescriptions – and usually their doctors supply enough for that purpose.

'My job...' Mr Shearer says.

'Yes, I can understand the worry there,' John says, 'but there's very little chance they'd find out. They've more chance of knowing if you go on like this.'

After a few seconds, Shearer nods his compliance.

John gets the appropriate form and fills it in. Then he puts an address list of clinics on the table by Mr Shearer's jacket. 'Go to any one of them on Monday,' he says. 'I'll give you a letter before you leave, confirming that I've notified the Home Office. You'll get treatment right away.'

Shearer groans and presses his hands to the sides of his head. 'Monday,' he shudders. 'I can't wait...'

John Blake leans close to him. 'I've got you down on the card as having severe back pain. I'm going to give you a shot for it. It'll be nothing like Dipipanone – you won't be quite up on top again – but it'll help.'

The drug John injects is pethidine. It has some of the properties of morphine and in addition it's useful in reducing the muscle spasms Mr Shearer is suffering. It will contribute nothing to his addiction, but it will merely make life more bearable until an addiction specialist can take over.

Within five minutes Mr Shearer is like a new man. He is calm and totally in control of his reflexes. He gets dressed and thanks John for his help.

'I get the feeling you were desperate,' John tells him. 'I shouldn't try that stunt again, if I were you. Withdrawal sticks out a mile, when you've seen enough of it. And a lot of casualty officers take the needle to addicts, if you'll forgive the pun.'

'It was pretty bad,' Shearer says as he tightens the knot in his tie. He is in no way the cliché addict; he is wearing brogue shoes, twill trousers, shirt, tie and sports jacket. And his hair is short. 'My contact upped the price. He can sell as much as he gets. I couldn't really afford the old price. So...' He spreads his hands. 'I took some aspirin when I started getting the shakes. I tried Veganin when my veins began to feel itchy. Then I drank about a gallon of sweet tea. Nothing worked.'

'Do many people know you're hooked?'

'My girlfriend knows, but she doesn't know how badly. I didn't know it was that bad myself. This is the first time I've run out of supplies.'

There is nothing in the plight of drug addicts or alcoholics that makes John Blake feel superior. He knows a professor of anatomy who drinks a bottle of brandy a day, an anaesthetist addicted to sniffing nitrous oxide, and a young physician with a morphine habit. John's father-in-law died of cirrhosis.

'When did you start?' John asks as he is scribbling out a note for the clinic.

145

'Six or seven months ago. My previous girlfriend started me. She was a nurse.'

John is sure the young man isn't trying to shock him and, in any case, he isn't shocked. Drug abuse among nurses isn't common, but it's not so infrequent that it can be called rare.

'She kept me supplied for a few months, then we broke up,' Shearer goes on. 'By that time I'd met other users; and one of them agreed to sell to me.' He smiles for the first time. 'I feel relieved. Maybe it's the jab.'

'Maybe it's deciding to cope with the trouble, instead of just accommodating it.' John isn't above using clichés when they embody the truth.

'Will I hold till Monday?' Shearer asks as John hands him the envelope with the note in it.

John goes to the lock-up cabinet and gets a small tub of high-dosage Librium. He gives them to Shearer and says, 'These'll make things bearable. One every four hours if you don't think you can hold out. Don't try doubling-up on the dose, even if you're tempted to. You'll just be sick.'

At the door Shearer thanks John again and goes off across the waiting room, looking as normal as anyone can.

The department is relatively tranquil now. Mr Bryant, the plastic surgeon, has finally vacated the theatre and his patient, Teresa, has been transferred to Women's Surgical. There are three weary-looking citizens in the waiting room and three others are receiving treatment. Phil Cowley is doing the rounds with a mop and bucket and Nurse McLean is replenishing cubicle supplies.

John Blake is about to call in one of the patients from the waiting room when the paediatrician, Dr Roarke, comes in. He has news about the case of Elizabeth Quigley, the child who was brought in the previous night with scalded legs.

'If you have tears, etcetera,' Roarke murmurs as they go into the office and sit down. He puts his hands flat on the desk and looks straight at John. 'Early this morning, I decided young Elizabeth had a postural abnormality. It was nothing very prominent; in fact I couldn't even decide where it was centred. So I had her X-rayed.'

John groans his apprehension.

'Healed fracture of the right humerus with misalignment,'

Roarke says. 'Hairline crack in the mandible. And something that might be a healed fracture of the right third rib.'

'So what's been done?'

Roarke sits back, folding his arms. 'A female detective visited the mother yesterday. She energetically denies ever having laid violent hands on her daughter. That much I expected. The bit that creases me is that she's trying to blame the bloody dog. It's too boisterous she says.' Roarke sighs. 'That child probably hasn't had a day without pain in her entire twenty-six months. And some kinds of pain make them mute. Nobody knows what's going on – except the torturer and the victim.'

'Are the police bringing charges?'

'Oh yes. Yes. But you know how these things can go. The social workers'll get on the case and shoot the magistrates full of their jargon and half-baked psychology. And now there's all this garbage about PMT as well. Sweet God.' Roarke looks at the ceiling and grunts derisively. 'Pre-Moronic Terrorism in this case.'

'Is there a husband?' John asks.

'No, she's single. From the sound of her, I'm surprised anybody got desperate enough to couple with the monster.'

John Blake is aware of a growing strain in Dr Roarke. He has seen it in other doctors whose objectivity has been eroded by prolonged involvement with other people's pain.

The door opens and Donald Ramsay comes in.

'Sorry to interrupt,' he says. 'I've got a lady out here I'd like you to have a look at when you get a minute, Dr Blake.'

Dr Roarke stands up. 'I've got to be going, anyway.'

As Blake and Ramsay are heading for the cubicles, Ramsay says he's noticed that Dr Roarke always seems to bring his news in person, rather than using the telephone.

John Blake nods. 'It's an excuse to get out of the ward.'

'Really? I've always had the impression he's a workaholic. The general consensus seems to be that he loves his job.'

They pause outside the cubicle where the lady is waiting. 'He does,' John says. 'But he's having to cope with too much horror these days. It's easy for us. We're with the sick and battered babies and the crippled and mutilated toddlers for a few minutes each, an hour at most. Roarke's got to stay with them and care for them, watch them going through all the pain and misery. He sees a lot of those kids die, too.' John points at the still-swinging door to the ambulance bay. 'That bloke's going to have a breakdown one of these days. Soon. All the little jaunts out to Casualty and the path lab are his subconscious way of delaying it, if you ask me. He's got an obsessive tendency to talk things out. It gets like impromptu Freudian therapy, sometimes. He never used to be that way.' John taps the side of his skull. 'It's accumulation. Pressure.' He jerks his head at the cubicle. 'What have you got?'

Ramsay lowers his voice. 'Lily Newton, sixty, single. She's got a really weird lesion on the right side of her jaw. Puckered and indurated, and it's as hard as brick at the centre.'

John Blake consults his watch. 'Another night-panic, I suppose.' Every experienced Casualty Officer knows that the human being's terror of death or catastrophe flourishes in the darkness and silence of the early hours. 'How long has she had it?'

'Three weeks. She says it started as a red lump, then it began turning in at the centre, and that's when the hard floor began to develop.'

They go into the cubicle. Miss Newton is the tidy epitome of a middle-class spinster. She is wearing a brown tweed coat and a matching hat. Her brown leather gloves are laid neatly on her lap. Her face betrays anxiety and she has the tired eyes of someone who has contained her fear for too long.

John sits down beside the patient and introduces himself. 'Let's have a look at this sore you've got,' he says, gently turning the woman's head. 'I won't hurt you, I'm only going to look.'

He uses his torch to examine the cratered lesion. It is close to her chin and it looks like a ruptured boil, with an inflamed border and a dull greyness at its centre. John picks up a thin steel probe from the instrument tray and touches the grey part very gently at first, then more firmly. It's hardness is transmitted along the shaft of the probe.

'Does it hurt very much, Miss Newton?'

'Lately it has,' she says. 'It throbs.'

'Is it throbbing now?'

'Yes.' Miss Newton's voice is shaky. 'Quite a bit, Doctor.'

John sits back. 'I suppose you've been worrying yourself ragged about it. You can stop all that, I'm sure.'

148

'But it *is* a growth, isn't it?' Soft tears are welling. 'I've felt it getting bigger. And it's so hard...'

John smiles at her and takes one of her hands between his own. 'Listen to me. It's a growth all right, but not the kind to worry you. You won't even need a doctor.'

Donald Ramsay is frowning at John. Like Miss Newton herself, he has been tentatively approaching the conclusion that she has a cancer.

'I'm going to give you an appointment card to come in to our dental outpatient department,' John says, and he is still squeezing Miss Newton's hand. 'That thing on your face is a wisdom tooth.'

'Never!' She is staring at John as she touches the lump, feeling it for the first time without fear. Donald Ramsay looks just as surprised.

'It happens,' John assures her. 'The tooth probably formed at the wrong angle, and it's spent years burrowing through the side of your jaw bone. That's the crown of it you can see, and all our dental surgeon will have to do is draw it, like any other tooth. You won't even have to open your mouth.'

'Goodness...' Miss Newton is fumbling in her bag for a handkerchief. Tears of relief are rolling down her cheeks. 'Oh, dear...' She finds the hankie and presses it to her eyes. 'I'm sorry...'

'Just you sit here and have a bubble,' John tells her. 'I'll be back in a few minutes with your appointment card.'

Miss Newton unfolds the handkerchief and puts it tightly to her face again. She cries silently, with heaving shoulders and sharp, up-and-down movements of her head. John smiles and leads Ramsay by the elbow to the door.

When they are outside, Donald Ramsay slaps John on the shoulder. 'Hot stuff, Squire. I'd never have picked that up without an X-ray.'

'Of course you wouldn't,' John says flatly. 'You lack the innocence for that kind of diagnosis.'

'What does that mean?'

'It means,' John says, 'that I looked at the lesion and kept my conditioned reflexes well under control. I'd seen nothing like it and I made no assumptions.' He's being mock professorial. The clowning is a sign of his own relief; at first sight, Miss Newton's lesion did look malignant to him. 'That's why my eyes weren't clouded. I realised, after a minute, that I was staring at the top of a little tooth.'

They get to the office and John reaches in and takes a clinic appointment card from the box behind the door.

'I guess some people are just born for the profession,' Ramsay says wistfully. 'Folk like me, we hobble along from blunder to blunder, while the real artists bestride the mysteries...'

'Terribly true,' John says airily. He fills in the card, then looks up at Ramsay. 'But it's not a gift that comes entirely naturally, you know. It takes a terrible lot of hard work to be a smart-arse.'

* * *

At 4.00 a.m. Detective Sergeant Halliday is in the sluice, standing beside Glenda Cross as she mixes him a draught for his ailing stomach.

'You're a good girl. I'll remember you in my next will.'

Halliday's face looks even more lined and pale than usual, and he has the laboured breathing of someone who has been walking too fast. He is near the end of a four-month stretch of night duty and he has been worn down by it. Like night-shift Casualty staff, he finds he sleeps twelve hours at a time and still wakes up feeling exhausted.

'There you are.' Glenda hands the detective the glass. 'Drink every drop.'

'What's in it?'

'Trade secret. It's got funny side-effects, but don't let that worry you.'

Halliday swallows the white liquid and predictably makes a sour face. 'God Almighty. It tastes like chalk and vinegar.'

'Damn,' Glenda says. 'You've cracked the trade secret.'

John Blake comes in and apologises for keeping Halliday waiting. 'We've just pumped two bottles of home-made wine out of an old man. He says he drank it because he got depressed. He'd have been better off taking paraffin, from the smell of it.' John hoists himself on to the worktop and looks expectantly at the policeman. 'Have you come to cheer me up, or what?'

'My job's making people miserable,' Halliday points out. 'I wanted to give you the latest on our rapist. Michael Crosby Esquire, psychopath.'

150

'I don't think I want to hear,' Glenda says. 'I'll be helping Sue to tidy up if anybody needs me.'

When Glenda has gone Halliday stands tapping his stomach for a minute, then he belches. 'I don't know what she gave me, but it worked.' He leans back against the sink and folds his arms. 'Crosby's going to be trouble. All the way. And the one that'll suffer most is Mrs Crumley.'

'Christ, she's suffered enough...'

'Don't expect any pity from Master Crosby,' Halliday says. 'It's a tear-stained case but it'll be a lot worse soon. That crazy bastard's made a statement that'd curl your hair. I'm beginning to wish we hadn't charged him.'

'What's he saying?' John asks.

'He's saying he was led on. Seduced. And he's furnished all the details, right down to the dirty talk Mrs Crumley allegedly used to switch him on.'

'But that's nonsense...'

'I know, I know. But it'll get aired in court. And do you know something? Crosby's evidence is filth, but it sounds convincing. Convincing enough to raise doubts in a jury.'

'Can't it be broken?'

'Like I said, he's a psychopath. I'm sure of it. And they make good liars, don't they? Once he'd got that story put together, he stuck to it. I've questioned him on it twice and so have two other officers. He's word perfect.' Halliday is silent for a moment, looking at the floor. 'I'll tell you straight, we could lose the case.'

'Have you any idea what that'll do to Doris Crumley?' John says. 'The psychiatrist tells me she's not doing too well and that comes as no surprise. If she goes into a courtroom and hears Crosby's muck, if she suffers all the humiliation and then gets hit with a judicial verdict that spells out she's a lying scrubber...'

'No need to paint it for me,' Halliday says. 'It's not something I like to contemplate. I haven't forgotten Sheila Smith.'

'Neither have I,' John says.

Sheila was a patient in a psychiatric ward at Anderson General. She had claimed that a male nurse from another ward had come to her bedside one night and assaulted her sexually. Sheila, a shy, nervous girl, had been persuaded by relatives to report the matter and the case eventually went to court. The jury decided that, in spite of the evidence of an eye-witness, there weren't grounds enough to find the male nurse guilty. Three weeks later Sheila killed herself. Eight months after the case the same male nurse was back in court, facing a similar charge, and this time he was found guilty. He was jailed for six months.

Halliday moves towards the door and starts buttoning his coat. 'I wanted you to know, anyway,' he says wearily. 'To be more accurate, I want to be sure you know we're not to blame for what Mrs Crumley might go through. A lot of folk'll give the police stick if we go down on this one, and it really isn't our fault.'

'I know,' John says. 'And you handled Mrs Crumley a lot better than some would. Not that it's going to matter much now.' John sighs. 'It hardly bears thinking about. The girl's got nothing to hang on to.'

'That husband of hers is a right prat as well. The last I heard, he was talking about a legal separation.'

The enormity of it all produces a wave of impatience in John Blake. He gets down off the worktop. 'I don't want to hear any more, Sergeant.'

Halliday opens the door. 'Maybe we shouldn't be too gloomy. Her evidence could swing it – but Crosby worries me sick. He's too good at playing the victim.'

They walk to the main door together and stand looking out at the dark for a minute; then Halliday shivers and steps outside. 'Bloody rape,' he murmurs as he goes off across the car park.

Sister Pringle is going round the department locking away supplies in cupboards and cabinets and making sure that all floor areas are as clear as they can be. Casualty will be closed from 7 a.m. until 9 p.m. as it is every Sunday. A team of technicians and cleaners will move in during the day and they will work for five hours. By the time they've finished, the department should be shining clean again and most of the equipment and lighting that has broken down or gone faulty during the week will be functioning properly once more. This once-a-week regime became necessary when it was realised that the sheer number of cases passing through Casualty was defeating the daily routine of maintenance. Cleaners still work each morning in Casualty, and technicians will come in at any hour if there is a major breakdown, but by Sunday the backlog of jobs is formidable.

Phil Cowley has mopped the floors yet again, and he has put all but one of the trolleys into the Emergency room. The place is beginning to look larger.

'That's how I like to see it,' Sister says to Phil. 'Open spaces. No clutter.'

'And no patients,' Glenda Cross calls from the plaster room, where she and Sue McLean have almost finished tidying.

Phil goes out to the ambulance bay and stands with his hands in his overall pockets, watching the dazzle of the puddles on the tarmac. Most of the time his troubles are predominant and there's little that comforts him, but this does, a few silent minutes hypnotising himself out of the aching territory that's his life-space.

When he was younger, and before sciatica had made it necessary for him to do a less strenuous job, Phil worked the night-shift in a factory. Even then, when he had been relatively happy, he would snatch minutes in the open air, especially when it had been raining. Away from the noise of the machines, staring off-focus at light on dark water, he always felt himself being restored, invigorated. That doesn't happen nowadays, but it's still a very pleasant thing to do.

He has been standing there for a couple of minutes when he hears the door behind him creak open.

'Oi.'

Phil turns and sees Glenda Cross.

'Coming in for a cuppa, are you?'

He smiles at her and nods.

They go to the sluice and Glenda busies herself making some coffee. Phil sits down on a small stool by the door and watches her.

'How's it going then?' Glenda asks eventually. Everyone on the shift knows about Phil's trouble, but Glenda's the only one who talks to him about it.

'The same,' he says, and he passes a hand over his hairless scalp. 'Lily's a bit better, I think. Got more colour.'

'No word from your wife?'

Phil shakes his head.

Phil's misfortune was made public, to his embarrassment, through the gossip of another porter at Anderson General, whose sister lives near Phil. Two months ago Phil's wife left him and went off to live in the Midlands with a man who had been Phil's friend for thirty years. Phil had always known that his wife had a restless nature, but he would never have guessed how truly desperate she was to be quit of the life they had made together.

That pain is severe enough, but there is another that regularly pulls Phil Cowley to the verge of despair. He has a daughter of thirty, a rather backward girl who has always lived at home. She had been sporadically listless and ill for a year, and until six weeks ago the family doctor was treating her for anaemia. But now the girl, Lily, is in another London hospital being treated for multiple sclerosis.

Glenda hands Phil a mug of coffee and pats his head, as she has a habit of doing. 'You're going to have to cheer up, you know. It's bad for you, all this moping.'

Phil's eyes are clouded, scanning his inner landscape. 'I don't reckon Josie'll be in touch, ever,' he says softly. 'I've wrote a couple of times, but she's turned her back on us. That's that.'

'Some women don't know when they're well off.' Glenda swings herself on to the edge of the worktop and rests her coffee mug in her lap. 'Just you forget her and get on with your life, mate.' Glenda's counsel is relentlessly chirpy, a deliberate counterpoise to Phil's melancholia.

'I think,' Phil says slowly, 'if I could be sure Lily'd be all right...'

'Now you know what I told you about that,' Glenda says.

'Yeah.' He smiles apologetically. 'It's all them stories you hear, though.'

'That's all they are, Phil. Stories.'

Glenda believes that Lily's illness was accelerated by her mother leaving home, though she would never add to Phil's anguish by telling him that. The girl was deeply attached to her mother, even though it's easy to infer, from what Phil has said about her, that Mrs Cowley had very little affection for Lily beyond simply caring for her. There is no known cause for MS, beyond a hardening suspicion that it is linked to an abnormality in the sufferer's reaction to infection. But it is known that emotional upheavals often precede the first clear symptoms.

'You reckon she'll get on her feet again, do you?'

Glenda stares at Phil. 'Do you think I've just been blowing through a hole in my neck? I checked up, Phil. I told you I did.'

He smiles, nodding. 'I just like hearing it, I suppose.'

'The treatment Lily's getting will stabilise her, she'll be back home with you soon. And she'll be on her feet, Phil. She'll have plenty of years of good, active life. More than you, I shouldn't doubt.'

It was Sister Pringle who did the checking on Glenda's behalf. Lily Cowley is responding well to a treatment called Protein Shock. High concentrations of protein substances – milk, bacterial vaccines – are injected in the patients, with the aim of raising the body's overall temperature; this stimulates the chemical processes of the system, improving its healing powers. In cases where this treatment is effective, the outlook is good. Lily will never be free of the disease, and as time passes she will develop more and more of the crippling symptoms, but the process will be gradual; it could be twenty-five or thirty years before the sclerosis finally threatens her life.

'Your daughter's being well looked-after,' Glenda says. 'You concentrate on getting yourself into shape. Are you sleeping all right?'

'Not bad.'

'You can have some pills, if you want. Just to help for the time being.'

'Thanks. I'll let you know.'

It doesn't surprise Glenda that Phil's marriage broke up. He has worked nights for over twenty years. The psychological stress on a woman whose husband rarely spends a night with her could be devastating. And there are a lot of well-charted personality defects that can develop in people who do their work at night and sleep during the day. Glenda has no intention, however, of telling Phil that he probably contributed as much to the breakdown as anybody.

There are small sounds of activity outside. Glenda hears the squeak of trolley wheels and goes to look. Sister Pringle is standing in the middle of the open area behind the bay doors with one hand clasped to her forehead.

'Just look at my floor!' she yelps.

As the ambulancemen are transferring their stretcher patient to a Casualty trolley, blood is dripping down both sides, making crimson star patterns on the tiles.

Glenda and Phil go across to help. Donald Ramsay, still

155

carrying his newspaper, is coming from the office with John Blake behind him.

'There's another one to come,' one of the ambulancemen says.

Ramsay is beside the trolley, lifting the blanket off the groaning patient. 'Jesus,' he says, 'a massacred Indian.'

'Krooklock job,' the ambulanceman tells him.

The patient is wearing only underpants, and he has temporary dressings on his arms, legs and head. They are all leaking blood. People bleed more freely if they have alcohol in the bloodstream, and there is a powerful smell of whisky from this patient.

'Help Dr Ramsay here,' John Blake says to Glenda. 'I'll see to the other one.'

As the dressings come off one by one, the first patient's injuries are revealed to be multiple and serious. Skin and muscle have been gouged out of his right arm in one long wound, from the elbow to the wrist. His left upper arm is swollen and the forearm has two deep cuts, like razor slashes. The injuries on his legs look as if they've been inflicted with a chisel; there are several of them on each leg: squareish wounds with badly torn edges on the shins, calves and thighs. His head wound is the least serious – a cut on the scalp that turns out to be quite small and superficial when the blood has been mopped away. It's inevitable that the man will need prolonged surgical care after the Casualty team have attended to the immediate business of containment.

'Who says the Indians haven't contributed anything to our culture?' Ramsay murmurs to Glenda as they ease off the sopping dressings and drop them into the buckets Phil has brought. 'They've given us a whole new field of trauma.'

With the exception of the slashes on his left arm, the patient's injuries are typical mutilations inflicted by a weapon that's been adopted, almost exclusively, by violent elements within the Indian community. The Krooklock, with its unique combination of metal bar and square-ended hooks, offers the assailant a wide range of weapons in one.

When Krooklocks were first used as weapons, police and hospital staff were mystified. The distribution, severity and shape of the wounds presented something quite new. There was wild speculation among police officers and doctors, ranging from theories about advanced, possibly imported weaponry, to suspicions that teams of young thugs were roaming the streets armed with hammers, batons and chisels. The victims always maintained they didn't know what had happened to them, thereby obeying the community rule that nobody would tell the police anything. The mystery was solved one night by two constables when they went to answer an emergency call and found a small gang battle in progress; the combatants were armed exclusively with Krooklocks.

The second patient is an Indian too, but he has only one injury, a bullet wound in his right shoulder. There is no exit wound, so John Blake assumes the bullet is lodged somewhere in the shattered articular cartilage and bone. The patient is much younger than the other man, probably in his late teens. He is conscious and wary.

'How do you feel?' John Blake asks him. 'Is there much pain?'

'It doesn't hurt,' the patient says.

John pinches the upper arm. 'Feel that?'

The patient shakes his head.

'Right. Just lie still and we'll get you X-rayed.'

In this case the radiographs will be taken from several angles so that the site of the bullet can be determined precisely. A tangle of nerves, known as the brachial plexus, lies just under the bullet hole and the absence of feeling in the wound and arm indicates that some of those nerves have been damaged. The subclavian artery is also nearby. Further damage, possibly disastrous, could be done if a surgeon attempted to remove the bullet without knowing its exact location.

John fills out the X-ray request and Phil Cowley wheels the patient away.

'I was looking forward to a quiet couple of hours,' John tells Sister Pringle as they cross to the other trolley.

'And me,' Sister says. 'We should know better by now.' She looks at the drying patches of blood on the floor and sighs.

'What's the assessment?' John asks Donald Ramsay, whose coat and hands are now covered with blood.

'Multiple injuries on arms, legs and head. But no internal damage.' While it's true that a person can die from even a single wound on the arm or leg, the general rule is that so long as there is no abdominal injury, a patient will survive however severe his wounding. 'Some enlargement of the liver, by the way,' Ramsay adds.

'He's an alcoholic,' a voice says from the doorway.

They turn and see Inspector Donnie Howard, self-styled pride of the Flying Squad, limping towards them in his shiny purple windcheater and jeans. As with everything else that adds to his legend, Howard sports his lameness with energetic pride. Four years ago, when he was barely thirty, he had his leg smashed in six places by an irate burglar wearing steel-toed shoes. He's been at pains ever since to live up to the image conferred by his unique war wound, and has an unequalled record of arrests against odds that would make any balanced man abdicate on the spot.

'My, my,' Howard says, coming to the side of the trolley and looking down at the battered patient. 'You've got a scratch or two there, Ahmad.' To John Blake he says, 'He's Ahmad Iqbal. The one with the bullet in him's called Sitti Mardhekar. Not worth a shit, either one of them.'

Donald Ramsay and Sue McLean have begun cleaning the wounds. Glenda Cross has sent a sample of the patient's blood to the lab for matching and now she's in the clean theatre laying out the necessary local anaesthetic, suturing equipment and dressings. A Dextran drip has been set up to tide the patient over until he is transferred to a surgical ward, where he will be given whole blood.

'What's the story?' John Blake asks Inspector Howard.

'Iqbal here's got a daughter,' Howard says. 'He's not what you'd call a traditionalist, really, except in that one area. He's integrated to the point where he can pick a winner ten feet from the back page of the *Mirror* and he can tell the difference between Bell's and Teacher's with fur on his tongue. But...' Howard shakes back his long hair and stabs his finger in the air above Iqbal's face. 'When it comes to marrying off his daughter, this one's orthodox as they make them. There's money in it that way, you see.'

'The young one was after his girl?' John says.

'After her? He'd caught her, been through her a time or two as well I shouldn't be surprised. Wanted to marry her, but Ahmad here wasn't having any. He told young Sitti to sling his hook. Sitti hasn't two rupees to rub together, so you can see his point, can't you?'

'What does the young one do?' Sister Pringle asks.

158

'Ponces for his sister most of the time,' Howard says casually. 'Anyhow, to cut a dull story short, Sitti went on seeing the girl, secretly. Pater here found out, and sent round a couple of his lads – he's got a garage, employs a lot of heavy young Sikhs and such – and the lads kicked skittles of shit out of young Sitti. As a warning. That was two weeks ago.'

John is nodding. 'And tonight was revenge night?'

'Right,' Howard says. 'Half-three, or thereabouts, Sitti climbs in through Iqbal's back window and gives him a massage with the Krooklock while he's still asleep. He took a knife to him as well, just for a bit of variety. Iqbal's missus started screaming the place down and when Sitti carried on hammering the old man, she got the gun out of the tea caddy and plugged him.'

'Who gave you the story?' John asks.

'Iqbal's missus. No hesitation. Told me the lot without prompting. That Sitti's lucky he's alive. She was aiming for his head.'

Phil Cowley and Donald Ramsay wheel the trolley through to the clean theatre. The patient isn't in shock, but he remains very quiet as the drip is put into his arm and Ramsay starts injecting the local anaesthetic around the perimeter of each wound.

'We'll be here for ages,' Glenda groans. She and Sue McLean stand by, ready to hand Dr Ramsay needle holders, threaded needles and dressings as he sets about the repair work.

'If the young one had put it off a couple of hours,' Ramsay says, 'they'd be doing this over at St Bride's.'

'If!' Glenda grunts. She looks at her watch. 'My mum'll be switching on my electric blanket just about now.'

In the office John Blake, Sister Pringle and Inspector Howard are having some re-heated coffee.

'Nectar,' Howard says, sipping carefully. 'With the accent on tar.'

They drink in silence for a minute, all of them fatigued and at that point on a shift when one more emergency would make them anxious over their ability to cope.

'You two seem to work together without much bother,' Howard observes as he sets down his half-empty cup. 'Some Casualty places I go into, you can smell the tension in the air.' He makes a tremor of a wink at John Blake. 'Sisters can be bloody murder to get on with, can't they?'

159

John nods, smiling. 'Not this one, though. Sweetness and light all the way.'

Mary Pringle smiles and flutters her eyelashes. 'I'm only thirty,' she says. 'My war-horse years are still up ahead.' She looks at Dr Blake. 'We get on because we don't try to score points off each other, isn't that so?'

'Yes,' John says, 'and because we've shared a lot of grim experiences. That kind of thing generates harmony, Inspector.'

Howard shakes his head. 'Not in the police, it doesn't. If a couple of our blokes share their grim experiences for any more than two months at a stretch, they end up at each other's throats.' He shrugs. 'That's the way it is in my outfit, anyway.'

'I think I'd better go through and give Dr Ramsay a hand,' John Blake says, draining his cup. 'You take it easy, Sister. Let Inspector Howard thrill you with some of his tales of daring.'

'I've heard them all,' Sister says. 'I haven't time, anyway. Got to get that floor cleaned.'

They file out of the office as Phil is bringing Sitti back from X-ray. John hooks the plates on the viewer by the office door and studies them for a minute.

'Nothing trivial I hope,' Howard says.

'It's serious enough to be taken out of my hands,' John murmurs. 'I'll call up Men's Surgical and hand him over to them.' He asks Sister to put a fresh dressing on Sitti's wound before he's transferred.

Inspector Howard has gone over to the trolley, where the young Indian lies placidly staring up at him. 'Feeling rough, are we, Sitti?'

'Not really,' the youth says. He even smiles slightly.

'Pity.' Howard goes back to where John is standing and pats him chummily on the arm. 'I've got a couple more villains to bully. I'll come back and talk to these two tonight. Nice seeing you again.' He nods to Sister and walks off towards the door. When he gets there he stops and raises one shiny purple arm. 'Don't forget the medical thought for today,' he calls.

John grins at him. 'And what's that?'

'A crushed finger's a sore thing, but a crushed thing isn't necessarily a sore finger.'

In the clean theatre, Donald Ramsay is progressing well with his repairs on Mr Iqbal. He has stitched the cuts on his left arm and is halfway through closing the large wound on the right arm when John Blake comes in to help. Between them they tie off a couple of severed veins, then draw the torn muscle together with soluble sutures. The wound is closed with fine silk; it will probably be re-opened later so that a proper cosmetic effect can be obtained.

'Just the legs now,' John Blake says when they have finally dressed the right arm. 'Bear up, chaps.'

Glenda and Sue are looking as if they could fall asleep any second.

John examines the left leg carefully, then swears softly under his breath. 'Splintered tibia,' he tells Donald Ramsay. 'Can't tell how extensive it is. He'll have to go to X-ray.'

They all step outside to stretch and yawn as Phil wheels the patient away.

'We could definitely have done without this one,' Glenda grumbles. She sits on a stool and slips off first one shoe, then the other. She puts the soles of her feet on the cool floor and sighs, then looks up at John Blake. 'Terrible what people do to one another in the middle of the night, isn't it?'

'Sex and money,' John says offhandedly.

Sue McLean frowns at him, failing to understand.

'The reason for so much of it, Nurse,' he says slowly, like a teacher trying to get through to an infant. 'It's a combination that causes a lot of trouble in the world.'

After a moment's silence, Glenda Cross nods. 'True enough,' she says. 'Sex and money's ruled my life for years.' She eases her swollen feet back into her shoes and stares grimly at her watch again.

Sunday

Mrs Mayhew, a part-time receptionist, unlocks the door to Casualty at five minutes past nine. She looks out across the car park for a minute, seeing shadows and telling herself sternly that there's nobody there. Three weeks ago she encountered a flasher – a sad soul really – who ran away in mid-flash, terrified by his own compulsion. Mild though the outrage was, Mrs Mayhew has trouble confronting the dark now.

In the office, Sister Pringle is behaving as if she's caught in a private thunder-storm. SNO Parker has been on the phone again, complaining that the maintenance staff had to move four trolleys and a defibrillator to get at a fuse box this morning. The department is supposed to be made ready for maintenance, Miss Parker pointed out, and would Sister kindly see to it that her porter does his job thoroughly in future.

'I'll swing for that flaming woman,' Sister promises John Blake, as she bangs open the register and engraves the date in it with a ballpoint that she wields like a scalpel. 'She *looks* for faults. Invents them when she can't find any.'

'That's what admin's all about,' John says. He is sitting in front of the desk, reading through a paper on the pharmacologic use of Prostaglandin E, a substance being used successfully in the treatment of heart disease in children. From time to time John has a yearning to be involved in the long-term treatment of illness and he compensates by reading long, complex treatises on current clinical practice. This particular report is a shade too difficult to follow at the moment, however. He puts the paper down and rubs his eyes slowly. 'Miss Parker retires in a couple of years. Hold that thought.'

163

'I won't last,' Sister snaps. She stands up, brushing non-existent fluff from her sleeves, and strides to the door. 'I'm going to look for a few maintenance faults. Give me a shout if you need me.'

John is alone for only a minute. Donald Ramsay comes into the office, still wearing his sports jacket, and throws himself unceremoniously into Sister's chair.

'You look shattered,' John tells him. 'You're supposed to get some rest between shifts, you know.'

'I went to bed as soon as I got home this morning,' Ramsay says. 'I slept for eleven hours, got up, showered, shaved and came straight back here. This is the way I always look when I'm really refreshed.' He scratches his chest idly. 'It's a quiet city out there tonight. We could have an easy time of it, for a change.'

Speculation about how busy they will be is a regular game in Casualty and the Sunday-night shift is the hardest to predict. On occasions they have gone the entire night without seeing one case. At other times the flow of patients has been as steady as on a winter Friday.

'They're just conning us,' John Blake says. 'They'll wait till we're all settled down with cups of tea and the Sunday papers, then they'll get out on the streets and start battering chunks out of each other.'

It's a fairly customary start to a Sunday shift. Donald Ramsay sits back and stretches, then crosses his legs and settles himself deeper in the chair. 'How are the kids, John?' he asks.

'Fine. Gareth's over his teething for the time being. George has stopped torturing the cat since it bit him.'

'And Sheila?'

'A bit low,' John says. His wife is a doctor, and although she elected to give up her work for a few years to raise a family, she's finding the drudgery of day-to-day motherhood harder to withstand than she had imagined. 'She'll be better when I get back on day duty.'

'I'll take her some flowers next time I'm round,' Ramsay says. 'Just to remind her she's a woman.' Once a month Donald Ramsay has dinner with the Blakes. He plays uncle to the children and lets Sheila lecture him on looking after himself properly.

John asks Donald how his mother is keeping. The question is a nicety, part of the social convention of exchanging news of families. Donald's mother has terminal cancer, and both men know there is no hope at all of her living beyond spring.

'She's high on Brompton's most of the time,' Ramsay says. I've never seen her happier.'

The Brompton Mixture – known to doctors and nurses as Brompton's Cocktail – is administered in the form of a linctus to patients with the more agonising forms of inoperable cancer. It is a highly addictive mixture; the main ingredients are morphine and cocaine and it's frequently given in large doses. Since more and more doctors have turned to the view that the prolongation of misery is no part of a healer's craft, Brompton's has been used widely. Given in sufficient dosage, it can even remove the kind of visceral pain that was once described as intractable. The patient remains alert and usually cheerful, since the addictive constituents of Brompton's eliminate any tendency towards depression.

'Tina's the one who worries me a bit,' Ramsay says. 'She broods about mother.' Tina is Donald's older sister. They live together in a flat in North London, close to the school where Tina teaches. 'She never gets off the topic.'

'It's only natural.'

'It's mother's euphoria she goes on about. Thinks it's too unnatural. She can't handle the idea that the old lady's a junkie. I've explained it's better like that, mother's got no pain, she's happy and she's come to terms with her illness. But Tina still broods. Last week, she told me she didn't like the idea of us letting the doctors shorten mother's life.'

'But they're not.'

Ramsay frowns. 'I must say, I thought that was what was happening. All that dope in her system can't be doing too much good...'

'Check the figures,' John Blake says. 'The hospices are proving that pain can carry off an old, failing life a lot sooner than drugs. Morale's got a lot to do with people surviving.' As always happens, their light social chat has led them back to medical topics. John hoists his briefcase up from beside the chair and starts rummaging in it. 'There's a paper here, somewhere. It'll interest you.'

Glenda Cross and Sue McLean are in the plaster room,

discussing their own lives beyond Casualty. Sue has recently become engaged, but she's not sure she likes it.

'Denis was never...' she searches for the word; *'restrictive'* before. Since he's got the ring on me, he's changed an awful lot. He goes out three nights a week on his own, but he doesn't want me doing it. And he's talking about me giving up nursing as soon as we're married. Likes the idea of having me to come home to, he says. I hadn't anything like that in mind. I told him so.'

Glenda is sitting on the plaster table, glumly nodding as Sue unfolds her misgivings. 'It happened to me when I got engaged,' she says. 'My nice, happy-go-lucky big boyfriend turned into my keeper overnight.'

'What did you do?'

Glenda looks at Sue. 'I'm not married, am I? I got shot of him double quick.'

'Was that long ago?'

'Ages. I was just a kid.' She pauses. 'I was your age.'

Sue McLean sighs and folds her arms. 'I don't know what to do. I'm not half as sure about Denis as I was six months ago. But on the other hand...'

'I'm not the person to talk to about it,' Glenda says flatly. She's made it clear on previous occasions that she has no intention of getting married. 'Neither is Sister.'

Like Glenda, Mary Pringle has no plans for marriage. Both women hope to move higher in their profession; they know that their single-mindedness would form a barrier to a successful long-term relationship. Neither woman has a steady boyfriend, and neither of them subscribes to the belief that a woman is incomplete without a husband and children.

'I'll tell you something,' Sue says after a minute. 'You might think it's silly...'

'As if you'd say anything silly,' Glenda says, laughing.

'No, listen. One big reason I *do* want to get married some time is that it terrifies me to think of being lonely when I'm old.'

'You should have a word with my Aunt Maisie.' Glenda leans close to Sue. Her face is serious now. 'She got divorced after being married for twenty years. She realises now they were the twenty loneliest years of her life.'

Sister Pringle puts her head into the room. 'What's the gossip tonight?'

'Love and marriage,' Glenda tells her.

Sister groans and goes away again.

At 9.25 Mrs Mayhew comes through from the waiting room to tell Sister there is a patient waiting and hands her the case card.

'She looks awful,' Mrs Mayhew says.

Sister says she will call the patient shortly. 'Chat to her, will you Mrs Mayhew?'

John Blake comes out of the office and Sister hands him the card. 'A Mrs Gold. Says she's hurt her back. Will I get her in?'

'Leave it to me, Sister,' John says. 'I'm bored.'

He goes to the waiting room and sees Mrs Mayhew sitting beside the patient, a small elderly woman who looks ill and distressed. 'Mrs Gold? Would you like to follow me?'

The woman stands with difficulty, grasping the chair in front of her and holding on to it for a second before she starts walking. She gets visibly paler as she comes close to John, who holds the door open with his foot and puts his arm around her for support. On the way to the cubicle Mrs Gold starts to sway, and John has to get behind her and hold her up.

'Nurse! Quick!'

Glenda Cross comes running and without being told, bends and lifts the patient's legs. They carry her to the cubicle and with an effort get her on to the bed.

Glenda stands back, panting. 'What's up with her?'

'Hurt her back according to the card. But it doesn't look like it to me.' John raises one of the woman's eyelids. 'Fainted clean away. With pain.'

Mrs Gold is coming round again. Her small, smooth face is regaining some of its colour.

'You're all right,' John tells her softly. 'You're on a bed. Just lie still until you feel stronger.' He notices that Mrs Gold's fingernails are badly bitten. Two of the fingers have hardly any nail-bed left.

After a minute Mrs Gold raises her head and looks at John and Glenda. 'Could I speak to the nurse?' The tremor in her voice could be pain or anxiety.

'Of course.' John leaves the cubicle and Glenda steps close to the side of the bed.

'I didn't want to go to my doctor,' the old woman says, and she averts her eyes.

167

'What is it that's wrong?' Glenda leans closer, holding one trembling hand. It begins to look as if the woman's embarrassment is as bad as her pain. She moves her mouth twice to speak, then loses the courage. 'You can tell me,' Glenda prompts.

Outside, John Blake has run to help Donald Ramsay who is struggling with a wild-eyed, skull-shaved youth who is trying to kick Ramsay's feet away from him.

'Stand back, Donald!'

Ramsay jumps clear and John runs past the boy. As he passes he shoots out his hand and grabs the back of the boy's collar, and keeps running. Helpless, the youth is propelled backwards and slammed against the office door. By the time he realises what's happened, John Blake is waving a cylinder spanner at him.

'Right then, hard man. What's this all about?'

John's puzzlement deepens as two police constables burst in from the ambulance bay and grab the boy. They carry him between them to the middle of the floor, then twist his arms behind his back and handcuff him.

'Should've cuffed the bastard in the first place,' one of the policemen says. He warns the youth with one big bunched fist as the other constable leads him away, then he crosses to where John is still holding the spanner. 'Sorry about all that, Doctor.'

'What's going on?'

'We arrested him for assault. We were bringing his victim here on the way to the station. He made a run for it when we pulled in.' The constable grins. 'Nice tackle, that. You don't expect to see a doctor wading in.'

'I've learned a lot about riot suppression in this job,' John says. He puts down the spanner. 'What kind of state's the assault victim in?'

'I'm not sure. I'll bring her in.'

'*Her?*'

The constable nods. 'Random assault. He's a right charmer, this one.'

A couple of minutes later, while John Blake, Donald Ramsay and Sister Pringle are comparing notes on self-defence, the constable comes back, leading a young girl by the arm.

'Oh dear,' Sister murmurs. 'The poor little thing.'

The frailty of the girl is instantly apparent. She is about fifteen, dressed neatly in a duffle coat, polo neck sweater,

168

trousers and knee boots. Her tidiness makes the injuries look worse. There are ugly purple bruises on her cheeks and chin, and her nose looks as if it has been bleeding. But what is most distressing of all is her expression. Everyone in Casualty has seen it before, the look of fright and dismay that seems permanently fixed. Until tonight, the girl has probably never even witnessed violence.

'I'll take care of her,' Sister says to the constable. 'Have her family been told where she is?'

'Somebody's going round to tell them.'

'Come on love.' Sister leads the child away to a cubicle.

'I should have hit him with that spanner,' John Blake says. He sees Glenda Cross come out of Mrs Gold's cubicle and he goes across to her. 'What's the big mystery?'

'Piles,' Glenda says. 'The poor old duck's been suffering with them for years. They've got pretty bad now. She has a partial prolapse.'

'It's the old story,' John says. 'Some people have got to be in agony before they'll even admit they've got haemorrhoids. I take it she's pretty heavily embarrassed?'

'Yes.'

'Well, it'll be best if you do the necessary. And don't let her walk home afterwards.'

Piles, although they form the basis of much coarse humour, are among the most painful of the common ailments. They are true varicose veins in the anal lining and they hurt so much because they occur at a part of the body which is especially well supplied with nerves.

There are several new ways of treating the condition, but injection is the one most appropriate in Mrs Gold's case. The solution injected is a mixture of phenol in almond oil. It's put directly into each of the inflamed veins, where it causes rapid shrinkage. Before making the injection and after, Glenda Cross will apply a cream that contains a local anaesthetic which will take away most of Mrs Gold's pain.

Sister has taken off the little girl's coat and helped her on to the bed.

'What's your name?' Sister asks softly.

The girl's lower lip is stiffened with bruising and she speaks carefully in a wavering voice. 'Diane.'

'Well Diane, I want you to know two things. That bully who hit you is going to be punished. He won't get away with it. The other thing is, you're with friends, good friends who are going to help you.' With any teenage patients who are frightened or in pain, it's Sister Pringle's habit to treat them as if they're younger than they really are. There's great comfort and reassurance in being treated like a child; even the tough, defensive ones respond to the technique.

With Diane, the response is immediate. Her chest heaves once and she lets out a long, high wail that leaves her breathless. Tears start to stream along her cheeks. Sister raises the girl and puts both arms around her, letting her cry against her shoulder.

'That's what you need, my lamb.' Sister pats Diane's back steadily as she sobs. 'Cry it all out, that's a good girl.'

Just as violence can cause an old person's will and personality to disintegrate, so sensitive young people can have their emotional growth curtailed. With them, heavy doses of kindness are the best first aid and Sister Pringle never forgets that. The other bruises can wait.

John Blake is on the point of settling down in the office to make another try with the paper on Prostaglandin E, when there is the sound of violent braking from the car park. Instinctively John is out of his chair before the car door slams. He goes running through the waiting room, startling Mrs Mayhew, and out through the main door.

A middle-aged man is running towards the door. He stops when he sees John. 'Can you help me?' he shouts frantically, not realising that John is out there for that very purpose. 'We'll have to carry him!'

There is a young man in the passenger seat. John can't see him too clearly as they lift him out, but he can hear the choking and wheezing. He registers the fact that the man's body feels hot through the material of his shirt.

'Get him over my shoulder,' John says, and he bends forward, taking the patient in a fireman's grip. He goes back to the department at a trot, with the other man behind him.

They go straight through to the treatment area. Donald Ramsay takes one look and sprints to the nearest trolley. He wheels it across and John lowers the patient on to it.

Breathless, John makes a rapid assessment of the man's

condition. His face is swollen and his lips are blue. On his arms and neck there are ugly red blotches; his hands are twitching and flexing as if they're being burned. He has great difficulty in breathing and his pupils are dilated. In spite of his collapsed condition the patient is fully conscious.

'Tell me what happened,' John gasps. 'Quickly.'

The other man is flustered and agitated. He keeps looking from the patient to John, expecting action.

'Look, he's very ill, but I can't do anything until you give me an idea what happened.'

'He took a tablet...'

'One?'

'Yes. One.' The man's agitation is growing. 'My son told me he'd a sore throat, so I gave him one of the tablets I had for my own throat trouble.'

Donald Ramsay is putting a plastic airway into the patient's mouth. 'Throat's swollen,' he grunts, trying to ease the end of the airway past the puffy tongue and palate.

John Blake is glaring at the patient's father. 'What were the tablets? Have you brought them?'

The man takes a plastic bottle from his jacket pocket and hands it to John.

'Penicillin!' John hisses.

'I didn't see any harm...'

John shoves past the man and starts pushing the trolley to the Emergency room. Donald Ramsay runs alongside, holding the airway in place.

Both doctors now know what's wrong with the man. He is suffering from anaphylactic shock, an allergic reaction to penicillin. His body chemistry is doing everything to reject the antibiotic but the nerve centres are unbalanced and he is actually being killed by his own defence mechanisms.

'How long?' John shouts to the father.

'What?'

'How long since he swallowed the tablet?'

The man frowns. 'About ten minutes ago. What's happened to him, anyway?'

John makes no reply. 'Epinephrene,' he says to Ramsay, 'intramuscularly.'

While Ramsay gets the injection, John raises the patient's feet.

171

His condition is worsening. He is looking frightened and John senses the mild tremor that precedes a convulsion.

'He'll need Benadryl too,' John calls to Donald Ramsay. 'And a saline drip after the injections.'

The drugs are designed to offset allergic reactions. In a case of anaphylactic shock they have to be given in huge doses, so saline is put into the bloodstream to prevent prolonged and harmful reactions to the drugs.

John has pushed the airway further into the man's throat and is assisting his breathing by rhythmically pressing on the chest.

'One each,' Ramsay says, handing one of the syringes to John.

The Epinephrene has to be given first. Ramsay injects it in the patient's left arm. John counts to ten after the needle has been withdrawn, then he injects the Benadryl. While he is doing that, Donald Ramsay sets up a saline drip and wheels it across.

'Two minutes,' John says, 'then start it running.'

Ramsay puts a clamp on the feed line from the saline bag, before sliding the needle into a vein in the patient's forearm.

The patient's father is standing well back from the trolley, moving from foot to foot. 'It *was* the tablet, was it? My wife said it must be, but I couldn't really see...'

'It was the tablet,' John assures him, without looking round.

'Will he be all right?'

'I've no idea.'

After seventy seconds by Donald Ramsay's watch, the patient suddenly starts to breathe more easily. The tremor in his legs and hands stop. The reversal is rapid, a cancelling of biochemical chaos as the support systems re-align themselves.

'Christ,' Ramsay whispers. 'It's working.'

He's entitled to be surprised. It is commoner for people to die from anaphylactic shock – usually within ten minutes of the onset.

John checks the man's pulse and respiration, then listens to his heart. He turns to the father. 'He'll be all right,' he says.

The man swallows. 'Thank goodness,' he says huskily.

'I'm sorry if I was a bit short with you. I was worried for a while that he wasn't going to make it.' John takes a deep breath and lets it out slowly. 'Promise me you won't give anybody your medicines again, will you?'

The man nods sheepishly.

172

Ramsay starts the drip and for ten minutes the two doctors monitor the patient's steady recovery. When John Blake is satisfied there will be no relapse, he turns to the father again.

'We'll have to keep your son in for a couple of days, just to make sure he's over this. Perhaps you'd like to pop back home and get his pyjamas and toothbrush and whatever else you think he'll need.'

The man leaves without saying a word.

Ramsay squeezes the drip bag gently and puts his face close to the patient's. 'I'm sorry about jamming the tube into your sore throat, but you'll have to keep it in for a while, until you get to a ward.'

The man gurgles something indecipherable through the airway. From the look in his eyes, it's probably an expression of gratitude.

Fifteen minutes later, when the facial swelling has practically disappeared and the patient's heart-rate and respiration are almost normal, Phil Cowley wheels him away to Men's Medical.

In the office, John Blake announces to Sister Pringle that he and Dr Ramsay deserve a drink.

'Coffee or tea?' she asks.

'Don't be silly.'

Sister sighs and hoists her bunch of keys onto her lap. She finds the right one and puts it in the lock of the cabinet beside the desk.

'Scotch?'

'If you insist.' John sits down. 'How did it go with the little girl?'

'She just left with her mother and father. I think she'll be fine. The parents panicked a bit when they saw the dressings, but they settled down after a minute or two. Nice people.' Sister unscrews the bottle cap and pours thirty millilitres of whisky into a medicine measure. She hands it to John and puts the same amount into another measure. 'What's the occasion, anyway?'

'You know what it is,' John says indignantly. 'We pulled a man out of anaphylactic shock.'

'Is that all? I might as well have a glass myself. I restored a kid's faith in the world.' She smiles. 'I told her skinheads and the like were put on the globe just to make the rest of us look better.' Sister pours a third drink and she's putting the cap back on the

173

bottle when Dr Ramsay comes into the office with Glenda Cross close behind him.

'What's this, then?' Glenda demands. 'Somebody's birthday?'

Sister groans and pours one more glass. 'Here. You lot can buy the next bottle.' She starts to pass the glass to Glenda, then hesitates. 'Hang on, you're supposed to have done something to deserve this.'

'That's right,' John says. 'We've saved a life and Sister's done some PR for the human race. What about you?'

Glenda puts on her stiff face. She draws herself up to her full sixty-three inches and says, in her SNO Parker voice, 'I relieved an old woman's Farmer Giles, that's what.'

The laughter explodes from them, echoing out across the department. It is the sound of catharsis, a spurt of joy from people too accustomed to meeting misery head-on.

It's a whole minute before they are under control again. When they are, John Blake takes a sip of whisky, then says that he really doesn't approve of people making jokes about painful ailments. 'I only laughed because the rest of you did. I know there are nicknames in medicine, it's inevitable. But I think, Staff, you could dream up a more dignified one for piles.'

'I don't know a better one,' Glenda says.

'Well, I do,' John says, and now it's getting hard for him to hold on to his pompous act.

'What?'

John savours the moment. He swirls his whisky and looks at his three colleagues in turn. Finally he says. 'The Grapes of Wrath.'

Out in her booth in the waiting room Mrs Mayhew shoots a worried glance at the treatment area. She shakes her head sadly. From the noise that's going on, she reflects, a person could be forgiven for thinking that discipline among the staff had broken down completely.

* * *

No further cases are brought to Casualty during the Sunday shift. John Blake manages to read his paper and most of the current issue of the *British Medical Journal*. Sister Pringle gets her paperwork up to date and Glenda Cross wins two pounds off Donald Ramsay at pontoon.

174

When daylight edges grey across the car park, Phil Cowley goes for a walk. He has Monday night off, so he'll do his housework during the morning, visit Lily in the afternoon and evening, and perhaps go out for a pint later on. Having planned the day, he feels better. Plans leave less room for surprises and Phil's not keen on surprises any more. As he walks he whistles softly. It isn't a tune, it's just a pleasant sound that makes him aware of himself – aware that he's still here in spite of his disasters.

At 6.45 a.m. John Blake feels he won't be tempting fate if he takes off his white coat and puts on his jacket. Donald Ramsay does the same and they go out together to stand in the ambulance bay, as they often do, watching the hospital get ready for the day.

Glenda Cross, Mary Pringle and Sue McLean are in the sluice, having a final cup of coffee. Inactivity has made them wearier than work does; as they drink they yawn periodically and blink the scratchiness from their eyes.

'My bed'll be like toast,' Glenda says. She has her cape wrapped around her tightly. Her hands emerge from it like the hands of a waif, clutching the steaming cup.

'I won't get near my little bunk before nine,' Sister mumbles over the rim of her cup. 'Buses!'

Sue is too tired to say anything. She's gulping the hot liquid, hoping it'll make her feel brighter for the bicycle ride home.

Mrs Mayhew stands for a minute in the doorway to the treatment area, watching the second hand on the white clock by the Emergency room. The silent department is like a sculpture of itself, miraculously accurate but unreal, innocent of movement or urgency. Mrs Mayhew yawns, willing the hand to move faster.

Out in the bay, with his jacket collar turned up against the wind, Donald Ramsay says, 'Three hundred and sixty-two.'

John Blake looks at him. 'You're doing it again. Being opaque.'

Ramsay is referring to the number of patients treated in Casualty during the weekend. In all 181 men, 128 women and 53 children under the age of 18 have received treatment. Among numerous other procedures the staff have applied 412 wound dressings and 23 plaster casts, transfused 23 litres of blood and

Dextran, administered 503 injections, and put countless stitches into hundreds of wounds. Nineteen attempted suicides have been saved since Friday night; two people have died in the department during the same period and two others have died after being transferred to wards.

Much of the treatment initiated in Casualty is being continued in other parts of Anderson General. In Cardiac Care, Terry Doyle is making good progress after his coronary attack. His wife will be able to feed him breakfast this morning and the doctors have promised that, if the rate of improvement continues, he will be allowed to get out of bed and sit in a chair within the week.

Alice Lawson, the pregnant girl who was admitted on Friday with a suspected iron deficiency anaemia – which has since been confirmed – is responding satisfactorily to treatment. Her blood count has improved and the swellings on her ankles and tongue have subsided. Her baby gives every appearance of being normal. Most encouraging of all, Alice has agreed to let the social worker get in touch with her family who, she admits, have no idea where she is.

Of the four men admitted with serious burns, one has died in the Intensive Therapy Unit and another died quite suddenly in Men's Surgical. There was very little hope that the man in Intensive Therapy would survive. He was burnt badly on his back and had inhaled toxic smoke; the capacity of his lungs to absorb oxygen and filter his blood was dangerously diminished. His liver and kidneys had also suffered damage and he finally succumbed to kidney failure and acute blood poisoning. The other man, who had been making progress, died of a pneumonia that invaded his lungs too rapidly to be controlled. The remaining two burns cases are making reasonable progress, but it will be months, after grafting operations and muscle-regeneration, before they leave hospital.

The rape victim, Doris Crumley, is in a side ward off Gynaecology. The consultant psychiatrist, Dr Lloyd, has noted on her case sheet that she has entered a phase of deep depression, characterised by immobility, silence and total loss of appetite. Dr Lloyd also suspects the gradual onset of an obsessive-compulsive disorder; on occasions when Mrs Crumley has believed she was alone, she has been talking to herself in a low, breathless monotone. It is too early to make a firm

176

diagnosis, but this is typical compulsive behaviour. No relatives have yet visited the patient. Dr Lloyd has intercepted a note from Mr Crumley, in which he tells his wife he could never look at her again. He also tells her she can't come back home. Dr Lloyd believes that Doris Crumley may have to be admitted to a psychiatric ward in due course for observation and psychotherapy.

The two-year-old child Elizabeth Quigley, who was admitted with scalded legs and was later found to have several older injuries, is in a ward with twelve other children. She can't walk, because of the burns on her feet, but she appears to be happy and obviously enjoys having the company of other children. When she is well enough to leave hospital she will be transferred to a children's home, where she will stay until a court decides whether or not she will be taken into permanent care, as Dr Roarke has recommended.

Teresa, the young woman whose husband inflicted twelve bites on her face, is in Women's Surgical. She has had her entire head encased in a protective dressing and only her eyes and mouth are visible. When her mother saw the dressing she had to be led out of the ward, crying hysterically. Teresa seems to have patience and she has accepted assurances that the plastic surgery was successful; in a year or two her scars will have disappeared. She has told the police that she doesn't want to bring charges against her husband.

'We're eight down on last week's count,' Donald Ramsay says. He flicks his cigarette end across the tarmac.

'We'll have to see if we can do better next week,' John Blake murmurs.

Ramsay digs his hands deep in his pockets, shivering as a breeze cuts across the ambulance bay. 'I'm off for four days, thank the Lord.'

'You've earned a rest, old son,' John Blake says. 'We all have. Casualty tends to drain the personnel faster than other jobs.'

'Right,' Ramsay smiles. 'Still, we've licked it for another weekend, haven't we? One more victory?'

John pulls the door open and they stroll back inside and get their overcoats. For a moment he has an urge to argue with Ramsay's last remark, but decided to let it pass. Donald didn't really mean it, anyway. People will say anything at the end of a shift.

'Victory,' John murmurs to himself as he goes into the office to wait for the early team. 'That'll be the day.'

There can be no abiding sense of victory in Casualty, nor even a sense of completion. The sick and wounded keep on coming. The weekend's arc of panic, chaos, triumph and disaster has been one tiny section of an eternal cycle. The staff don't function as victors – their job is to do permanent battle without any hope of conquest. Even so, the work is exhilarating and endlessly challenging. Casualty people are happy to go on battling against the tide. At best, they achieve containment. Or, as John Blake once put it, a fluctuating kind of control.